HEROIC HEARTS

JD MARCH

Copyright © 2018 JD March

All rights reserved.

ISBN-13: 978-1725720572
ISBN-10: 1725720574

Heroic Hearts

Tho' much is taken, much abides; and tho'

We are not now that strength which in old days

Moved earth and heaven, that which we are, we are;

One equal temper of heroic hearts,

Made weak by time and fate, but strong in will

To strive, to seek, to find, and not to yield.

(From Ulysses by Alfred, Lord Tennyson..

Praise for *The Devil's Own* books

"First time author JD March's *Dance with the Devil* is a dynamite beginning to a new series, 'The Devil's Own', from Five Star that will have fans placing orders for volume two months ahead of publication. March's here, Johnny Fierro, is a conflicted gunfighter that fans of Elmore Leonard's outlaw heroes will recognize and cheer for—even when they know he's wrong." — **True West Magazine**

"…there's plenty of action… for fans of Zane Gray or Max Brand…" — **Booklist**

"Can the prodigal ever fit? A tough novel about a half-breed outcast son who came home" — **Dusty Richards**, two-time Spur Award winner and Wrangler Award-winning author of *A Time To Kill.*

"Johnny Fierro, bitter *and* deadly. A combination readers will love to hate." — **Monty McCord**, Peacemaker Award-winning author of *Mundy's Law.*

CONTENTS

Acknowledgments	i
Chapter One	1
Chapter Two	16
Chapter Three	23
Chapter Four	30
Chapter Five	40
Chapter Six	59
Chapter Seven	73
Chapter Eight	87
Chapter Nine	97
Chapter Ten	110
Chapter Eleven	120
Chapter Twelve	132
Chapter Thirteen	145
Chapter Fourteen	157
Chapter Fifteen	169
Chapter Sixteen	180
Chapter Seventeen	190
Chapter Eighteen	205

Chapter Nineteen	215
Chapter Twenty	224
Chapter Twenty-one	239
Chapter Twenty-two	250
Chapter Twenty-three	263
Chapter Twenty-four	273
Chapter Twenty-five	284
Chapter Twenty-six	293
Chapter Twenty-seven	303
Chapter Twenty-eight	314
Chapter Twenty-nine	325
Chapter Thirty	339
About *The Devil's Own* series	359
About JD March	362

ACKNOWLEDGMENTS

This series would never have been written without the unwavering support of four people — CC who taught me to tell a story and started me off on this path; Whistle for hours of proof reading and innumerable suggestions; Anna for her loyal support, encouragement, and being a technical wizard and the queen of formatting; and Shelley who has urged me on and inspired me throughout. I will always be indebted to them.

CHAPTER ONE

Guy Sinclair wrapped his bandana tighter around his face in an effort to keep from breathing in the choking dust kicked up by two thousand bawling cattle. He stared into the shimmering distance through stinging eyes, longing for this journey to end. They'd been on the trail for seven weeks, and he'd had enough.

Had enough of the noise, the dust, the smell, and he reckoned if he had to look at another plate of beans he might shoot the cook.

His brother, Johnny, was scouting ahead with Manuel, the trail boss, keeping a watchful eye for any signs of Indians. Back at the family ranch near Cimarron, the vaqueros had regaled Guy with vivid tales of the dangers of cattle drives – men swept away in raging rivers, cattle stampedes, and skirmishes with Indians. But now he was wondering if the tales had simply been tall stories for, so far, the drive to Kansas had been singularly uneventful. Although they'd seen broken arrow heads and old tracks, there hadn't been sight nor sound of Indians. It hadn't rained, and all the cattle had done was kick up huge clouds of dust.

He swiped the sweat off his neck and shifted in the saddle trying to ease the ache in his back. The chuck wagon couldn't be too far off now for surely that was the scent of coffee in the air? He was looking forward to resting up for the night, grateful that at least he didn't have to ride night herd. Earlier in the drive, when his brother had cheerfully suggested that Guy could do with the experience, this being his "first cattle drive an' all," Guy had enjoyed shooting down that idea. Being a part-owner did bring some privileges. Grinning at the memory, he pushed his horse on.

Much later, as he forked in a mouthful of stew, Johnny came and squatted next to him.

"I reckon it went well today. We should hit Abilene in less than a week now," Johnny paused, and peered hard at Guy. "You look done in, Harvard. I figure you'll be glad to sleep in a bed again."

Guy raised an eyebrow. "What, and leave all of this?" He gestured toward the grazing cattle, and the men crowded around the chuck wagon. "A soft bed instead of a bedroll? Whatever gives you that idea?"

Johnny swatted a fly away from his neck. "Well I guess if you like this so much, you won't be interested in lighting out ahead of the herd tomorrow." He rose to his feet, grinning as Guy shot his hand out to grab him and pull him back down.

"Lighting out ahead?" Guy kept a firm grip on his brother's arm.

Johnny laughed. "Yeah, I thought that would get your attention. I been talking to Manuel and he reckons they can bring the herd in easy now. You and I can ride ahead to look for the best price and sort out the business end. We could be in Abilene by the day after tomorrow if we ride hard. Just think, soft women, soft beds and hard liquor!"

Guy rolled his eyes. "I should have known you'd be thinking about women."

Johnny winked. "We been on the trail a long time." Johnny scrambled back to his feet. "We'll head out at day break so you'd best check your guns and saddlebags. Take plenty of spare ammunition. We been lucky so far on this trip, but there are Comanche in this territory and they sure as hell ain't too friendly."

Guy frowned. "You think we'll see any?"

Johnny shrugged. "There's a chance. Like I said, we've been lucky so far, and I guess I never expect a run of luck to last for long. We'll be keeping a sharp lookout, that's for sure, and we won't be slacking."

They headed out at dawn, having packed a few essential supplies in their saddlebags. Johnny had stowed extra ammunition in a pair of bags slung across the pommel of his saddle, muttering to Guy about leaving nothing to chance.

They kept up a good pace, but slowed regularly to give their mounts a breather. Johnny stopped occasionally to crouch on the ground examining tracks. Each time he'd remounted looking unconcerned. But this time, instead of remounting, he scanned the horizon through narrowed eyes.

"A problem?" asked Guy.

Johnny nodded slowly. "Maybe. These are fresh tracks."

"Perhaps it's other cattlemen pressing on to Abilene, like us."

Johnny shook his head. "Nope. These horses ain't shod." His voice was tense. "Come on, let's get moving."

Johnny's horse spotted them first. Its head came up and it stared intently at some rocks off to the right. Then Guy and Johnny saw the slightest movement. Johnny cursed softly. "Comanches. Don't stare, just keep looking straight ahead. Make like you ain't seen nothing."

A heavy weight settled where Guy's stomach used to be. Somehow he hadn't believed the men's tales about the Comanche—encountering Indians happened to other people, not him. But now the words rang a chill reminder that this was wild country and nobody knew it better than the Comanche. "What do we do?" Damn silly question really, but he had to say something.

"Keep right on riding toward that group of boulders by the trees. It'll give us some cover and then we stand and fight."

Guy set his jaw and tried to shrug. "Maybe they won't bother us."

Johnny laughed like Guy had made a very bad joke. "They'll bother. The Comanche always bother. They're probably out hunting. Or maybe they escaped from one of those reservations. But I guess this is a small group we got here. There ain't too many of them I reckon."

Too many for what? Probably a damn sight more than two. "You've faced Comanche before?" He swallowed hard as he tried not to stare at the rocks where the Indians were hiding.

Johnny glanced at him, but his face was remote. "I've faced Kiowa and Apache. And yeah, I fought Comanche. Once or twice. And they're the toughest sons of bitches I've ever met. Usually they travel in bands of a dozen or so. But I don't reckon we got anything like that number here. Hopefully not enough to box us in." Johnny paused, his brow furrowed as he seemed to mull it over. "Indians are tricky bastards. They'll sit for hours waiting for their enemy to make a wrong move. They're watching for any show of weakness. Then they go in for the kill. But if they figure that we ain't spotted them, and seeing as how there's only two of us, this bunch may go straight for an attack.

"When we get to the rocks, get under cover but grab our horses. I'll take care of the Indians while you tie them out of sight. We sure as hell don't want to lose them out here. I don't fancy being left afoot."

Guy swallowed hard. "I don't want to lose my scalp either. Are you sure this will work?"

Johnny snorted. "Sure? No, I ain't sure. But I reckon we got a fair chance. I got to keep you alive. Our old man would be pissed as hell at me otherwise."

Guy gritted his teeth, irritated that Johnny thought he needed to look after him. The idea was a little insulting. He resisted the urge to peer back over his shoulder.

Johnny looked over at him. "They're still on our tails, if that's what you're wondering. I reckon they're sizing us up at the moment and that tells me there can't be many of them. If there were, they'd attack us without a thought. I only hope they don't make a move before we're a mite closer to them rocks. Ain't much cover out here."

Guy could see his point. It was a gently rolling landscape of tallgrass prairie with a few stands of blackjack oak and only occasional low-lying rocks. But ahead of them was a higher outcrop of rocks and a denser stand of trees that would provide some cover. "Surely they won't have guns, will they?" Guy found the thought comforting. He visualized men in war paint brandishing bows and arrows.

Johnny gave another hollow laugh. "If you're hoping all they got is bows and arrows and axes and knives, you could be sore mistaken. There're lots of men who'll sell guns to Indians. They got a particular liking for Spencer rifles." He shook his head. "Mighty fond of Spencers is Indians."

That killed the comforting thought stone dead. The newspapers back East were right—the West was a savage place inhabited by savages. Well, he'd been in battles before. Too many battles. It was merely that the rules were different out here. Or maybe it was more a case of there being no rules out here.

"You checked your guns last night?" Johnny looked at him quizzically.

Guy rolled his eyes. "Yes. My pistol and rifle are both loaded and ready." Although Guy had felt at home with weapons in the war, civilian life was a different matter. He'd spent too many years in Boston to adapt easily to carrying a sidearm. Even so, since coming home to Cimarron, he'd very quickly caught the habit of keeping his weapons primed.

The crackle of gunfire echoed as bullets kicked up sand and gravel near Guy's horse, causing the animal to skitter sideways in fright.

"Run for the rocks," Johnny yelled, already with his head down by his horse's neck as he spurred the animal to a breakneck gallop.

Another volley of bullets kicked up dust. Guy followed Johnny's lead, crouching low to present a smaller target. He weaved as well, knowing from the war that it could throw off a pursuer's aim. He reached down for his rifle, drawing it from the scabbard ready to go into action the second he threw himself from his horse. More bullets were kicking up grit all around him. But he was almost at the rocks. Johnny, a length ahead, flung himself from his horse and rolled into an eroded hollow basin protected by a low spread of boulders. It was a good place to make their stand.

Guy made a grab for the reins of Johnny's horse and pulled it into the shelter of the trees. He tethered the horses before running, bent low, to join Johnny who was keeping up a covering volley. As he threw himself down, his heart thumping, he felt a bullet snatch at his hat. Suddenly a Comanche rose from behind a rock and started to move forward. Guy swung his rifle up, took a quick sight and fired.

From the higher ground where they crouched behind the boulders, Guy could see only the one Indian. He was a good two hundred yards off and lower down, but the bullet caught him full in the chest. He staggered and then Johnny got a shot into him even before the Indian could drop, but when he did drop, he lay still.

"How many do you think there are?" Guy swiped sweat out of his eyes as he looked across at Johnny.

Johnny shook his head. "Maybe five or six. They ain't putting up a smoke so they must be some ways from their camp. Or they're a lone band of Comanches."

The land beyond them shimmered in the heat. Guy screwed his eyes up trying to see if anything was moving out there. He caught a flash of an Indian moving but the fellow dropped down again before he could take aim.

"That's how they close in on us," Johnny muttered. "Watch and learn. And you'd best learn real quick. You get a glimpse of them maybe, but then you'll see they drop away. They're sneaky like that. But you'll see just the slight movement in the grass as they edge forward. And I tell you, they sure as hell fight different from the soldiers you fought in that war of yours."

A bullet sprayed dust just ahead of where they lay. Then another ricocheted off a rock with an angry snarl; the flattened bullet so close that Guy jerked away, his heart hammering in his chest. It had been too damn close. He swallowed hard. "Will they try to keep us pinned down and wait for nightfall to launch a full attack?"

Johnny shook his head. "Doubt it. I don't reckon they'll hang about too long when there are only two of us. As a rule, Indians don't attack at night. They reckon if they get killed, their souls will be lost and won't ever find peace. But the Comanche are different. They do a lot of their raiding at night." He grunted in apparent frustration. "Damn Comanches. There's some Indians, some tribes, well, a man can reason with them. But not the Comanche. No, they won't wait for dark; they'll be creeping up on us right now."

Even as he spoke, Guy saw one move forward, but no sooner did he point his rifle at the Indian than the man dropped down out of sight. Then all of a sudden another one appeared. He'd been lying, hidden in the tall grass. He darted up and started moving toward them. Guy swung his gun to fire and then cussed as the man dropped out of view again, while yet another Indian rose and moved forward.

Guy set his jaw. Johnny's advice *"watch and learn"* rang in his ears. And yes, he could see their technique now. He settled down to wait and so the next time one started up he held his fire. He simply waited, carefully watching the general area where the Indian dropped.

Another of them started up, crouching as he moved, but

Guy let him come until he dipped back down. Instead, he waited patiently for the first one to reappear. His patience was rewarded. As the Indian rose up, he and Johnny both fired. Johnny's reaction was lightning fast and he shot him in the chest. But before the man could fall, Guy had worked the lever on his rifle and hit him again.

"You're learning real quick." Johnny grinned across at him. "I always reckoned you was handy with a rifle."

Johnny narrowed his eyes. Without even taking breath, he fired off a round at an Indian who appeared no more than forty feet from where they lay. The man dropped like a stone.

Johnny's eyes were screwed up, peering through the shimmering air to where the Indians' ponies were huddled together in the distance. "I reckon I count seven ponies. D'you make it seven?"

Guy shaded his eyes and again tried to swipe the sweat out of them, struggling to count through the heat haze. "I think it's seven. Maybe only six."

Johnny grunted. "Well, we bagged ourselves three Comanches, so that leaves three or four out there. We'd best reckon on four." Johnny sighed. "And Guy, if the worst comes to the worst, don't let 'em take me alive. And I'll do the same for you."

Guy jerked his head around to stare at his brother, but Johnny's face was remote, his eyes once more scanning the country ahead of them.

They both stared intently at the land, looking for any sign

of movement. But for now all was still. Too still. And it was almost silent too. Guy couldn't hear quail or warblers – they'd taken fright at the gunfire. The only sound was the chirping of crickets.

They lay sprawled on their fronts for what felt like hours, the intense heat causing salty sweat to run down their faces, in their eyes and into their mouths. Johnny lay still as a statue, with an impassive face and watchful eyes. Guy peered through the haze. The shimmering landscape played tricks on his eyes. At times he could swear he saw movement, but then realized it was merely an effect of the light. His shirt was sticking to his back and sweat was building up inside his pants making him itch. But he knew if he moved to scratch, he would probably get a bullet through the head for his pains. And if the heat wasn't enough to contend with, there was the forced inactivity itself. Never mind not being able to move to scratch, Guy could feel every muscle cramping up. He hated lying there feeling so helpless. Johnny was right – it was a very different method of fighting from the battles he'd known as an officer in the Union army.

Surely there was something they could do? But no, they had to play the Comanche at their own waiting game.

Their patience was rewarded when they saw a stir in the long grass a couple of hundred yards from them. They settled to watch, their rifles ready and their pistols and knives in easy reach.

Guy saw a flicker of movement off to the left. A Comanche had been moving through the prairie grass for the last half-hour, creeping, crawling, out of sight most of the time, but always getting closer. Guy grit his teeth. The next time the bastard moved...

Settling himself into the sand, and shuffling into a comfortable position, Guy braced his elbow and took a careful sight and waited. The Comanche moved but didn't raise his head. Still, Guy waited. Then the warrior lunged into view and Guy squeezed off his shot. The Indian went down hard and never even twitched.

Johnny's rifle cracked at the same time, picking off an Indian who had been approaching from their other side. "Two to go, I reckon. But don't let your guard drop thinking there are only two left. That's when a man gets himself killed, reckoning he's on top of the job." Johnny paused and flashed him a quick grin. "But then again, maybe I'm teaching my grandmother to suck eggs."

Guy found himself grinning back, inordinately pleased by the subtle compliment.

And then the waiting game started all over again. The only thing to be said was that the ferocious heat was less intense now. Dusk would come rapidly and suddenly, and Guy wasn't sure if that would be a good thing or bad. Would they have a chance to escape under cover of darkness? Would the warriors confound Johnny's expectations and wait and then attack during the night, or would they mount a sudden attack at dusk. But at least now the odds were evenly stacked.

A shot cracked through the air and Guy fired back in the

general direction, desperate now for some sort of action. Any action. But the muzzle of his rifle must have showed a touch beyond the rocks at the edge of their hole, because an Indian fired again, hitting the rocks and spattering them with stinging rock fragments.

Suddenly the Indians charged, their knives flashing in the sun as they leaped across the low boulders. Guy dropped his rifle and grabbed for his pistol. But the Indians were upon them and kicked the gun out of reach, as Guy rolled over to avoid the Comanche's slashing blade. Guy seized his own knife and took a vicious swipe at the figures. There was a cry of pain and a body crashed against him. He jerked his knee up, slamming it into his attacker and throwing him off. He could hear Johnny cursing loudly and repeatedly, and the crack of his pistol.

The Comanche came storming back on Guy now, his knife in his raised hand, but Guy threw himself at his attacker, and caught him with another slash of his own knife.

But it wasn't enough. The Comanche head-butted Guy's midriff, throwing him off balance. With a winded grunt Guy fell, sprawled out, even as the Indian came again at him. The warrior had blood on his arms and chest but it didn't slow him. For what felt like an eternity, Guy wrestled with his attacker, trying to slash at him with his knife. Breathing hard, Guy jerked his knee again, catching the Indian hard in the groin. Guy followed through with a sharp jab at the man's stomach and then swiftly brought his knife up thrusting it at his attacker's chest. The Indian let out a strange rattling sigh.

And suddenly it was over.

Guy lay on the ground, sucking in great shuddering breaths even as Johnny's pistol cracked once more.

He pushed himself up into a sitting position. Johnny lay close by, panting hard, and blood trickling into his eyes from a cut across his forehead.

Johnny's Indian lay sprawled, shot straight through the middle. Guy reached over and struggled to retrieve his knife, still fighting for breath. Johnny met his gaze, a broad smile across his bloodied face. "Reckon we showed them a thing or two."

In spite of his exhaustion, and the grit and dust making his eyes smart, Guy grinned. "Reckon we did at that, and a damn fine job we made of it."

Moving slowly, they stumbled to their feet and looked around. The light would be fading soon and the question was what they should do next. Johnny pointed toward a sweep of rolling hills, flushed with gold in the late sun. "Let's head for them hills. We should make 'em before night falls. It'll be a better place to camp, and right now I've a mind to put as many miles between us and them Indians as we can."

Guy nodded. "I have no problem concurring with that sentiment. Let's move on out."

Johnny looked at him, furrowing his bloody brow. "Damn it, even after fighting Indians you still use damn tricky words. You just can't help yourself, can you?" Johnny chuffed out a snort of laughter. "Come on, Harvard, let's go."

CHAPTER TWO

They made camp a few miles further on, in a thicket of trees. Johnny set about laying concentric circles of branches around their base. "Leastways we'll hear anyone approaching," he muttered and then threw Guy a sharp look. "But no fire tonight. We eat our supplies cold."

Guy nodded. It was a wise decision, but despite the warmth of the evening he couldn't stop shivering – same as after a battle in the war. Travis, the camp cook, had packed them some of the previous night's stew. It would have been good heated through, it might have warmed him up. Instead, he sank down and leaned against a tree and forked in the cold food, his hands trembling slightly as he did so.

"You did OK today, Guy." Johnny's soft drawl broke the silence. "But I reckon fighting Indians must have been a lot different from the fights you were used to in that war of yours."

Guy carried on forking in his food. He had no intention of being drawn into talking about the war. He never wanted to talk about the war. Ever. And for the life of him he couldn't understand why so many men who'd served liked to get together and talk about old times.

Johnny rolled a cigarette, and made a small sigh of pleasure as he struck a match to light it. "Damn, but I been wanting that all day. And I'd best make the most of it because I can't have one after dark. If there are any Indians out there, I sure as hell don't want them to see the glow or catch the scent." He nodded at Guy. "Yeah, you did good. You held your nerve. I guess that's because you were a soldier. Cavalry, wasn't it?"

Guy hunched over and speared a piece of meat. God only knew what Johnny would say if he knew some of the things the cavalry had done. Or what Guy had done... And if there was one thing he was certain of, it was that Johnny wouldn't understand. "What you said earlier about not being taken alive, what would they have done to us?" Maybe if he changed the subject, Johnny would leave the war alone.

Johnny shot him a quick glance, and was silent for a second or two. "Indians is fond of torture, but the Comanches are better than most. They got a real talent for it. And they enjoy it." He took a drag on his cigarette. "And if you're very unlucky, they hand you over to the women. They're even better at torturing their prisoners. Hell, they can make their menfolk look like amateurs."

"Women? The women get involved in torture!" Guy was astounded.

Johnny nodded. "Yeah, women. Surprising, ain't it? They

can keep a man alive for days, and trust me, you don't want to know the things they do. We aren't just talking about scalpings here."

"Surely they wouldn't torture you though. Would your being part-Apache not help? Can you speak Comanche?" At least he'd distracted Johnny from the war.

Johnny shrugged. "A little, but not much. It's different from the Apache language. I know far more of that. I picked it up from my mother. But being part-Apache wouldn't have done me no favors. The only thing that might help a fellow is how well he stands up to the torture. They admire courage. If a man can show no fear at all, they've been known to let him go. I've heard they reckon then that the prisoner's magic is more powerful than their magic." He took another drag. "The thing is, you can't hardly blame them for hating white men. They came in and stole the Indians' country. And as for rounding them up and forcing them to live on reservations..." Johnny shook his head. "Who the hell thought that up? These are people who need to be free to roam and hunt. It's their nature. They got their own ways of doing things. Their own beliefs and gods. And they don't understand white man's way of doing things, any more than you understand theirs. But you all seem to forget the Indians were here first. This is their land. It ain't right to go marching into someone's land, destroying their homes. And look at your army killing the buffalo, so you can starve them into giving up. Making the women and kids starve. What kind of army does that? What kind of government orders that sort of thing?"

The words struck a chord that was too close to home. Guy swallowed hard, and his hands started trembling again as he tried to push the memories of the war away. Johnny had turned the conversation back toward the army. Was it deliberate? Still, he could deflect too. "Do you feel yourself to be more Mexican or Indian than American? The way you say 'white men', I can't help but wonder where your allegiances lie."

Johnny held his gaze, not speaking for a second, and raised an eyebrow. "I don't really feel much of anything. I guess my allegiance, as you put it, is to me. I don't reckon I got much Mexican in me. I'm what you might call a mongrel."

Guy frowned as he recalled his step-mother. "But Gabriela was half-Mexican..."

Johnny let out a harsh laugh. "That's what she told our old man, yeah. But I reckon that she was more Pueblo than Mexican. She might have had a touch of Mexican blood, but not much. I guess she told him a pack of lies so he wouldn't realize she was pretty much all Indian. The Apache half of her would put most folk off – nobody likes them on either side of the border. By saying the other half was Mexican she probably figured it made her seem more respectable.

"All I know is that it means I don't really fit in either side of the border. But that's another thing, that border between here and Mexico... There's another case of your countrymen taking what ain't rightfully theirs."

Guy took a swig of water from his canteen. "You could say the same thing of the Spanish. They invaded it originally."

Johnny nodded. "Yeah, and a lot of those Mexicans descended from the Spanish treat Indians like dirt too. Same as gringos do." He huffed out a sigh. "Still, our old man is OK with Indians. They don't seem to bother him. He always treats them right, same as he does our vaqueros. He treats them with respect and doesn't behave toward them any different from if they were Anglo. I like that. There ain't many like him."

"Yes, I'd noticed that about him too." Guy shivered and pulled his coat around him. The temperature had dropped considerably since sunset. "I must say that the two of you are getting along much better these days. You don't have nearly as many fights."

Johnny nodded slowly. "Yeah, I reckon you're right. I'm feeling more settled. It's easier now." Johnny flashed him a sudden smile. "Well, easier since he got over his temper about us going to Utah. Boy, he sure yelled at us over that. I thought that pulse in his temple was going to explode he was so mad at us."

Guy smiled at the memory. "He was worried sick. Coming back from his trip to find us gone, and to hear that you'd been dragged off in handcuffs to stand trial there for murder, must have been something of a shock, to say the least! Once he calmed down, he was fine. He even listened to what you had to say. Now that's progress." He stared down at his hands. They'd finally stopped shaking.

He looked up, aware that Johnny was watching him. "You OK now, Harvard?" Johnny's voice was soft. "It's a hell of a thing fighting Indians, and like I said, you did real good. I was impressed at how well you handled that knife too. But I'll bet you never had to use one like that until today. I guess in your war the fighting was with guns and canons, or maybe swords. You never talk about it though. Hell, you've never even told me what rank you were. I'm guessing an officer. Did you see much action?"

Guy bit his lip. He couldn't ignore the direct question. He had to say something. "By the end of the war I was a major."

Johnny grinned. "Well, that figures. I couldn't imagine you in the ranks. Maybe I should salute you in the future." Johnny shuffled back to lean against a tree. "Still, you must have been awful young for a major."

Guy could feel his shoulders tensing up and a bead of sweat inched its way down his forehead. His hands were shaking again. And damn it, Johnny was looking at him expectantly, waiting for more.

"I... I was in the cavalry. I served under Sheridan. And yes, I saw some action. An awful lot of young men achieved high rank very quickly. Battlefield promotions often..." He hesitated, damn it, he didn't want to discuss this. "But it wasn't anything like fighting those Indians today. Although I suppose that the one thing they have in common is that people end up dead."

"So where about did you do your fighting? What sort of battles were they?" Johnny leaned forward, wrapping his arms around his legs.

"I don't want to talk about it!" He snapped the words out before he could stop himself. Avoiding his brother's quizzical gaze, he shook out his bedroll and pulled it over himself. "I'm turning in."

"Sure, Guy." Johnny spoke very softly. "And don't worry, I'll keep a watch tonight."

CHAPTER THREE

Johnny struck a match and lit another cigarette. He grunted in irritation and stubbed it out again. Night was closing in and he sure as hell wasn't going to risk giving away their presence to Indians or anyone else who might be abroad that night.

He eyed the dark outline of Guy's back thoughtfully. Of course it was only natural for any man to be shaken up by a run-in with Indians, especially one who'd spent a great deal of his life out East like Guy had. But judging from his reaction, the fight had triggered something deep inside of Guy which he'd been keeping well hidden, bringing back unpleasant memories which had everything to do with the war and nothing to do with Indians.

Frowning, he went and pulled his rifle from the scabbard on his saddle before sitting back down and leaning against a tree. He'd never seen Guy so nervy before. He was always calm and controlled. But thinking back, Guy had never talked about the war either. Johnny had often wondered whether Guy had, in fact, spent the war far behind the lines, out of danger, but it seemed that his assumption had been wrong.

He shook his head. If he was honest it was none of his business. But even so, he hated to see Guy so distressed. Turning his collar up, he pulled his pistol from the holster and shuffled back against the tree, trying to get comfortable. It was going to be a long night.

"Put it out! Sergeant! Put it out!"

Guy's shout jerked Johnny from a fitful doze at dawn. Guy was striking out in his sleep and Johnny called out softly. "Hey, Guy, it's OK. We're fine."

Guy sat bolt upright and stared at Johnny, his eyes glazed and seemingly unknowing.

"You were having a bad dream. That's all."

Guy shook himself. "A dream? Yes. I was dreaming..." Guy ran his hand across his face. "Dreaming, yes. I was dreaming about those Indians..." He looked away, not meeting Johnny's eyes.

Johnny nodded slowly. "Yeah, sure." Like hell he'd been dreaming about Indians. Johnny rose to his feet, wincing in pain. "Damn, I'm stiff. I been awake most of the night keeping an ear open for trouble. I reckon we might as well make an early start." Johnny glanced at the sky. "The sun will be up soon and I'll be a damn sight happier when we reach Abilene. Breakfast had best be jerky on the hoof. Let's get moving."

The terrain was flat so they rode hard all day, only easing their pace to rest the horses. Late in the afternoon they could see huge herds of cattle ahead. Johnny pointed. "See that, Harvard, the cattle are held outside the town while the deals are done. That's what Manuel will do when ours reach the outskirts. He'll hold 'em there until the cattle buyer inspects them. Then we send word to bring them in to the railhead to be loaded onto the cars."

Guy raised an eyebrow. "I knew it was the main market, but I had no idea there would be this many cattle. It makes you wonder if anyone will want to buy ours with so many coming in."

Johnny grinned. "Trust me, they'll want them. All those people back east have to be fed. Come on." Urging his horse on, he set off toward the town.

Abilene certainly lived up to its reputation as one of the busiest towns in the West. And although Johnny would never have owned to it, he hated it. There were far too many people. He hated towns at the best of times. Hated having so many people thronging around him. He could never relax because he always expected someone to recognize him, and that led to trouble more often than not. But maybe the worse thing about Abilene was having to check his gun in on entering the town.

"Do many Western towns make you check in guns?" asked Guy as they collected tokens from the office where they handed their weapons over.

Johnny shrugged. "Yeah, some of the rougher towns do. Here only law officers are supposed to carry weapons." He paused until the door of the office slammed shut behind them. "But an awful lot of fellows will still have concealed weapons on them." He winked at Guy, knowing full well that his brother would have noticed that he'd only checked in one pistol.

They left the horses at the livery and headed across to the hotel which Guthrie had recommended. Johnny grinned at the memory. Before they'd set out from the ranch, their father had droned on and on about what he expected of them. Hell, he'd all but written down a list of orders! But when he'd done with issuing all his commands, he had told them to stay at Drovers' Cottage which offered the best accommodation and was an excellent source of contact for the commission men and the cattle buyers. He'd also recommended the best places to eat. Johnny had been tempted to ask him if he could recommend a bordello too, but figured that would have been a touch paper to the old man's short fuse.

Johnny pushed open the door to their room even as Guy scooted in ahead of him to bag the best bed. Guy threw himself down on it. "Wake me in a week, when the men arrive with the herd."

Johnny rolled his eyes. "Hell, Harvard, don't you want a bath or a drink?"

"Next week," muttered Guy, "or the week after."

Shaking his head, Johnny headed out into town. A bath first and then a woman. The business of selling the herd could wait until tomorrow.

He found a girl in a small saloon some distance off the

brash and noisy Texas Street. It was scruffy, but quieter than the other places he'd looked at, and it doubled as a bordello. It sure as hell wasn't as classy as Delice's place back in Cimarron. And the girl didn't smell as good as Delice's girls either, but everything was in the right place so there wasn't much point in brooding on it. He'd needed a girl after so long on the trail and she fit the bill. It felt sometimes like he was ruled by his dick because it sure wasn't picky.

Afterwards, he pulled his jacket on and tossed the girl some coins. Then he felt a twinge of guilt and put a few notes on the battered table by the bed. What a way to have to make a living.

She lay naked on the bed, watching his every move. She was old before her time – same as him. Both of them whores in their way. She whored out her body while he'd spent years whoring out his gun.

Sadie had once told him that she liked to talk after he poked her. Did this girl want him to talk to her? Was that what girls wanted after he'd done with them?

"You been working here long?"

Her tired eyes widened. They were a sludgy gray. Not green. "A year or so." She shrugged, then narrowed her eyes, like she didn't trust his interest. "Why? What's it to you?"

He forced a smile. "Oh, I just wondered." He gestured around the room with his hand. "I figured maybe there's better places you could be."

She laughed at that but she didn't sound like she thought it was amusing. "Yeah. Sure. I could be a high-class girl working in some real fancy place earning good money. But you know what, I turned all those places down so I could be here getting poked by drunks, gamblers, and cowboys off the trail. And if I'm very lucky some of them knock me around. No, I don't want to leave here – I'd really miss getting my nose broke."

Johnny bit his lip at her bitter voice. Life was shit, and they both knew it. Some people had it so easy and then there were people like her. Lots of people like her. Who the hell decided who should be dealt a losing hand? God? The devil? "I'm sorry. Really. You got a name?"

"My name? It's Daisy. But I got to tell you, not many men ask me that. The only talking tends to be telling me what to put where." She sat up and pulled a thin robe around she shoulders. "Thanks for asking. Makes me feel I'm almost human."

Sharp blades of guilt stabbed at him. Sometimes it felt like those blades could pierce his soul. He fumbled in his jacket and pulled out a handful of notes and pressed them into her hand. "Do me a favor. There'll be a stage heading south this week to Cimarron. This will cover your fare. There's a bordello there. Tell the owner, Miss Martin, that I sent you. She'll take care of you. Promise me you'll do that."

She scoffed. "Cimarron? I've heard a lot of stories about that place. That's a rough town, just like this one is. I'm guessing whoring there will be the same as it is here. There'll always be cowpokes and drifters to give me a broken nose. A bordello ain't going to be no different from a saloon. What's so special about that bordello?"

"Miss Martin's special." He paused, as the truth of his words hit him. "Yeah, she's really special. She makes all the difference. She don't take no nonsense from any of the customers. She looks after her girls and none of them gets treated rough. I promise it'll be better." He looked around at the grubby room. It smelled of piss and sex and sweat, and hadn't seen a coat of paint in God only knew how many years. "Much better. It's clean and you'll be well-fed and I swear nobody will knock you around. You'll go?" Why? Why did he care so much that this girl, who'd simply opened her legs for him, should have something better than this place? Dios but he was loco at times.

She didn't speak for a few beats and then shrugged. "Yeah, OK. I'll give it a go. After all, if it ain't no better it don't make much difference. Might as well be poked in Cimarron as here. You want to do me again?" She reached out and felt his dick through his pants. "Kind of as a thank you for asking my name. And the money."

His dick stirred again. She rubbed harder. He shook his head. "I really got to go..."

She cupped his balls in her other hand, squeezing them gently as she carried on rubbing his dick. He shrugged himself out of his jacket.

CHAPTER FOUR

He didn't return to the hotel until the following morning. He burst into their room to find Guy stretched out on the bed, snoring. Johnny dragged him from his bed despite Guy's protests that he needed more sleep.

"Come on, Harvard, let's get the business side sorted out. And then, if you like, I'll take you to see where Bill Hickok spends most of his time."

"Hickok? Of course! I'd forgotten that he was marshal here. I'd love to see the man himself – he's quite a legend. Rather like yourself! Would he recognize you?"

Johnny shook his head. "I doubt it. I don't recall ever meeting him. Mind you," Johnny rummaged in Guy's saddle bags for a shirt and threw it to him, "he'd probably recognize what I am even if he doesn't know who I am."

Guy pulled the shirt on. "Do you think so? I would have thought he'd only recognize a gunfighter from the way he wore his gun."

Johnny shrugged. "A lot of shootists keep their guns hidden, so a man can't rely on that. But I think professionals have a certain look about them, it's something that only another pro would recognize. Something about the eyes, I guess. From what I hear, Hickok's a man who spins a lot of yarns about himself. I reckon half his stories are a load of bull but I do believe he's a damn good shot." He cast a critical eye over Guy who was busy tying a string tie. "Well, at least you look smarter than me. Maybe someone will do business with us. They'll probably all reckon I'm one of your ranch hands."

"Well, I'll certainly be interested to see Hickok – but later." Guy tugged on his boots. "Come on, let's go and sell cattle!"

Although the cattle business in the town was on the wane, there were still plenty of opportunities for trade. Guthrie had been right – lots of buyers could be met at Drover's Cottage. It was popular with wealthy cattle owners and was an oasis of comfort in the rough town.

Johnny and Guy avoided the saloons, preferring to discuss deals in the more peaceful environment of the hotel verandah over the next few days.

The majority of the ranchers staying there were from Texas. They'd driven their cattle up the Chisholm Trail to the railhead. And while the owners relaxed at Drovers Cottage, the cowboys kicked up a storm in town, blowing their wages in the saloon, at the gaming tables, or on the numerous whores who plied their trade. It was another reason for Johnny to avoid the main town. He sure as hell didn't want to be recognized. It was bound to lead to trouble.

But there were a fair number of southerners there too. They spoke differently, and dressed differently from the Texans. They weren't as loud, and appeared very gentlemanly in their behavior. Or so Johnny reckoned. But he noticed that Guy went out of his way to avoid them, always moving toward the Texans, or men from the other states. It puzzled Johnny because Guy was normally open and friendly with everyone. The war had been over for a few years and he hadn't figured Guy to be the sort of fellow to carry a grudge.

He asked Guy about it when they were getting ready to have dinner with a rancher who'd turned out to be an old friend of Guthrie. "I'm not avoiding them," snapped Guy. "Neither do I carry a grudge. Why should I have a grudge, for God's sake?"

Johnny shrugged. "I dunno. You tell me."

"We'll be late. You'd best catch up with me." Guy strode from the room letting the door slam behind him.

Johnny huffed out a sigh. Damn it, but Guy could be an irritating son of a bitch at times. Ever since they'd fought the Indians he'd been acting strange. He'd been having bad dreams too – he'd sure as hell woken Johnny up more than once in the past few days. Shaking his head, he followed Guy down to dinner.

Guthrie's old friend, Saul, turned out to be easy company,

although Johnny left most of the talking to Guy. Hell, it was what Guy did best and it left Johnny free to keep a watchful eye on the other diners. At times like this he couldn't help but wonder if he'd ever be able to relax in company. But maybe it was good that one of them was watchful, because he noticed that two men sitting at a nearby table seemed to be taking a great interest in them. Their heads were close together and they kept glancing at Guy, setting Johnny's senses on full alert. If he was honest they didn't look to be a threat. They looked like businessmen, not gunmen, but out west a man couldn't be too careful. It was how he'd survived all these years, and he wasn't about to start changing his habits now.

The men didn't approach them until after they finished their meal. Saul had said his goodbyes and left Johnny and Guy drinking coffee.

"Major Sinclair?" The taller of the two men raised an eyebrow and extended a hand. "It is Major Sinclair isn't it?"

Guy flushed and half-rose to his feet. "I'm sorry, do I know you? I don't quite recall..."

The man nodded, smiling broadly. "I'm Robert Curtis, and this"—he gestured toward his companion—"is my old friend George Lowell. We met you back in '64, initially on the first night of the battle at Trevilian Station. But then we met again when you were at General Sheridan's camp outside Woodstock. We were attached to Custer's crew. We had a grand evening, quite a feast too. Damn, but we ate well on that campaign!"

Guy nodded, and cast a quick sideways look at Johnny.

"Ah, yes, of course I remember now." The tips of his ears were red and he shifted from foot to foot.

Lowell grinned. "We insist you join us for drinks. It'll give us a chance to catch up on old times." He glanced dismissively at Johnny. "Perhaps your man could leave us. I don't think he'd be interested in our old war stories and reminiscences."

Guy flushed a deeper red. "Actually—"

Johnny cut across him. "I'll leave you to it, Mr. Sinclair, and see you in the morning." He bit back a smile at the astonished look on Guy's face. But hell, it would save him the embarrassment of having to introduce Johnny as his brother. He suspected that these men weren't the kind of men who would be impressed by Guy having a half-breed for a brother. He nodded at the two men. "Gentlemen, enjoy your evening."

The creaking of the opening door jolted Johnny awake. He'd been dozing in the chair, knowing he wouldn't sleep until Guy returned and he could finally lock the door. "You're late, Harvard. Have a good time did you?"

Guy huffed out a big sigh. "For God's sake, why did you wait up for me?"

Johnny smothered a yawn. "I wasn't waiting up. But you know me – I need to watch my back and I sure as hell can't relax until this door is locked." Johnny hauled himself to his feet and turned the key in the lock and then threw himself down on his bed.

Guy snorted. "It certainly seems as if you were waiting up for me."

Johnny rolled his eyes and ignored the comment. "Did you have a good time with your soldier friends?"

"They're not friends," snapped Guy. "Merely old acquaintances. And why, for heaven's sake, did you let them think you were one of my employees?"

Johnny raised an eyebrow at the accusing tone. "I figured that it might be awkward for you having to explain a half-brother who's part Apache, that's all. They looked to be the type of men who don't think much of Indians. Makes no difference to me that they probably thought I was one of your ranch hands." He shrugged. "Anyway, I reckoned you'd enjoy an evening with them. Seems to me that old soldiers always like swapping stories and talking about the past."

Guy glared. "I don't wish to reminisce about the war." He tugged his boots off. "With them, you, or anybody else. Goodnight."

Manuel had pushed the herd hard and arrived sooner than Johnny expected, so by the time he and Guy had lined up a prospective buyer, the herd was grazing outside of town ready for inspection. After that, all that was left to do was see the herd loaded at the stockyard. As a reward to themselves, Guy had reminded Johnny that he'd promised a visit to the Alamo Saloon where Bill Hickok was the central attraction.

Now Johnny found himself sitting at a corner table regretting his rash promise. Did all gunfighters hate saloons? Or was it only him? All he knew was he hated them at the best of times. Hated the noise, the smell, and the people.

Even though he was supposed to have left his gun fighting days behind and no longer hired out, he still couldn't relax. And although he knew that he didn't want his old life back, his past had a way of creeping up on him. So now here he was with his back to the wall, watching the room for any sign of trouble, because old habits die hard.

It was easy for Guy – there was nothing in his past that could come back to haunt him. He was a respectable citizen – a son of whom any father could be proud.

He watched Guy snake his way across the crowded room holding two glasses of beer in front of him like weapons. Johnny bit back a smile as a burly cowboy collided with Guy, splashing the beer over his brother's jacket. The cowboy boomed out an apology and proceeded to clear a path, hefting people out of the way, allowing Guy to reach their table without any further spillage.

Guy sank onto a battered bentwood chair and shoved the emptier of the glasses at Johnny, before raising his own glass in a mock toast.

Johnny took a long swig and cast a sour look at Hickok's table, where the big man was telling some complicated story of which he was the hero. "He sure likes the sound of his own voice."

"Does he always carry two guns?" asked Guy.

Johnny glanced at the two ivory-handled pistols which Hickok wore in a wide red sash. "His Navy Colts? Yeah. See the way he wears them with the handles turned forward, that's because he uses a twist draw."

Guy leaned forward, apparently trying to take a better look at the guns. "Is that the best way?"

Johnny rolled his eyes. "It ain't that simple. If it was the 'best' way, we'd all wear our guns like that. It's whatever works best for the shootist. But," he looked again at the two Colts, "I always reckon that wearing two guns is kind of brash."

"So the second gun is only for show?" Guy frowned.

Johnny shook his head. "In his case no. From what I hear he's damned accurate with either hand, and he's fast. And equally important, he's got a cool head." Johnny took another swift look at Hickok. "Truth to tell, I'd be interested to see who's faster – him or me."

Guy paled and jerked forward. "You're not going to put that to the test are you?"

Johnny grinned. "No, I ain't. Top guns never look for trouble with each other if they got any sense. If they did, they sure wouldn't live long! I'm just curious, that's all. Although" he paused and glanced once more at Hickok's table, "someone I knew, who'd seen him in action, said he reckoned I was faster." He pushed his glass around the table. "Anyway, you've seen him now. And I'll be glad to get outta here. Out of Abilene and away from all these people."

Guy rolled his eyes. "The trouble with you, is that you are essentially unfriendly. You'd never have fitted in at my clubs back east. You are not a sociable person. But now you've left your old life behind, and are supposed to be a respectable rancher, you really must try to adopt a friendlier demeanor and make more effort to be pleasant."

Johnny took a long slow look around the customers in the saloon and then swiveled back to eye his brother. "Pleasant? To this bunch of wastrels?" He shook his head and reached into his jacket for the makings and proceeded to roll a cigarette. He might as well add to the cloud of smoke.

"You don't know they're wastrels." Guy glanced around, his gaze resting briefly on a couple of drunks sliding from their chairs and sinking under a table. "Well, not all of them, at any rate. I imagine a lot of them are here to do exactly what we're doing – gawk at Bill Hickok."

Johnny grunted, and took a drag on his cigarette. "I ain't gawking, he don't impress me. But, never mind about him. You're too trusting, that's your trouble. You're like our old man. He's got lousy judgment when it comes to people. And no, I sure as hell wouldn't fit in at your clubs out east, and I wouldn't want to. And I wouldn't have fitted into your Yankee army either. Can you see me taking orders from anyone?"

Guy's easy smile faded. "Why do you always bring up the army?"

Johnny frowned. "I don't always bring up the army. Was just saying, that's all." He gulped his beer back as he glanced at the door. "But if you don't want to talk about the army then you'd better drink up. Your two friends from the other night just walked in."

Guy jerked his head around to look at the fellows. "I told you, they're not friends and I want to get out of here now." He pushed his chair back, leaving his drink unfinished, and stalked out of the saloon.

CHAPTER FIVE

It was a relief when the cattle were loaded onto the cars at the railhead. Johnny had seen more than enough of Abilene and was eager to start the long trek back to the ranch. He hoped, once they left town and headed home, Guy's mood might improve too.

"When we get through Indian country, you and I could take a couple of the vaqueros and go on ahead. We'd make faster time. And I reckon the old man would be glad to have us back to help out. He's short-handed while we're on the drive." He figured it was the best way to get Guy back in a good mood.

It worked too. Guy jumped at the prospect of getting home ahead of the crew. So, once they reached safer territory, Johnny, Guy, and two of the more experienced men, left the main party to follow on behind, tasked with the job of keeping the spare horses, supplies, and chuck wagon safe.

As it turned out, his plan pleased their old man too. Guthrie welcomed them like returning heroes, clapping them on the backs.

"It was Johnny's idea," Guy said when their father

congratulated them on their speedy return.

Guthrie smiled broadly at Johnny. "It was a fine idea, son. It's always hard when we have so many hands tied up with a cattle drive. It means extra work all around for the men who are left here, but the work piles up even so. Believe me, they'll be doubly pleased to see you back.

"Anyway come on inside and tell me how you got on."

The old man hadn't been wrong when he said the work had piled up. For the next few days Johnny worked from dawn to dusk, falling into his bed immediately after dinner. So, later in the week, when he'd finished his last chore of the day with time in hand, he breathed a sigh of relief and figured maybe he'd treat himself to a soak in the tub.

He enjoyed a leisurely ride home to the ranch. As he reined in Pistol by the barn he glanced at the house and groaned. An unfamiliar buggy was outside and that meant visitors. The last thing he wanted was to be forced into small talk with strangers.

He threw his right leg across Pistol's withers and jumped down, then led him into the barn. Maybe he could sneak into the house without being noticed and hide out in his room until supper time.

He gave Pistol a rub down and a quick feed, before pocketing his spurs and cat-footing across the courtyard to the side door of the hacienda. He eased it shut behind him and sidled through the back hall, hoping to make it to the stairs unheard.

The murmur of voices came from the living room. He could hear Guy's measured tones, and a voice he didn't recognize talking louder than anyone else. "Of course, I knew the Reverends John Smithett and John Burrell well. I am proud to say that they always treated me like one of their own. I regularly visited each of them at the Old North Church in your home city before the war. A very beautiful old church. Doubtless that was your place of worship when you lived on Beacon Hill."

"Yes, my mother's family had their own pew. And of course I remember both of those gentlemen well."

Dios. That sounded like real dull stuff.

"Unfortunately my ministry in Boston was far too brief. I would have liked to have spent more time there. But God's will must be done, and the church moves its ministers around. After Boston, I was sent to minister in the south. To Virginia. My family had its roots there. It was so tragic when the war occurred. So unnecessary. I believe you fought in the war for the Union—"

"That was a long time ago." Guy cut across whoever was talking.

"I heard tell that you were in the cavalry with Sheridan's men. You must have seen action in the south."

Tiptoeing, Johnny edged to the bottom of the stairs. He grinned. Almost home and dry.

"There's my other son now. Johnny, come and meet Cimarron's new Reverend and his wife." Guthrie's voice sounded kind of strained.

Johnny sighed softly. Just when he'd thought he wouldn't be spotted, trust Guthrie to see him through the open door. He hated making small talk to strangers. He hadn't got Guy's easy manner. Though judging from Guy's tense shoulders and ramrod straight back, he wasn't enjoying it either. Johnny forced his mouth into something approaching a smile and headed in.

The Reverend could have done with losing a few pounds and then some. He had the kind of self-satisfied air that so many of his type had. God only knew why he should look so pleased with life, because his skinny wife wasn't doing him no favors. She had a face that would turn milk sour.

A flicker of relief crossed Guy's face. "Well, I'll leave you with my father and brother. Please do excuse me; I have some rather pressing business to attend to." Guy may have sounded polite, but he had the look of a man who couldn't wait to escape. Seemed he wasn't too taken with the unexpected visitors. And who could blame him.

Johnny bit back a sigh and moved forward to be introduced. "Sorry, I just got in from the range. I'm really not fit for company." He gave what he hoped was an apologetic smile as his father waved him into the room.

"Don't worry about that, son." Guthrie shot him a strangely pleading smile. Kind of like he was desperate for some company now that Guy had abandoned him. "I'd like to introduce my younger son, Johnny. Johnny, this is Reverend Hausmann and his wife. Luther Vonn retired while you were on the cattle drive. The Reverend has taken over the ministry of the Episcopalian church in town."

Mrs. Hausmann didn't look none too impressed by the old man's "younger son." She inclined her head, but her lip curled, and she looked like she'd stumbled over a rotting coyote.

But her husband had no trouble making his thoughts known. "Ah, so this is the black sheep of your family, Mr. Sinclair. We've been in Cimarron for only a short time but we've already heard many tales of this young man's sinful ways, and we have been praying for his soul."

Guthrie's mouth dropped open; if it stayed that way he'd be catching flies. Still, it was worth being insulted just to see the old man lost for words. Johnny bit back a grin. "That's real thoughtful of you, Reverend. I reckon the more people praying for my soul, the better. It needs all the help it can get."

Guthrie made an odd choking noise. Johnny tried his broadest smile and moved swiftly to pat his father vigorously on the back. "You okay there, Guthrie? Sounds like you got something stuck in your craw." He gave the old man a wink before turning back to face the Reverend Hausmann and his vinegary wife.

"So, what do you think of Cimarron, Mrs. Hausmann? Are you settling in? I'm guessing from your talk with my brother that you're from out east. You must find this to be a lot different from life back there."

She sniffed, still looking like she'd come across something real unpleasant. "I think the west is a very sinful and wicked place, young man. From what we've seen, it's full of desperados and gunmen." She gave Johnny a long hard look. "As my husband said, we are praying for your soul."

Guthrie's mouth tightened, and the nerve started pulsing in his temple, same as always when he was getting riled. He opened his mouth to speak, so Johnny cut across him. There was no point in letting Guthrie lose his temper, the man would only regret it later. "Well, like I said, Ma'am, I need all the help I can get."

The minister glared at Johnny. "A soul is not a matter for levity, young man. I should think it would do you good to attend our services with your family." He shot an oily smile toward Guthrie. "I understand from my predecessor, Mr. Sinclair, that you and the rest of your family are regular attendants at the services. Perhaps you should ensure in the future that your younger son attends with you."

Guthrie glared. "Johnny was brought up in the Catholic faith; that is why he doesn't attend services with us."

The Reverend patted his forehead with a large handkerchief and waved his hand like that didn't matter none. "Mr. Sinclair, I have made inquiries, and I understand that your son doesn't attend the Catholic mission either. That is why I firmly believe he is need of the guidance that my church can offer him."

Guthrie was starting to go a real funny color and it sure didn't look healthy. Johnny interrupted again. "That's real thoughtful of you, Reverend, and if I decide to change faith I'll bear it in mind. So, I guess you got a lot to do moving into new territory. Do you have any plans? Other than worrying about my soul?" Johnny smiled innocently.

"The good Lord always finds work for me to do." The Reverend smiled smugly.

His wife chipped in. "Cimarron is full of sinners. We have also discovered that there is a house of ill repute in the town."

Johnny furrowed his brow. A house of ill repute? What the hell was that? "Oh! You mean the bordello. Well, yeah, the town has got that and a couple of saloons."

"We shall ensure that it is closed down." Mrs. Hausmann looked very pleased at the notion.

Johnny stared at her. "Closed down? Why?" What the hell was wrong with folks that they had to interfere in other people's pleasures?

"Because it is sinful. Those dreadful fallen women are a stain on the town's good name." She flushed red, like even the mention of those women was an embarrassment.

Johnny cocked his head to one side and looked at her. Her mouth was a thin, tight line and she'd gotten deep lines from all her frowning. "Ma'am, you ever been in a bordello?" He tried to look innocent when he asked.

She flushed an unpleasant brick color, kind of like the color of the mesas in Utah and Arizona. But before she got the chance to answer, her husband, who'd also turned a kind of odd color, chipped in. "We have neither of us, ever ventured into such a den of iniquity! What sort of people do you take us for, young man? I find your levity ill mannered."

Guthrie made another kind of choking sound. Johnny tried to look apologetic. "No offence intended, Reverend. I only wondered how you know it's so evil if you ain't ever been inside one. The girls are real nice."

The man struggled to his feet, breathing heavily at the effort. "One doesn't need to venture into Hell to know that it's full of sinners. My wife and I have overseen the closure of such sordid places in other towns; Cimarron will be no different. Mr. Sinclair, thank you for your gracious hospitality. But I venture to say, that having met your son, you should ensure that he attends church regularly."

Guthrie rose to his feet. "Thank you, Reverend Hausmann. I will be sure to pass your message on to Guy. I am sure he will appreciate your concern for his soul."

Hausmann turned an even deeper shade of red. "It was not your elder son—"

Guthrie beamed at him. "Well, we mustn't keep you from the Lord's work. Thank you for calling." And with that Guthrie swung his arm around the man and propelled him to the door. "Good day, Reverend Hausmann. Mrs. Hausmann."

Guthrie slammed the door shut on them, and turning to Johnny, exploded into laughter. "What a poisonous couple! You handled them brilliantly, Johnny."

Johnny jerked his head up in surprise. He'd been half-expecting the old man to bawl him out for not being polite. He felt a warm glow inside, like he always did when the old man praised him. But even so, there was a niggle of worry at the back of his mind. "Can they do that?"

Guthrie sank down on the couch, still laughing. "Do what?"

"Close the bordello down?" Surely people couldn't close a place down just because they didn't like it? Could they? "I mean, they pay their taxes, they ain't doing anything illegal, are they?"

Guthrie shrugged. "I suppose if the town council made it an offence against the bylaws, maybe they could get it closed down. But the Hausmanns would have to get the majority of the council in favor of such a move. I should think the councilors have more important things to worry about."

Johnny muttered an oath under his breath. People could be real tricky at times and he didn't trust the Hausmanns at all. But maybe Cimarron wouldn't bend over backwards to help them. Maybe enough men used the bordello not to want to see it disappear. Dios. This was all he needed. He sure as hell couldn't lose Delice. Or the girls. They were friends. And there wasn't nobody going to hurt his friends.

"I'll tell you one thing, Johnny." Guthrie beamed across the room. "When I first arrived in this territory, the Mexican authorities said people who wanted to purchase land out here had to become Catholic. So, like everyone who bought land at that time, I converted, but like most other cattlemen out here, I've reverted to the faith I was brought up in. But having met the Revered Hausmann, I think I might have to abandon our Episcopalian church and take up Catholicism again. Either that or go Methodist!"

The brief flare of a match lit the darkness before dying, leaving only the faint whispering glow of a cigar to light the night.

He'd been out there a while now. He'd stalked out before they'd hardly finished eating. Hell, Guy had almost forgotten to thank Peggy for a nice dinner like he usually did. He'd hesitated in the doorway, thanked her briefly, and then gone outside.

Guy had sat through dinner looking like he had a broom handle up his butt. And hadn't said a word.

Not a single word. He hadn't joined in with any of the talk about the new reverend. Instead, he'd pushed his food around his plate and looked like he'd rather be anywhere other than with his family.

Johnny chewed on his lip as he paced around the room. The old man sat in his favorite chair with a book resting on his knee. But whether he was reading the book was another matter altogether. Either Guthrie took even longer to read something than he did, or he wasn't reading it. He sure hadn't been turning the pages.

Johnny paused in his pacing and peered out into the darkness again. All men had secrets; he of all people should know that. Hell, Fierro had far more than most anyone. But he reckoned that his brother was carrying some secret about his time in the army, and the secret was weighing him down. It was as if the run in with the Comanches had set something off, and it didn't look like it was going away any time soon.

Johnny shook his head. He'd seen the look on Guy's face immediately after the Reverend had mentioned the war. And he'd seen how Guy couldn't get out of the room fast enough.

He'd reckoned that Guy was entitled to his secret. But as it was eating away at him, maybe the time had come to talk about it. Time to ask Harvard why he never talked about the war or the army. Hell. Guy was always pushing Johnny for stories about his past, but he never said a damn word about his own. Johnny sucked in a breath. Yeah. The time had come.

He moved swiftly to the liquor cabinet and poured a generous measure of tequila and a measure of Guthrie's best malt before turning toward the door which opened out onto the terrace.

"Leave him be." Guthrie looked up from the book that Johnny figured he hadn't been reading.

Johnny shrugged. "I thought he could use a drink."

Guthrie gave him one of those looks. The kind that said he didn't believe a word of it. "You're spoiling for a fight. I've been watching you."

Johnny grunted in irritation. "I know you been watching me. I could feel your eyes on me. And I ain't spoiling for a fight, as you put it. I'm going to take him a drink, that's all."

Guthrie raised an eyebrow. "And I said leave him be."

Johnny rolled his eyes. "Is that an order?"

The old man didn't answer; simply gave him another of those looks.

Johnny leaned against the cabinet and raised an eyebrow. "We told you we had a run-in with some Comanches on the way to Abilene, and we kind of made light of it to you. But I might as well tell you, it was rough. And it was a close run thing." He paused, watching his father pale. "You know how tough those sons of bitches are. But Guy, he did OK. And I told him so too. But that fight, it's like it stirred something up in him. Something to do with the war. Then in Abilene he met some fellows he knew in the army and that's kind of made things worse. And today, when that Reverend mentioned the war, Guy couldn't get outta the room fast enough. You must have noticed. You couldn't hardly miss it! But something's eating away at him and I want to know what it is. Don't you?"

"I think it's his business, not ours." Guthrie sounded kind of even. Like he wasn't going to rise to anything.

"You didn't answer the question." Johnny slammed the two glasses down on the table next to him, the liquid splashing over the polished oak.

Guthrie's jaw tightened just a touch. "It's not uncommon for men not to want to talk of their experiences in war. I believe that if Guy wants to tell us about it, he will. Otherwise it's none of our business."

"How the hell can you say it's none of our business? He's your son, damn it! And anyway, how come it's fine for Guy to not talk about things but you're always poking your nose into my past? You're always asking me questions. Fishing." He bit his lip. He sounded like some little kid, but hell, it wasn't right that there seemed to be one rule for Guy but a totally different one for him.

"That's different." The old man sounded wrong footed. Like he was real put out about being called on his own behavior.

Johnny cocked his head to one side and narrowed his eyes. "Different? Exactly how is it different?"

Guthrie laid the book down and drew in a deep breath. Then he paused, like he was stalling for time or maybe just trying to control his temper. "It's different," he spoke slowly, like he was making a point. "Because although you were born here, I never had the opportunity to know you. You were so young when your mother left and took you away." He paused and shook his head, looking kind of sad. "I expected you to grow up here. You should have grown up here. But you didn't, and so naturally, when you came home after all those years away, I wanted to find out all about you. Get to *know* you." He stressed the word know, like it was important. "Guy I knew. Although he was only seven when I had to send him away to stay with his aunt and uncle in Boston because of the Indian raids around here, I corresponded with him. I knew what was going on in his life." The old man hesitated again. "But you were a stranger when you arrived here. It's different."

Johnny stared at the floor, scuffing the toe of his boot back and forth, leaving a mark in the dust. For a second he almost bought the old man's line. Funny to think that he'd been born here. If only he could remember something from those early years. But the only memory, and even that wasn't really a memory, was his mountain. All he knew was that when he'd first arrived at the ranch, and had stood at his bedroom window looking out, it had looked familiar, and that he felt a pull to it. But otherwise, he might as well have been born in Mexico because he sure couldn't feel any other ties to the ranch. And the fact that he was born here didn't matter none right now. It didn't alter the fact that Guy was obviously in a hell of a state about something and was being real secretive about his past. And Johnny couldn't help but wonder why.

He looked back up at his father and cocked an eyebrow. "Well as you know him so much better than me, I guess you know where he served and what he did in the war."

Guthrie flushed red. "Obviously he informed me when he decided to join the cavalry, but... but communications were difficult at that time."

Johnny laughed softly. "So what you're really saying is you don't know anything about his war service at all. Or you do know something and for some reason you don't want to tell me. But the fact is I want to know a bit more about Guy and I reckon he owes me some answers. So, I'm going to go and have a talk with him, whether you like it or not." Johnny picked up the glasses and with a brief nod headed out to the terrace, Guthrie's sigh echoing in his ears.

It took a few heart beats for his eyes to grow accustomed to the darkness. If it hadn't been for the smell of cigar smoke he would have sworn he was alone. Then he saw the glow of the cigar as Guy turned.

"Brought you a drink." Johnny held the glass of malt out but Guy didn't move to take it.

"I didn't ask for one." Guy's tone was cool.

Johnny sighed. "No, you didn't. But I figured you could use one." He tilted his head, wishing he could make out Guy's face better in the darkness. "At dinner it seemed like you were someplace else." Johnny hesitated. "If I'm honest, it's like you been someplace else ever since our fight with them Comanches. Then there was the business with the army fellows who you'd met in some battle. Trevilian was it? Something like that, anyway. And when Hausmann started on today about the war, hell, you almost ran out the room. So, I can't help but wonder what's going on. As you seem to always want stories about my past, I'm kind of curious about yours and the war." Johnny waited to see if the tone of his voice would get a rise out of Guy.

He didn't have to wait long.

"If I had wanted to talk about the war, I would have done so. Frankly, it is none of your business." Guy's tone was icy enough to freeze an ocean.

Johnny laughed humorlessly. "Yeah, well, that's all fine and dandy. But it seems to me that you want it all your way. You been pushing and pushing me since I first came here, wanting to know about me and all sorts of things that ain't your business. You been acting like you had a right to know, being brothers an' all. But that only cuts one way then?" Johnny paused. "Hell, anyone would think you're trying to hide something or maybe that you're ashamed of something."

Guy hissed in a breath. Johnny allowed himself a small smile. Yep. Seemed like he'd touched a nerve. But what the hell could Guy be covering up? He was an honorable man – Johnny was certain of that much about his brother.

"So." Johnny held the glass out. "Have your drink and then you can tell me all about it."

"I don't want the drink. And neither do I intend discussing my past with you. It's my business and that's an end of the matter." Guy blew out a cloud of smoke which hung in the air briefly before stealing away on the light breeze.

"But you like discussing mine?" Johnny laughed softly. "All those stories I told you. And you haven't given anything back. Not a single thing. And I can't for the life of me figure out why." Johnny paused, shaking his head slowly. "What are you hiding? I can understand that you don't want to dwell on the war, but this goes beyond that. Surely you can tell me something."

Johnny waited. He'd got time enough to wait. And it always worked. Men always wanted to fill silences.

"Leave it alone, Johnny. It's none of your damn business and that's an end of it." Guy turned to head back into the hacienda.

Johnny stepped in front of him, blocking his path. "Where's the harm, Harvard? I only asked for you to tell me something about your war service. What's wrong with that?"

He could see Guy's eyes now. There was enough light spilling out from inside to light Guy's face; a face filled with despair? Guilt? Anger? Shit, he couldn't even begin to figure what Guy was thinking.

Guy narrowed his eyes. "I'll thank you to get out of my way. I pack quite a punch in case you've forgotten."

Johnny sighed. He hadn't forgotten. The memory of Guy's punches after the shoot-out in Bitterville weren't a thing any man would forget. It had surprised him that the Eastern dandy could hit that hard. "No, Guy. I ain't forgotten. But I reckon you've forgotten some of the stories I told you. Things I've never told anyone else." He met Guy's gaze and then played what he hoped would be his trump card. "Stories I told you because I trusted you."

Guy bowed his head. He took another drag on his cigar and then shrugged. "I was in the cavalry and we saw a lot of action. Battles... like the Battle of Trevilian Station. That was chaos. Absolute chaos. Thousands of cavalry men in hand to hand fighting."

"Chaos? I guess war must always be chaos." Johnny spoke softly. Maybe now Guy might open up a bit.

"We had the superior numbers, possibly a third as many soldiers again as the Rebs. We were tasked to make a raid along the railroad and destroy the road at Gordonsville before carrying on to Charlottesville to destroy a supply depot."

Guy paused, shaking his head. "There were about nine thousands of us when we started out. It was quite a sight. Two divisions of cavalry and four batteries of horse artillery. It ended up as an all-out cavalry battle which raged over two days."

Johnny leaned back against the wall and waited. The silence stretched out, filling the night.

Guy sighed heavily. "Although the first day went in our favor, the second day went against us. On the first day, Custer was surrounded by the forces of Hampton and Lee, so we attacked Hampton's men to relieve Custer and pushed them back several miles. The next day we didn't fare so well. We destroyed railroad track before attacking Hampton's position. On foot. All of those lives lost... And it was all for nothing." His voice was bitter. "The Rebs repaired that railroad track within two weeks."

Guy paused again, his head down, like he was lost in memories. "Are you happy now? That's all you're getting. There is nothing more to say." Guy turned away, looking up at the night sky. There were no stars and no moon. It was as dark as Guy's mood.

Johnny studied Guy's profile in the darkness. Something was gnawing at the man, but what? He didn't believe that it was only the memories of a battle. Not that that wouldn't be enough to upset most men – it would. But, no, there was more to Guy's mood than that. He knew he shouldn't push this, but he was certain that Guy would feel better if he would only talk about whatever was eating him up. But would Guy say any more than he'd just said? Somehow, he doubted it. Unless he could push him a little more in the hope Guy would let something slip. Would it work? Only one way to find out. "You lost a lot of men? Friends, maybe?"

"Of course I lost friends. And comrades." Guy swung around almost like he wanted to hit Johnny, his voice bitter. "Sheridan lost more than seven hundred men in the two day battle. Either killed or wounded. We left many wounded men behind. Are you happy now?"

Johnny sighed. Seven hundred. That was a lot of men. "And this place, Woodstock, those army fellows mentioned. Where was that?

"I don't wish to talk anymore about it." Guy downed his drink. "It's unimportant."

"No." Johnny shook his head. "It's not unimportant, as you put it. I'm interested to know about it."

"And I said it wasn't important."

"I only asked where Woodstock is. What's wrong with telling me that, damn it?"

"I've told you something, you should be happy now. And beyond that, I think you should mind your own damn business." Then Guy stepped around him and strode into the hacienda.

Johnny swung himself up to sit on the low wall which ran around Peggy's rose garden. Despite the heady scents hanging in the warm night air, it felt as cold as tomb. Happy? Nope, he sure wasn't happy. And neither was Guy. The only question was why?

CHAPTER SIX

He gave the fence post one last savage blow, driving it deeper into the ground. Damn it, but he was sick of fence posts. Sometimes it felt like his entire life revolved around posts and fences. Either sinking them or mending them or stringing wire. When he'd accepted his father's offer of a share in the ranch, he'd figured his life would involve riding, rounding up and driving cattle. That was what cowboys did, or so he'd thought. So much for that idea. He stepped back and slowly stretched from side to side trying to ease the ache between his shoulder blades.

His shirt clung to his back, and beads of sweat trickled down his face. He ripped his gloves off, and took a hefty swig from his canteen before slumping down on the ground, leaning against a gnarled tree trunk. Driving in damn fence posts wasn't going to block out the memory of how he'd screwed things up with Guy. And he had screwed things up, for ever since their conversation on the terrace Guy had been very cool.

Johnny poured a splash of his water over his head and then

shook it like a dog. Thinking back, he couldn't believe how badly he'd handled things. He, of all people, knew that demanding answers wasn't the way to go about getting people to spill their secrets. But it was like someone else had been in control of him, and he'd been aggressive instead of being cunning and employing his more usual methods of sniffing out information.

But if he was honest about it, the way Guy was acting bothered him, a lot.

After all they'd been through together since he'd come home to the ranch, after all the confidences that Johnny had shared, Guy hadn't trusted him enough to tell him anything about his own past. And of course, the dumbest thing was that if Guy had told him something when he first asked about the war, Johnny wouldn't be so fired up to find out more. He'd have said something to try and show he understood, and then he'd have backed off and left it alone.

Trouble was, with Guy being so damned secretive, it was pretty clear that he was trying to hide something. And because Johnny had lumbered in like a great buffalo, he'd simply put Guy on the alert and that was going to make uncovering the truth harder. But what the hell could he be trying to cover up? He could understand a man not wanting to talk about war and killing, but his gut was telling him that something else was eating at his brother.

Johnny shook his head. It was a real puzzle, and he couldn't figure it at all.

But Guy was hurting. And he hated that. Hated it as much

as he hated that Guy didn't trust him.

Still, if he was going to find out what was troubling his brother, he'd need to be a damn sight more devious. He needed to get Guy thinking that he'd lost interest in talking about it. And maybe then Guy would drop his guard. But in the meantime he'd try to find out more about that damn war to figure out what the whole mystery was about.

Trying to get comfortable, he shuffled into a different position against the tree. It didn't help. Dios, but he was aching and sitting here wasn't doing him no favors. Sighing heavily, he swiped the sweat off his face and hauled himself back to his feet. Time to head back. Hopefully there'd be something decent for dinner. Maybe Carlita would be cooking. And that meant decent food – Mexican food. Not the bland gringo food that Peggy turned out.

And when he'd eaten, he could get to plotting. Hell, it was what he did best.

He hadn't even got the energy to take his boots off. And if he had to sink another post he might just shoot someone; probably the old man. He'd spent the whole week fencing in a new area of graze they'd bought when Porter's ranch had been split up and sold. Maybe Guthrie had figured if he was all worn out, it would keep him from hassling Guy. If that had been his father's plan, it had certainly worked. He'd hardly had the energy to stumble upstairs each evening, never mind figuring out what the hell Guy was covering up. He couldn't say that Guy was avoiding him since they'd talked, but he was sure keeping his distance. And making sure that they were never on their own together. Kind of like he was scared rigid that Johnny would start in on him again.

So he made a point of being extra friendly with Guy. All relaxed and casual like he'd forgotten all about their discussion. And he even started all sorts of talk about nothing at all. What was it they called it? Making conversation, that was it. Guy had looked surprised at that. But he'd answered politely. He'd even explained who the two "reverends" were that the interfering old goat, Hausmann, had mentioned. Seemed they'd each run the church Guy had gone to when he was a kid in Boston. One of them had even been involved in some sort of court case. Kind of odd to think of religious men stirring up so much trouble they ended up in court. Weren't they supposed to spend their time tending their flock, or on their knees praying? Well, maybe that was what they should do, but in Johnny's experience most of them didn't. No. They were mostly interfering old buzzards, like Hausmann, who couldn't mind their own business.

And then, because of all the talk about the church in Boston, he couldn't help but wonder what Guy had been like when he was a kid. Would they have gotten along if they'd grown up together at the ranch? Would they both have been different to how they'd turned out?

He tried to push the thought away. The thought that there

had been somewhere safe all along for him when he was a kid. Safe from Mama's men. But it didn't do to think on that because otherwise he got to wondering about why she hadn't sent him home. Surely a loving

mother would have wanted her son to be safe? He shook his head. He had to stop thinking like that. She'd done the best she could and that was an end of it.

He should clean his guns. He hadn't done it for days because he'd been so worn out each night from the damn fence posts. But knowing they needed cleaning made him fret. He couldn't relax until they were done. He could get called out any time and he sure as hell didn't want his gun letting him down because he hadn't cleaned it regular. To hell with that. If someone wanted his reputation they could damn well earn it.

The other thing he should do was go into town and see if Delice was all right. He hadn't had the chance since he returned home from the cattle drive. He wanted to make sure the Hausmanns were leaving her and her girls alone. What was it with some people that made them think they were better than others?

He fished out a bottle of gun oil from the big chest of drawers. The chest was kind of ornate, all carved with birds and trees. And not carved too well. He reckoned he could do it better himself, but it was handy for storing his boxes of bullets and rifle shells. Maybe that was why it was so big. Surely no man would have enough clothes to fill it? Well, except maybe Guy. He'd never known a man have as many clothes as Guy. And most of them were kind of odd – so many ties, gloves, and fancy shirts. Johnny shuddered, spilling a bit of the gun oil on the bed cover.

Johnny shook his head as he took his fighting gun to pieces. He'd never figure out Guy's odd taste in clothes and gloves. It must be an Eastern thing.

With luck he could get into town on Friday or Saturday. Go and see Delice and check up on things. Maybe she'd know about this damn gringo war that Guy had been in. She was kind of smart. Smartest person he'd ever met, even though she was a woman. Yeah, that would be the best thing. Go talk to Delice – always provided that the old man didn't have him doing the books on either of those nights.

He finally escaped on Saturday, heaving a huge sigh of relief as he and Pistol loped down the long driveway. The old man had wanted him to spend the evening doing the books, but maybe it was the look in Johnny's eyes which had made Guthrie back down. If his father hadn't backed off, Johnny might just have shot him. God only knew he'd been trying to settle since coming home, but at times all the boring day-to-day routines crowded in on him, and he felt like he was being corralled same as the horses. And at times like that, he needed to escape from his father's disapproving frown.

Once he was out of sight of the ranch, he pulled Pistol back to an easy lope, wanting to enjoy the warm evening.

He spied a litter of kit fox pups playing, enjoying rolling

over and play-fighting, while their mother stood guard close by. The pups glanced across at him, hesitating only briefly before carrying on with their game. Watching them helped leach some of the tension out of his shoulders and he rode on with a smile.

Cimarron was already lively when he rode in. Jarring music was belting out from the saloon where a bunch of men were gathered, talking by the door. And over by the small parade of shops there were folks out for an evening stroll, stopping to look in the windows whenever something caught their eye. He tethered Pistol and ambled over to Stoney's office to scrounge a cup of coffee before he headed to the bordello.

Stoney was poring over a pile of wanted posters which covered his desk and most of the floor. Johnny made a show of trying to step around them, but managed to scuff some of them up and leave muddy marks on them.

"Dang it, Fierro! Watch where you're putting your big feet." Stoney glared at him.

Johnny shrugged. "If you cover the floor with damn posters, folks can't help but step on them." Johnny attempted to perch on the side of the desk, but succeeded in sending another pile cascading to the floor. He grinned at Stoney's pained expression. "Any chance of a cup of coffee?"

Stoney grunted. "If it gets you out of my office quicker, help yourself. Provided you can do it without spilling the water. No, on second thought I'll damn well do it myself. I know you'll only mess the place up." Stoney pushed him to one side and set about brewing some of his foul smelling coffee. "So, to what do I owe the honor of a visit from you on a Saturday night? Thought you'd be straight off into the bordello."

Johnny grinned. "I figured I'd come and see an old friend. Kind of catch up on the town gossip. And I don't have to pay for the coffee here. So, what's been going on in town? What with the cattle drive and all, it feels like years since I was last here. The old man don't ever let up on me."

Stoney handed Johnny a steaming mug of coffee. "He'll turn you into a rancher yet, boy. Reckon you should give up fighting it." Stoney slurped his coffee noisily as he sank back into his chair, sending yet more posters flying. "We got a new reverend in town. Have you met him?"

Johnny pulled a face as he took a sip of the bitter coffee. "Yeah. He showed up at the ranch with his sour-faced wife. Has he been making waves?"

Stoney snorted. "Making waves! You bet he's been making waves. He's a real pain in the ass and he's busy poking his nose into everyone's business. Interfering son of a bitch."

Johnny eyed the posters curiously, thumbing through one of the piles. "You looking for someone in particular, Stoney? You got posters here going back years."

Stoney shrugged. "I was hoping I might recognize a fellow I had in the cells this week. I know damn well he gave me a false name. Jones!" Stoney shook his head in disgust. "You'd think he could come up with something better than that."

Johnny bit back a smile. "Stoney, hate to tell you but some folks are called Jones. Maybe it really was his name."

Stoney's eyes narrowed. "I know some folk are called Jones, but I don't reckon he was. He was as crooked as a corkscrew and had a mean streak a mile wide. The sort of man who'll never look you in the eye for long. Big fellow with fair hair, and a scar on his face and on his arm. And I know he's trouble."

Johnny huffed out a sigh. He wasn't interested in Stoney's former prisoners. "I didn't come in only for coffee. I wanted to ask you if you know anything about the gringo war between the states. Anything about Sheridan's unit?"

Stoney tensed and then shook his head. "Nope. I had other things on my mind at that time. I didn't pay the war much heed." The expression in his eyes warned Johnny against saying anything else about those years. Thinking on it now, he figured it would have been around that time that Stoney was hunting the men who'd killed his family. Johnny nodded casually, like he accepted the words at face value. He didn't want to stir up bad memories for Stoney. Maybe a change of subject was for the best. "So, what'd this man do? Why d'you lock him up?"

The change of tack worked; a flicker of relief showed on Stoney's face. "Oh, he was drunk and stirring up trouble. Then he went on the rampage and smashed up the bordello. I figured he needed some time to cool—"

Johnny jerked upright, spilling his coffee down his jacket. "Damn it, Stoney! Why the hell didn't you say so before? Did he hurt anyone? Are Delice and the girls all OK?" He could feel a knot of fear in his gut.

Stoney snorted. "Thought you'd have already heard about it most like."

"But Delice, is she all right?"

Stoney looked at him, his brow furrowed. "Course she's all right. She's a whore. You know how tough they are. They can handle a few knocks."

Johnny glared, swinging himself back to his feet. "She's a friend, Stoney. Not a whore. A friend."

Stoney rolled his eyes. "Still a whore. Anyway, she seemed fine to me. If she had any sense she'd get some muscle in there. Never knew a whorehouse which didn't have a couple of men around to take care of trouble makers. But she always thinks she knows best. Damn woman."

Johnny stalked to the door. "I'll bet she'll be real touched by your concern, Stoney. You're all heart."

Stoney slammed his coffee mug down on the desk. "Well, tell her to get some protection in. Maybe she'll listen to you – she sure as hell wouldn't listen to me. I ain't got time to babysit a bunch of whores, and if there's regular trouble there, the town will close the place down. I already had a delegation of 'good citizens' in here complaining about it."

Johnny slammed the door shut behind him and strode toward the bordello at the end of the street, blood pounding in his head. If he found the brute responsible, he'd kill him. Dios, he hated men who made war on women. It was as low as a man could sink. And God alone knew, there were some men only too quick to knock a woman around. An image of his mother sprang to mind, wringing her hands and standing wailing with her nose bleeding, her lip split and a swollen eye.

He pushed open the door of the bordello and then stopped short, shocked by the look of the place. Stoney hadn't been exaggerating when he said the place had been smashed up. Several lamps were broken, and the piano had been pushed against the wall with half of the top caved in. Chairs were missing, presumably too smashed up to stay in the main seating area. Even the chandelier had sections missing, although it had now been secured in place to prevent it falling from the ceiling.

The girls all looked strained and tired, like they'd spent most of the day working on their knees cleaning, rather than their more usual kind of work which they did on their backs.

Sadie came toward him, but without her usual hip-swinging walk.

He swallowed hard. She had a bluish-purple bruise across one side of her face, a swollen lip, and one eye was half-closed. He reached his hand out, and touched her chin very gently. "Sorry, honey, I only just heard about this. Are you OK?" Damn stupid question. She was obviously a long way from OK.

She smiled, but without her usual spark. A half-hearted smile, but leastways she was trying.

"I'm fine, Johnny. Really." She gave him another not very

convincing smile. "It was all a shock, that's all. I guess we ain't used to trouble in here. It's a real quiet place normally. You know how it is, Madam don't stand for no nonsense in here from the cowpokes."

Johnny raised an eyebrow. "Seemed she didn't do such a good job with this one."

Sadie's good eye widened in surprise. "Didn't you hear? She knocked him cold. She hit him over the head with a bottle of rye whiskey."

The tightness in his gut eased a touch. He grinned. "You're kidding?"

Sadie returned the grin, and then winced. "Nope. Honest. She knocked him out. He was flat out on the floor when the sheriff come for him."

Johnny glanced around the room. Delice was nowhere in sight. He felt another pang of concern. "Where is she, Sadie?"

Sadie shrugged. "She took the night off."

Johnny frowned. Time off? Delice? She never took the night off. "So, where is she? In her own rooms? I'll go look for her."

Sadie shook her head vigorously. Seemed that was a big mistake because she winced. "No. She don't want to be disturbed. Anyway, she ain't there." Sadie bit her lip, like she'd said too much, and winced again.

"Sadie, it seems to me you should be the one taking the night off." Johnny patted her shoulder gently. "So be a good girl and tell me where she is, because I need to talk to her."

"She really don't want to see any customers tonight, Johnny. She'd have my hide and my job if I let anyone see her."

His pang of concern was growing, stabbing at him now. "Is she hurt? Is that it?"

Sadie shook her head. "No, not really. But she was dead set on being left alone tonight and not wanting to see any customers."

"Sadie, I ain't a customer, I'm a friend. Now, tell me where she is. Please."

"Johnny, you'll cause me to lose my job. I really can't—"

"Sadie, tell me, there's a good girl. I won't tell her how I found her. I promise."

Sadie shook her head slowly and then shrugged. "She's out in the garden."

Johnny frowned. "The garden? I didn't know there was even a garden here."

"It's all walled in. Real private like. It's kind of like her special place and we're not supposed to tell people about it. I don't know why. You can get to it through a door out back – it's always kept locked and hidden by a curtain. But don't tell her I told you where she was or how to find her. I need this job." There was a note of desperation in her voice and just the slightest wobble of her swollen lip.

Johnny patted her shoulder again, and rolling some dollar notes slipped them down her cleavage. "Don't worry. I won't tell her."

He went through to the back of the bordello, looking for the door to the garden. He'd never even imagined that the place would have a garden. Although, to be honest, his mind was usually on other things when he visited.

He found the door hidden by a long tapestry and in the shadow of an ornate cupboard. The oak door had big bolts, strong enough to keep out an army. Pushing it open, he stepped into a peaceful, courtyard garden. The walls were covered in climbing plants. And in the center was a small pond with a statue in the middle. A long stone seat was sited under a wooden framework covered in more plants. It was a real restful spot. But then he stopped dead in his tracks and his mouth dropped open at the sight of Delice, dressed in a pair of man's pants, digging hard at the root of an old tree.

The pants were held up by a piece of rope tied around her waist, and she was wearing a working shirt with the sleeves rolled up. He shook his head in disbelief. "Delice?"

She whirled around at the sound of his voice. The spade made a dull thud as it fell to the ground. He could see some discoloration on her face, but even more worrying was the flash of anger in her emerald eyes. "Who the hell told you that you could come in here?"

CHAPTER SEVEN

Johnny shook his head, sighing softly. "That ain't much of a greeting. I only came to see if you were alright. I'd have come sooner but I—"

"I asked who the hell told you I was here." Her eyes looked even greener than usual and she stood with her hands on her hips looking as mad as hell.

"Nobody told me you were here. I was worried about you so I came looking—"

Her eyes narrowed. "Sadie. It had to be Sadie. You have her wrapped around your little finger. None of the other girls would have dared to tell you. I warned them they'd be fired if they ever told anyone about this place."

He could do narrowed eyes too. And he reckoned he could glare better. "Nobody told me—"

She raised an eyebrow, which said she didn't believe him. "Lying really doesn't become you. You'd never have found this garden by accident. The door is always locked and it isn't overlooked from the public areas. So, back to the matter in hand, namely Sadie."

So that was why he'd never known about the garden. He reckoned he knew the bordello pretty well, but now, looking around the courtyard, he saw that not a single window looked out onto it, other than the ones from Delice's own rooms. "Sadie shouldn't be working tonight. You should have given her the night off." Maybe attack was the best form of defense.

Delice folded her arms. "That's a very poor attempt to deflect me. But it might interest you to know that none of the girls has to work tonight unless they choose to. They're serving drinks to regulars and will be shutting up shop early. So, back to Sadie."

Johnny held up his hands. "OK, OK! But give her a break, Delice. She's in a bad way."

He could have sworn that Delice's mouth twitched ever so slightly. "Hmm. I'll think on it. It doesn't alter the fact that the girls are forbidden from mentioning my garden. This is my private space. And speaking of my girls, there is the matter of Daisy." Her voice had a sort of edge to it.

He stared at her. "Daisy? Who's Daisy?"

"Who's Daisy?" She didn't sound too impressed. "You mean you've forgotten her so soon? And there I was supposing she was the love of your life."

Yeah, a real sharp edge to her voice. Sharp enough to cut him. But Daisy? Who the hell was Daisy? "Oh, Daisy!" He grinned, suddenly remembering the girl in Abilene.

"Yes, honey, Daisy. Who you so thoughtfully sent to me for a job."

"She deserved a break. Her life was hell in Abilene. I thought you'd help her out." He felt a twinge of concern. "She needed a change."

"That's as may be. But I would prefer that you didn't send all your cast-off whores to me for work. I choose my girls very carefully and I do have standards to keep up. I am not running a charity. Broken noses are not in the job description."

"She was very good at her job." He snapped the words out. He couldn't believe that Delice would have turned poor Daisy away. Shit, and he'd sent the girl here thinking she'd do alright.

"Well, nobody would know better than you if she was up to scratch." Delice's voice was very cool.

"So what happened to her? Where is she?"

Delice bit her lip and suddenly seemed to find her spade real interesting. "Didn't you recognize her out there earlier?"

He grinned. "So you did give her a job."

Delice sniffed. How could anyone say so much with just a sniff? "Just don't make a habit of it. I cannot give work to every stray whore you come across on your travels. The building isn't big enough!

"But enough of business. I value my privacy, Johnny. So perhaps you'd like to leave now. I have more pressing things to do than standing here making idle conversation with customers." She picked up her spade and turned back toward the tree stump.

Dios, but she knew how to rile him at times. "Customer? I thought we were friends?" He stepped forward and wrested the spade from her hands. "Damn it, Delice, sit down and talk to me." He looked a little closer at her face. Yes, there was definitely a bruise there. His gut felt like it was tying itself in knots at even the thought of someone striking her. "You ain't in no fit state to be digging." Dios, the man who did this was going to live to regret it. But not for long.

He took hold of her arm and propelled her toward the stone bench ignoring her squeak of protest. Pushing her firmly down onto it, he then perched on the end. "Now, never mind going on about Sadie or Daisy. Tell me what happened here. That's far more important."

She shrugged. "There's nothing to tell. One of the customers got out of hand." She avoided his eyes.

"He did a hell of a lot of damage for only one man. And why the hell did you keep serving him drinks when he must have been getting as full as a tick? I reckon you'd have known better than that." Johnny eyed her curiously. She was too smart to have done anything so dumb.

She suddenly seemed to find her hands real interesting, and then sighed softly. "I made an error of judgement, I suppose." She shook her head slowly. "But it was very strange, because there was no indication that he was getting drunk. I certainly didn't notice him have many drinks, but then, quite suddenly, he started smashing the place up."

Johnny chewed on his thumb, before letting out a slow breath. "So you don't reckon he had that much to drink?"

She shook her head.

Johnny frowned. "Well, if he didn't drink much, then he either can't hold his liquor or he was faking. You reckon he could have been faking being drunk?"

She stared across at him, her brow furrowed. "But that makes no sense. Why should he fake being drunk?" But he could hear the doubt in her voice.

Johnny shrugged. "I dunno. Tell me more about him. What was he like? You reckon he was a miner from Elizabethtown, or maybe a cowboy or a drifter?"

Delice hesitated before speaking. "He wasn't a miner. And he didn't look like a cowboy either." She paused, frowning. "If I recall correctly, he was wearing an old army coat, not the clothes of a cowboy. And he certainly wasn't a drifter. He looked too clean and well fed."

"Was there anyone else with him?"

She shook her head. "He was alone. I'm sure he was alone. No, I guess I simply judged this one wrong and didn't notice that he was getting drunk. I was somewhat preoccupied."

Johnny looked at her sharply. "Preoccupied? With what?"

She pursed her lips and waved her hand like it didn't matter none. "Oh, I received an unpleasant letter telling me how the town would be a far better place without my presence. Apparently I am a stain on the good name of Cimarron."

Johnny snorted. "From the new reverend, I guess. The Reverend Hausmann, interfering son of a bitch."

Her lips twitched. "I believe that was the man's name. Have you met him?"

"Yeah, I met him and his sour-faced wife. Apparently they're real worried about my soul. And they had the nerve to tell me that they'd closed other bordellos down and this one wouldn't be no different. Quite a coincidence that someone smashed it up, immediately after you get a letter. And you know something, I don't believe in coincidences. Hausmann's a nasty piece of work. I was coming out to warn you about him, and to ask your advice about something else, but then I found out about the trouble here. Damn it, Delice, a place like this needs protection. You should have a couple of bouncers around to take care of any trouble makers."

She made a sort of pffftttt noise. "We don't need any bouncers, thank you. We have managed perfectly well before, and we will continue to do so."

Johnny scoffed. "Oh yeah, you're doing just fine and dandy without protection. Place looked real smart when I came through."

"There is no need to be so sarcastic." Her eyes flashed as she shot him her coldest look. "And anyway, we do have a man around. We have old Clem."

"Old Clem!" Johnny let out a snort of laughter. "Old Clem ain't going to handle any trouble for you. He sure as hell won't see sixty again. He does a good job as a barkeep, but he ain't up to doing much more than that. If you can't find some protection, I'll do it for you."

"I am quite capable of hiring and firing my own staff. Including girls who talk too much to the customers—"

"Oh, shoot. You ain't going to fire Sadie, so stop pretending you are. Fact is, Delice, you need a couple of guns in here. Men who put the fear of God into anyone thinking of causing trouble. Never knew a whorehouse that didn't have some muscle around the place."

"And you've certainly known more than most anyone." She had that tone in her voice that she always used when she was trying to score points. "But, for all your years of whoring, I very much doubt that you've ever known a bordello such as this. I believe that we are a cut above the usual class of bordello. Having armed men around distracting my girls does not suit my style. I am running a far more elegant and discreet establishment."

Johnny sighed and leaned back with his arms folded. She narrowed her eyes a touch more. "And it is one of the reasons why I have never permitted gunfighters over the threshold. If you recall, you were only admitted because Ben pleaded on your behalf. And, aside from that, I do have my profits to think about. I have no intention of frittering money away on superfluous sundries such as protection. I run a tight ship and cannot abide wanton extravagances."

"Are you done?" Johnny raised an eyebrow. "I mean, you can carry on all you like, and use all them fancy words, but the fact is you got a smashed up bordello and some old devil of a reverend who won't think twice about stirring up the town to get you closed down. And look at this." He reached out to gently touch her face where the bruise showed through the pallor of her makeup, but she jerked away from his hand. "You telling me that you don't need someone around to look after you?"

She shot him an odd look, like she didn't know what to make of that. Then she made another of her pffttt noises. God only knew what they were supposed to mean. "We have managed just fine until now, and we will continue to do so. You sound like Stoney the way you're carrying on. I've already had to listen to him ad nauseam. He became very repetitive after a while."

Johnny ran his hand through his hair; the damn woman would drive him loco before she was done. "Dios, Delice! What's wrong with your friends being concerned about you? Whether you like it or not, you need someone around to keep an eye on things. Just accept that Stoney and I know better than you over this." He eyed her in concern because she was sure turning a real funny color now. Maybe it hadn't been the wisest thing to say. But damn it, she was being stubborn. It seemed Stoney's words earlier in the evening had been fairer than Johnny had allowed for.

Her jaw clenched real tight for a second and she looked like she was trying not to yell at him. "I am sure that you mean well, Johnny, but if you'll excuse me, I have a tree trunk to dig at." She sounded as if she was talking through gritted teeth. She picked up her spade and made to go back to her digging.

"No, you don't!" Johnny grabbed the spade away from her. "You sit there, I'll do this."

Her eyes flashed again. "Give me back the damn spade."

"No! You just sit back and take it easy. You ain't in no fit state to be doing this."

She opened her mouth, but he cut across her. "Like I said, sit down and quit yapping." She looked at him in silence for a few beats and then sat back on the bench.

He really put his back into the digging, but damn if it wasn't harder work than sinking fence posts.

"Johnny, I think you should know—"

He threw her a glare over his shoulder. "I said quit yapping, Delice."

Despite the cool of the evening, it was hot work. He stripped his shirt off and threw it down onto the bench where she sat, with her arms folded, watching him.

The damn roots went real deep. Every time he managed to clear the earth from around a sizable section, as soon as he put the spade under it to lever it up, more soil would cave in on top. After he'd been digging around the root for what felt like hours, she spoke again. "Johnny, I really think I should tell you that—"

He glared at her again. Every bone in his body felt like it was gonna snap in half. "Delice, I told you to sit there and keep quiet. This ain't women's work." And wasn't that the truth. He couldn't remember ever working this hard doing anything. How the hell did she ever think she was going to shift this tree stump?

Damn woman had no sense at all.

And then, quite suddenly, the root gave beneath him, sending him toppling backward to land at her feet where he lay for a second heaving in great breaths of air. He looked up at her, still breathing hard. "You must be crazy, Delice. You'd never have gotten that root out in a hundred years. I reckon it's been in the ground that long!"

She eyed him for a few seconds, her head tilted to one side like she was deciding what to say, and biting on her lip as if trying not to laugh. "Very impressive, honey. But do you think that you could put it back now because I didn't want it dug up."

His mouth dropped open. Couldn't have stopped it if he'd tried. "What d'you mean, you didn't want it dug up? You were digging the damn thing up yourself."

Her lips twitched again. "No, I wasn't digging it up, I was digging at it."

He swiped the sweat out of his eyes. "What d'you mean, you were digging at it?"

"Honey, like you said, I couldn't get that root out in a hundred years, but when I want to let off steam I come and dig at it. It's very therapeutic."

Thera-what? Mierda, if only she'd talk English. He grunted, and hauled himself to his feet before slumping down heavily on the bench next to her. He aimed a kick at the tree stump. "Delice, if you want it put back, you can do it yourself. You should have stopped me if you didn't want it dug up."

She raised an eyebrow. "But you told me to be quiet every time I tried to stop you."

"You could have ignored me." He grinned. "You usually do! Anyway, look at it this way, it'll make good firewood and keep you warm next winter."

She picked up his shirt and threw it to him. "There's always that. And it was very entertaining watching you. I guess I'll have to plant something there now. Maybe a rose." She moved to stand up and then turned back to him. "Earlier you said you wanted to ask me about something. What was it?"

He scratched his belly and tried to remember what the hell he'd wanted to ask her. He shook his head as he pulled his shirt back on. For the life of him he couldn't think what— "The war! I wanted to ask you what you knew about the war."

"The war? Which war for heaven's sake? The Trojan war, the Napoleonic Wars, the Wars of the Roses, the Hundred Year War?"

Johnny furrowed his brow. "There was a war over roses? What sort of people fight over roses? Come to that, what sort of people carry on a war for a hundred years?"

She smiled. "I shouldn't worry about it; it was a very long time ago. But which war were you wondering about? There have been quite a few. Maybe the Mexican French war?" She raised an eyebrow like it was a question.

Johnny snorted. "Hell, I know all about that one. Damn Frenchies. No, it was the gringo war between the states."

"Ah! The War for Southern Independence or the War of the Rebellion! It seems what you call it depends on which side you were on." She furrowed her brow. "But honey, if you want to know about that war, you'd best ask your brother. He fought in it, didn't he?" She paused, and pursed her lips. "Although, on reflection, you might get a rather biased viewpoint. He's hardly an impartial observer."

"Yeah, well, that's the thing. He won't talk about it. It's like he's covering something up. And whatever it is it's eating away at him. So, I wanted to try and figure out what it might be about. He was in Sheridan's unit, a cavalry unit, and all I know is that he was serving in it in 1864." Johnny shrugged. "Thought you might know something about it."

She didn't say anything for a second. She sighed softly, and paused, watching him buttoning up his shirt. "Honey, if he won't speak about it, maybe it's something better left alone. Maybe he has a good reason for not wanting to talk about it."

"He was always quick enough to want to know about my past." He snapped the words out before he could stop himself. He could feel the heat flushing his face.

"So is it that which annoys you the most? Is it simply that you think he owes you an answer, or is it that you're concerned about him?" Those green eyes looked at him searchingly. Almost like they were looking into his soul.

Johnny laughed softly. "You always get straight to the point, don't you?" He shrugged. "I guess, if I'm honest, it's a bit of both. Yeah, it irritates the hell out of me that he was always wanting answers from me but don't give nothing back. But I also hate to see him so wound up over something. Whatever it is, it's like it's eating away at his guts. And if I don't know what it is, I can't help him."

"And you want to help him." She said it kind of even, like it was simply the truth, not a question.

"Yeah. I do. He stood by me when it mattered. I guess I'd like to do the same for him."

There was a small line between her brows. "Honey, maybe it's something which he feels you wouldn't understand. Or something that he feels you might disapprove of. Has that occurred to you?"

Johnny stared at her. "Guy wouldn't do nothing wrong. He always tries to do the right thing by everyone. He's not like me. He's a really good man."

He could have sworn there was a flicker of something in her eyes. Sadness? Something, anyway, that he couldn't figure.

She gave a slight shake of her head. "I still think that maybe it's something you should leave alone."

Johnny eyed her curiously. "D'you know something about it that you ain't telling me?"

Her face gave nothing away. It was like it was closed off. When she spoke her voice was kind of blank. "I merely think that you should respect his wishes."

If only he could read her. Did she know something about

that damn war? He shook his head. One thing was certain, she wouldn't tell him nothing unless she wanted to. He shrugged, like he wasn't bothered by her words. "I'm going to find out what's bugging him. One way or another I will find out." He tried to roll his shoulders to ease the pain that was thumping in his neck and back. "Dios, I'm beat. I been sinking fence posts all week, I really didn't need to go digging up tree stumps."

Her lips twitched. "That's what I told you. You didn't need to—"

He cut across her. "OK! You made your point. But right now, I reckon I'll head on back. Too tired for anything, even if the girls weren't shutting up shop early. But take my advice, get in some heavy hired help. Or I'll do it for you, and I reckon you'd rather choose your own staff."

Her eyes were flinty now. "I run my business the way I think fit. Goodnight, Johnny."

He grunted as he staggered to his feet. "Stoney was right about you. You do need someone to talk some sense into you. If there's trouble here too often, the town might shut the place down."

"I run things my way, Johnny. And if the town shuts me down, my girls and I will move to Santa Fe. I've been thinking that maybe a change would do us all good."

CHAPTER EIGHT

Sunday lunch was a bad-tempered affair. The old man saw to that.

Johnny spent the morning cleaning his guns while the rest of the family went to church. He was aching so much after digging out the damn tree stump that he'd barely been able to straighten up to walk down to breakfast. Dismantling his guns seemed like the easiest job he could find to do. And it would give him the time to work out what the hell he was going to do about Guy, and about Delice. He could barely believe she could be even thinking of taking off for Santa Fe. And that in itself was odd; she wasn't the kind of woman to give in without a fight. 'Specially to the likes of people like the Hausmanns.

Guthrie, tucking into a big helping of biscuits and gravy, had suggested that Johnny might like to do the books while the rest of them were at church. Johnny had enjoyed shooting that idea down. And, surprisingly, the old man had backed off.

But by the time the family arrived back from church in the buggy, Guthrie looked fit to bust. He'd stomped into the house muttering about the damn Reverend, while Guy helped Peggy down, both looking glum. Johnny grinned. "Fun service, was it?"

Peggy glared at him. "Well, your name cropped up more than once."

"During the sermon." Guy cut in before Johnny could think of anything to say to Peggy. "We were lectured about the sinners in our midst. Including you."

Johnny's grin broadened. "You don't say! I made it into the sermon? Oh boy, I really must be beyond redemption."

"It's no laughing matter, Johnny." Peggy snapped the words out. Her face was red and she looked like she was fighting back tears. "Everyone was staring at us, and afterwards, outside, they were all making nasty comments. It's horrid having to listen to people being so cruel about you. Susie Tandy was smirking and whispering and pointing at us when the service was over." Peggy dragged her bonnet off and banged it against the side of the buggy. "She's such a cat!"

Johnny sighed, and stretched out a hand to cup her chin. "Peggy, honey, it don't bother me none, so don't let it upset you. Susie Tandy is as full of hot air as her fat father. Give 'em a few days and they'll think of something else to gossip about. It's what people are like."

"And Henry Carter had a go at Uncle Guthrie about you. How you were always visiting places you shouldn't." Her face flushed a deeper shade of scarlet as she spoke.

Johnny bit back a smile. No wonder the old man was all

riled up if he'd had an earful from Carter and had to listen to Hausmann carrying on in the pulpit.

"See! There you go again. Why can't you take it seriously, Johnny? You never take anything seriously!" Peggy burst into tears and ran into the house, smacking Johnny's hand away.

"Mierda!" Johnny shook his head. "What the hell is she so worked up about?" He shook his head again, he'd never understand women.

"It was quite a vindictive rant from the pulpit." Guy's tone was mild. "And sadly, Peggy took the criticisms to heart. I guess she's at an age where the opinion of people she likes to think of as friends, count. And Father was in such a foul mood on the drive home that it made matters worse."

Johnny laughed humorlessly. "So, I'll bet I'll be in for it at lunchtime."

"I'd like a piece of your bet." Guy turned and headed toward the hacienda. He paused in the doorway. "And Johnny, try to keep your temper when he starts in on you. He'll calm down so much quicker if you don't rise to it."

He figured the safest course of action would be to say nothing over lunch except please, thank you, or pass the potatoes. He should have known it wouldn't work. The old man was simply waiting for Peggy to clear away, and the second she left the room, he started in.

"Do you have any idea how much comment your behavior arouses?" Guthrie's vein was already pulsing in his temple. That was always a bad sign.

Johnny ducked his head briefly before looking at his father. "No, but I guess some folks haven't got anything better to do than gossip. I don't set out to cause them to talk, in case you're thinking I do."

"Well, thanks to your behavior, your family had to suffer the indignity of listening to that pompous man lecturing us from the pulpit on your sinful ways. And then..." Guthrie's face was coloring up real good. "Of all things, I then had to put up with Henry Carter telling me how much time you spend in the whorehouse. Have you no regard for your family's feelings?"

Johnny raised an eyebrow and sighed softly. "I thought you and Carter fell out some time ago, so why do you care what he says? What I do in my free time ain't anybody's business."

"It becomes our business when Peggy has to hear about such things." All the dishes shook as Guthrie banged his fist down on the table. "It's not right that she hears about it. Your sordid private life is being dragged into the public domain. That makes it our business. God only knows what your grandparents would have thought of your behavior."

Johnny paused, his fork halfway to his mouth. What the hell had caused the old man to start on about dead people? "What? What have my grandparents got to do with this? I thought they were dead."

The pulse was going faster now. Any second the old man's head would bust open.

"Luckily they are dead so they are saved the pain of hearing about your unsavory habits. Until now, I have turned a blind eye to them. But I cannot continue to do so once Peggy is affected."

Johnny shut his eyes briefly. He would try not to lose his temper, but hell, what crap the old man came out with at times. He spoke softly, hoping maybe it would calm the old man down. "Guthrie, Peggy ain't some little kid. Do you really think she don't know about whorehouses? Heck, she's grown up on a ranch. Can't be much she don't know about what male animals get up to.

"I'm real sorry that you're so riled up about all of this. And I'm sorry that you had to listen to it. But it ain't anyone else's business. I reckon you'd be better off telling that old goat Hausmann to keep his nose out of our affairs. You said yourself what a poisonous man he is. Well, now you seen him at work. Sure as hell ain't much Christian charity in him." He hadn't yelled at all. He caught Guy's eye and Guy nodded like he reckoned Johnny was doing fine.

"I don't want you visiting the bordello anymore." Guthrie's lip curled. "Or as the pastor called it, the den of iniquity. And while I think he is poisonous, this family will not give him fodder to enable him to humiliate us in public. Therefore, you need to curb your bad habits. You waste far too much time and money in there. You'd be better off finding a wife if you can't control yourself."

Johnny pushed his chair back with a clatter. There was a limit to how much crap he'd take, and the old man had gone over it. Even so, he'd keep calm. Wouldn't yell, but it sure was tempting. He hesitated. Counted to ten, and then spoke real soft. "You make the rules on how we run the ranch and that's fine by me. But my private time's my own. We been through this before, and we had a deal. I ain't a kid. You can't tell me what to do. I'll live my life the way I choose. If you don't like it, I'll go board in town. And I've done talking about it."

He resisted the urge to bang the door as he walked out of the house, but damn it the old man had gone too far. And the pity of it was they'd been getting along so much better of late.

He was saddling Pistol when Guy came and leaned against the door of the barn. "Well, I have to say I thought you kept your temper very well."

Johnny gave a short laugh as he tightened the cinch. "Yeah, well, I was following your advice. But he ain't got the right to tell me what I can and can't do. It's not like I even grew up here."

Guy shrugged. "Maybe he feels that as it's his house it's his rules."

Johnny shook his head. "He and me had a deal. I keep my end of deals and I expect other folks to do the same. Dios, Guy! I ain't a kid. He'll be trying to find me a wife next."

Guy grinned. "Well, it would save you a great deal of money! And reduce the risk of you catching something very unpleasant."

Johnny grunted. "Delice runs a real clean whorehouse. And, speaking of Delice, someone smashed her place up this week." He turned away from Pistol to face Guy.

"A dissatisfied customer?" Guy didn't sound like he took it seriously.

Johnny narrowed his eyes. "I ain't funning, Guy. Delice and some of the girls got really knocked around by the bastard. And the place is a wreck."

Guy frowned. "I'm sorry that anyone was hurt. But I guess that it's a professional hazard. Although," he rubbed his beard thoughtfully, leaning against the partition of Pistol's stall. "I always thought she ran a very controlled operation there and got rid of potential trouble makers before anything started. She's slipping."

Johnny sucked in a deep breath. "She's slipping? Is that all you can say? She's got bruises on her face, Harvard. And I am real pissed about it."

Guy sighed softly. "Johnny, I'm sorry that she got hurt. I'd be sorry that any woman got hurt. And I think hitting a woman is unforgivable. But, we don't live in a perfect world, and I guess that women in that business do get hit sometimes. I am not condoning it. But I imagine it goes with the territory."

Johnny ducked his head and kicked at the straw around his feet, trying to swallow back the sour taste of bile. "Goes with the territory, huh?" He looked back at Guy. "Yeah, well, Stoney had the man in jail to cool off." Johnny paused and flicked a fly away from his ear. "And I'll tell you something else. I reckon the fellow was put up to it. Maybe by Hausmann, maybe by someone else. But given that Hausmann wants to see the bordello closed, it's a bit too convenient that some fellow smashed the place up."

Guy raised an eyebrow. "I find it hard to believe that, unpleasant as he is, Reverend Hausmann would get someone to smash up the bordello. I think you are being fanciful."

"Fanciful?" Johnny glared. "From what Delice said, the man didn't have enough to drink for it to have caused him to go on the rampage like he did. And I tell you something else," Johnny paused. "If I find him, he's gonna wish he'd never been born."

Guy swallowed hard. "What are you going to do to him?"

Johnny eyed him steadily, not letting any emotion show on his face. Didn't answer for a few beats, and it was getting to Guy, because the man swallowed hard again. Johnny spoke softly, still keeping his face blank. "Kill him."

Guy's mouth dropped open, and for a second it was like he couldn't think of a thing to say. "But... But... I mean, you'll get yourself hanged, Johnny. She's not even badly hurt. You can't kill a man for hitting a whore."

"A whore?" Johnny tilted his head to one side. "Does it make a difference, Harvard?"

Guy glared, and sighed loudly. "What I'm saying is that you can't kill a man for hitting someone. For hitting anyone."

Johnny raised an eyebrow. "I can, and I will. I ain't

standing by to let him treat women like that. I'll tell you something else, Delice reckoned he was an army type. He was wearing an old army coat. Maybe he was one of your soldiers."

Guy's mouth was a thin line and there was a nerve ticking in the side of his face. His face was white; but whether with shock or anger Johnny really couldn't tell. "What on earth has his being in the army got to do with anything? You are always harping back to that. And anyway, anyone can get hold of an army coat."

Johnny shrugged. He hadn't really intended to say anything about the army. And seeing the look on Guy's face, he wished he hadn't. The slightest mention of it upset Guy. He figured he'd best steer the talk away from the army. "All I know is he's going to regret making war on women."

Johnny tried to block out the mental picture of that bruise on Delice's face. Even thinking of it got him all torn up inside. He huffed out a sigh. "I've got a few chores in town, and I want to have a word with Stoney. I'll catch up with you later. Maybe the old man will have calmed down by the time I get back."

He could see some of the tension ease out of Guy. Yeah, that was the way to play it. Act uninterested again. Act. That's all it would be. One way or another he intended to find out what Guy's secret was. "See you later." He led Pistol out of the barn and sprang into the saddle. With the lightest touch of his spurs he headed off toward Cimarron.

Pistol was glad of the chance to stretch his legs and made short work of the journey to town. Johnny reined him in on the outskirts, and then cocked his head at the sound of singing and chanting coming from somewhere in the town itself. Surely it wasn't from the church? He was sure that they didn't hold their services in the afternoon.

He pushed Pistol into a trot, but pulled up short as he turned into the town's main street. At the far end of the town, outside the bordello, a bunch of women with banners were making one hell of a racket. And even from where he sat he could see from the signs on the banners and hear from the chanting, that they were protesting against the presence of a "den of iniquity" in the town. And they were making damn sure that everyone knew why they were there.

Johnny ground his teeth and cursed Hausmann. He could easily imagine the man being delighted by this turn of events. Yeah. He'd bet the Reverend would be real pleased with himself. Son of a bitch. If ever there was a man who deserved a bullet it was Hausmann.

CHAPTER NINE

He tethered Pistol at the hitching rail by the general store and stalked over to Stoney's office. Pushing the door open, he saw Stoney looking through a pile of documents, sitting bolt upright at his desk, and not slouched back with his feet up the way he normally did.

Stoney glared. "Don't say it. Don't say a damn word, Fierro." He jerked his head in the general direction of the street. "They been out there for the past two hours. And while you've been enjoying some fancy Sunday lunch in comfort, I been having to deal with half the town folks complaining." Stoney spun his chair away from the desk before getting to his feet and pacing around his office. "I've had 'em in here demanding I shut those damn women up, and then I've had others in demanding I shut the bordello down. They're going on and on about the stain on the town's good name. Hell! What good name? Cimarron's well known as a rough town, but they all seem to have forgotten that. And then they started on at me about how the trouble in the bordello will spread to other businesses. So right now, Fierro," he narrowed his eyes, "right now, I ain't in the mood for anything from you."

Johnny eyed him steadily. Stoney was as fidgety as a horse with a burr under its saddle. "Dang, but you're real pretty when you're angry!" Johnny let out a snort of laughter at the shock on Stoney's face. "Hell, calm down, you'll bust the buttons off your shirt." Johnny pulled up a chair and threw himself down onto it. Stretching his legs he rested his feet on Stoney's desk. "Dealing with unreasonable people, well, it's the sheriff's job, ain't it?" Johnny shrugged. "And let's face it, this town is full of unreasonable people. And the ones that aren't trouble want to make sure you're earning your money and their taxes ain't being wasted."

Stoney grunted. "I get paid to deal with law breakers. Not nursemaid whores, or deal with other folks being all agitated and unreasonable. What difference does it make if there's a whorehouse in the town?"

Johnny didn't bother answering. Figured Stoney wasn't really expecting one. "Anyways, that ain't why I'm here. I wanted to know if you'd remembered anything else about that man you had in your jail." Johnny chewed on his thumb briefly. "I spoke to Delice and he sounds like he might have been putting on a show. You sure he was drunk?"

Stoney stopped his pacing, and cocked his head to one side. "What? What the hell you talking about now?"

Johnny leaned forward, resting his feet back on the floor. "The fellow you had in jail. The one who busted up the bordello. That's what I'm talking about."

Stoney grunted. "You want to know about the drunk?" He jerked his thumb in the direction of the singing. "Right now I'm more interested in that crowd of do-gooders. Why do you think I'm going through this pile of paperwork? Trying to figure if there's a way I can get them to shut the hell up. They're sure as hell disturbing the peace with their God-awful singing." He slumped back down in his chair, running his hand through his hair. "I don't know how drunk the man was. OK? I threw him in the cell and left him to cool off. Now what am I going to do about those damn women?"

Johnny paused while he thought about how tricky women could be. "They got the vote in Wyoming."

Stoney's mouth opened and then closed again like he couldn't think of a thing to say. Then he took a deep breath. "Who got the vote in Wyoming? And what the hell does that have to do with anything?"

"Women." Johnny rested his foot on his knee and spun the rowel on his spur. "They gave them the vote in Wyoming."

Stoney furrowed his brow. "Why?"

"They reckoned it would make more women go and live there. I was up in those parts one time and I sure noticed there was a shortage of women." He shook his head slowly. "Always had to queue up for the whores too. Weren't many of them neither."

"So it didn't work?" Stoney cocked an eyebrow. "Not that it surprises me. But I don't see as how that's got anything to do with this. You saying we should give them a vote and they'll shut up?" He paused, scratching at his beard. "Why the hell would anyone think women would care about voting?" He shook his head. "It won't never catch on. Women only like giving men hell. That's all they care about."

Yeah, Stoney sure had that right. Johnny nodded. "That and trying to catch a husband in the first place. And my old man's all in favor of that. Shit, today he told me to give up the bordello and find myself a wife if I couldn't control myself." Still couldn't believe that the old man had said that. Like he would want a wife. To hell with that.

Stoney snorted with laughter. "No woman with any sense would have you. But you ain't helping me solve my problem. I mean, surely this ain't really my job? Dealing with a bunch of noisy women? And if they don't like their men folk heading to the bordello then they should open their legs more often."

Johnny nodded, idly thinking of Sadie's soft fingers stroking him... "I tell you, I'd rather have Sadie than the likes of Mrs. Henry Carter. I saw her out there. What man wouldn't rather have Sadie than any of those women out there?" He rubbed at his shoulder, it was still aching from digging up that damn tree stump. "Anyway, never mind the damn women. This ain't solving my problem, which is who the bastard was who smashed up the bordello."

Stoney jerked forward. "You seem mighty interested in him. You wouldn't be thinking of looking for him, would you? Because let me tell you, Johnny, I won't have personal scores being settled in my territory. Things get done legal when I'm around. I mean it. As far as I'm concerned he spent a couple of days behind bars and that's an end of it. Leave it alone."

Johnny shrugged.

Stoney narrowed his eyes and looked hard at Johnny. "I mean it, Fierro. I'm the law around here and I mean to uphold it. And if that means throwing you in jail, I damn well will."

Johnny raised an eyebrow. "Sure, Stoney, whatever you say. I was just wondering, that was all. Anyway, did you find anything in all them papers you're looking through about how to shut up them women?" He nodded toward the pile of documents, hoping to steer Stoney's thoughts onto something else.

Stoney shot him a look which said he didn't trust him at all, but Johnny just smiled, all innocent like.

"No, I didn't. Well, apart from disturbing the peace. But one thing you don't know, is because of all them women making so much noise, and all the damn complaints, I heard that the mayor's holding a meeting in a few days' time to discuss the bordello. So you'd better tell Delice to make damn sure there ain't any more trouble in there in the meantime."

"What sort of meeting?" He didn't like the sound of that. Once people started having meetings to complain about something, it usually brought trouble.

Stoney rolled his eyes. "About introducing a town ordinance banning the bordello. That's the trouble with some people, they ain't never happy unless they're causing trouble for others. What is it with folks that makes them think they can stick their noses into other people's business? And where's the law that says we all got to see things the same way? Damn people. And that Mayor Tandy... Talk about putting a jackass in charge."

"You're getting worked up again. They ain't worth it, Stoney. I'll go and have a word with Delice." Johnny eased himself out of the chair. His back was still paining him. Damn tree stump.

"Mind you tell her to get some protection in." Stoney shot him a sharp eyed look. "Maybe if I can tell the town that she's got a couple of bouncers in to stop troublemakers, they'll be less likely to be wanting to close the place down. And then, maybe, I can get back to some proper sheriff duties."

"Sure, I'll tell her." Johnny waved his hand and headed back into the street.

He hesitated briefly. The women were still chanting and singing. He shook his head; if their husbands had any sense they'd drag their wives home and set them to cooking a meal. Or cleaning the house. He wouldn't let any wife of his carry on like that. A wife... Dios, but Guthrie had a nerve suggesting that he find himself one. And heck, the old man didn't have too good a record with wives; he was the last person to be suggesting Johnny should settle down.

But right now, he was more interested in talking to Delice. Maybe she'd have come to her senses and organized some protection. He sighed softly. Yeah, that was about as likely as finding a talking horse.

He strolled along toward the group of women, the chink of his spurs announcing his approach. The women's singing fizzled out like a cigar in the rain. Johnny smiled and nodded to them, tipping his hat. "Ladies. You picked a real good day for a sing-song." He waved his arm toward the cloudless blue sky. "Yep, a real pretty day. And, if I may say so, you're in fine voice. I could hear you from back outside of town. Listening to you made my day, and brought a smile to my face. I do love to hear a group of people singing because they're so glad to be alive."

The women stared at him, like he had two heads or something. Henry Carter's wife's mouth was opening and closing like a fish. Seemed she had about the same amount of brains as her husband.

"Now, I'd love to stand and pass the time of day with you all, but I'm going in here. So, if you wouldn't mind standing to one side, please."

"Mr. Sinclair. Or Mr. Fierro, whatever name you call yourself." The sour voice was all too familiar.

He turned toward Mrs. Hausmann with his broadest smile. "Well, how nice to see you again, Mrs. Hausmann. I call myself Sinclair these days, but whatever you feel most comfortable with is just fine by me. And how's your husband? Settling in are you?" He cast his eyes over the women. "Oh, but my, you've already got yourself a nice group of friends." He beamed at her again.

If anything, her expression grew even harder. "Mr. Fierro—"

He grinned. "Fierro it is then, that's fine by me, Ma'am."

Her eyes narrowed. "Are you venturing into this den of iniquity on a Sunday? Have you no shame?"

Johnny scratched his ear, his brow furrowed. "Sorry, Ma'am, I don't think I rightly get your point. Are you saying it would be all right for me to go in here any other day of the week?"

He kept the puzzled look, biting down the desire to laugh at the look of sheer fury on her face.

"Young man, it is a den of iniquity on every day of the week and brings shame on the good name of Cimarron. But that a young man, who has been graced with the chance of a better life and the opportunity to put his sinful ways behind him, should venture in here on God's Day of Rest ensures his place in hell."

Johnny tilted his head to one side, and nodded slowly. "Well, yes, Ma'am, I take your point. If I see that young man inside I'll be sure to mention it to him. Now much as I'd like to stand here and pass the day with you, I got pressing business to attend to." He tipped his hat again. "Good day, ladies, enjoy your singing."

He pushed open the door and moved swiftly into the bordello. There didn't seem to be no customers, but that was hardly surprising. He figured there weren't many men in the town who'd have the cojones to venture in if they had to get past that group of sourpusses.

The girls were sitting around not doing much of anything, but they brightened up when they saw him. They pressed around him in a cloud of scent and rustling petticoats. They were fluttering their lashes and running their hands over his chest and shoulders, like they were desperate to get their hands on a man. He grinned at them. "Enjoying the singing, girls?"

They all started talking at once, sounding like a flock of noisy starlings. He put his hands over his ears briefly before trying to get them all to hush up. "Girls, I'm real touched by all the attention, and although I could easily handle you all at once, I'm sorry to say I'm here on business. Is Delice around?"

Sadie, who'd pushed in front of all the others, pouted. "You could come upstairs first, Johnny. I ain't seen you properly in ages because of you being gone for so long on that cattle drive. I got things to show you."

Relieved to see that the bruise on her face had faded and her lip wasn't as swollen, he brushed his hand lightly over her breasts. "I seen them before, Sadie. And although normally I couldn't say no to an invitation like that, I really do need to speak to Delice."

Sadie's pout looked closer to a sulk. "You could see her later." She pulled a face and then gave a long deep sigh, which made her breasts almost burst out of her bodice top which was barely holding them in check even without all her sighing. "She's in the office." Then she licked her lips slowly. "Come and see me after, Johnny. I'll show you a good time."

He grinned and slapped her on the rump as he headed down toward the office.

He tapped on the door, but didn't wait for an answer before pushing the door open. Delice was busy writing but she put the pen down and sat back, folding her arms. "Did I say to come in?"

He shrugged, and pulled up a chair. "I wanted to check if you'd thought any more about getting some protection in here."

She didn't answer straight off. She watched with narrowed eyes as he slumped down in the chair, stretching his legs out and crossing his feet.

"Do sit down." Her tone was real cool. "Make yourself at home."

He shook his head at her. "There's no call to be like that. Anyway, I need to sit down — I'm still aching from that damn tree stump."

"If you recall, I never asked you to dig it up." She shot him a sharp glance. "And no, I haven't thought any more about protection. We don't need it."

Johnny sighed softly, shaking his head. "Don't be so stubborn. I was over at Stoney's just now and he told me that the town's having a meeting this week, to discuss closing you down. You need to take steps to show that it's a well-run operation and that it don't need to be shut down."

She pursed her lips, tapping her fingers lightly on the desk.

"It is a well-run operation. I have no intention of defending my record to anyone. I am certainly not going to pander to them because we had one man cause some trouble."

Johnny glared at her. "Damn it, it ain't a case of pandering to them or not. It's simply showing them you got things under control so you don't give them a reason to close you down. It's common sense."

"I am not going to lower myself to arguing with a bunch of mindless sheep, who are only worked up because of the distasteful manipulation of their emotions by the Reverend Hausmann. If it wasn't for his interference, none of this would be happening."

"Dios, Delice! You are a stubborn woman. I know it wouldn't be happening if it wasn't for Hausmann getting them all worked-up, but this ain't your style to cave in to the likes of him. You got more fight in you than that. Don't give him the satisfaction of winning. All you got to do is employ a couple of bouncers, and then Stoney can tell the meeting it's all under control here."

She leaned forward and picking up her pen, dipped it in the ornate silver inkwell that always sat on her desk. "I shall do no such thing. If the town wishes to close me down, so be it. I told you, I have been considering moving to Santa Fe, and maybe this will prove to be the necessary impetus."

Im-pa-tuss? What the hell was that? She was as bad as Harvard. Life would be so much simpler if only they'd speak English. Hell, he spoke English and it wasn't like it was even his first language.

He dragged his mind back to the matter in hand. She was sitting watching him, looking kind of amused like maybe she knew what he'd been thinking about. But Santa Fe? She was still going on about Santa Fe! Mierda! Even so, he couldn't believe that she really wanted to move there. Why would anybody move to Santa Fe? Maybe he should just ignore her comments about moving. She couldn't mean it, could she? But then, she was pig-headed, so maybe she'd do it just to be awkward.

"You don't really want to go to Santa Fe." He thought maybe if he said it like he was stating a fact, she'd agree with him.

"I want a change of scenery. I am tiring of Cimarron. I find the people tedious and provincial."

So much for her agreeing with him. He didn't know what provincial meant, but it didn't sound good. "You'd hate it there." He tried to sound like he knew what he was talking about. "All those people, and it's real expensive." He didn't know if it was expensive, but she always seemed to be fussing about her profits so maybe it would make her think twice.

"Although property there is more expensive, I think that Santa Fe would be a sound investment."

Hell. She sounded serious. But maybe she was just funning with him. Maybe. But then again, maybe not. He never could read her. And that wasn't fair because she was way too good at reading him. He sighed softly. "Well, I reckon you shouldn't jump into anything. All this fuss will calm down, you'll see. And seeing as how you're kind of set up real well here, it would be dumb to start over somewhere new. Expensive too. Fitting out a new place." Yeah, that was it. Plant some seeds of doubt about the cost. And in the meantime he had to somehow figure out a way to stop the town closing her down.

Shit. Like he didn't have enough to do already. He eased himself to his feet, wincing at the ache in his back. Damn tree stump.

"I could take care of finding a couple of bouncers for you, if you like?" He eyed her hopefully. Maybe she'd still listen to sense.

"No thank you, Johnny. I have no intention of wasting my money. Now, if you'll excuse me, I am very busy."

She dipped the damn pen in the ink again and started writing, like he wasn't even there. Shaking his head he left her office, banging the door behind him.

So, it seemed he'd got his work cut out. He'd have to find out more about this meeting and discover who was going to vote which way. Maybe he could bring some pressure to bear on anyone voting for closing the place down. And he'd have to make damn sure that there wasn't any more trouble there in the meantime.

He stalked onto the street, and leaned against the wall even as the ghost of an idea started to form. He grinned to himself. One thing was certain; the Reverend Hausmann wasn't going to win this battle. He'd met his match in Fierro.

CHAPTER TEN

He hesitated outside and then turned back to the bordello. The town meeting was only a few days off, so if he was going to put his plan into action there was no time to waste.

Sadie's pout disappeared as fast as a frost in the morning sun when she saw him. Grabbing her by the arm, he hustled the giggling girl up the stairs and into one of the rooms set aside for the customers.

"Oh my! You sure are in a hurry, Johnny. But then it's been such a long time since you saw me, I knew you'd be back." She draped herself over him, her hands trying to undo his belt while she lifted her knee to massage his cock through his pants.

Reluctantly, he pulled away from her embrace. "Not so fast, honey. Before we get to that I need some answers."

The pout came back. "Answers? Answers to what?" She eyed him doubtfully. "Madam almost had my hide for telling you about her garden. You said you wouldn't tell her."

Johnny shook his head impatiently. "I didn't tell her, but

she ain't stupid. Anyway, forget about that. I need some answers, Sadie, and I need them now. Never mind worrying about Delice. I want to know the names of all the customers who come in through the side door from that little alley that runs alongside of this building."

Sadie paled, and licked her lips. "I don't know what you mean. Why do you think anyone comes in through there?"

"Because there ain't any other reason for having that side door onto the alleyway unless it's for customers who don't want it known that they come in here. That door ain't overlooked and that alleyway is real private. I used it myself one time, and I ain't dumb, Sadie."

She shook her head. "We ain't allowed to talk about customers, you know that. And it ain't fair of you asking me."

Johnny ran his fingers lightly over her shoulder. "Nobody ever said life is fair. You of all people should know that."

"I ain't telling you nothing. I don't want to lose my job. Madam would fire anyone who talked about the customers. She's told us so often enough. It's one of the rules here. And she's really strict about it."

He pulled her a little closer, and ran his finger lightly down over her neck and then slowly down her cleavage. "Come on, Sadie, you know you'll tell me. Delice won't find out." He slowly massaged her breast and rubbed at her nipple through the thin fabric of her bodice. He leaned in closer and breathed softly on her neck behind her ear before kissing her very gently there. She moved her head more to one side as if to encourage him, a soft moan escaping her lips. He pulled away. "I'd be really sorry to have to always leave you for Jeb Lutz in the future and make one of the other girls my regular one. I know how much you hate having him poke you. Still," he shook his head sadly, "I guess if you don't want to help me, then he's all you got to look forward to in the future. And he don't even tip well."

He gave her breast one last caress before moving away with a shrug. He turned toward the door, steeling himself against her wobbling lower lip. "Yeah, it's a real shame, Sadie, because you were always my favorite girl. Still, maybe you could persuade Jeb to take a bath more often."

Sadie grabbed hold of his arm, tears welling up in her eyes. "I can't tell you. Honest, I would if I could but I daren't. It's no good saying Madam won't find out, I don't know how but she always knows everything. I swear she's got eyes in the back of her head."

He moved his hand back to her breast, rubbing his palm back and forth across her nipple and stroked her neck very gently with his other hand. "Come on, Sadie, you can tell me. I promise I won't tell anyone."

She shook her head. "But I can't. I'll lose my job and then what will I do? I need this job, Johnny." Her lip wobbled more and another tear made a bid for freedom, coursing down her cheek.

He bit back an irritated sigh. "Look, if Delice fires you, you can come and work at Sinclair ranch. OK?" He tried to block out a mental picture of the old man's reaction to Sadie showing up at the ranch for a job, with her ample breasts spilling out of one of her low cut tops. Shit! Guthrie would go loco and that wouldn't be a pretty sight.

She furrowed her brow. "You mean come and work there as a whore?"

Dios! "No, Sadie, I don't mean as a whore. We don't hire whores on the ranch. What I mean is you could work in the kitchen or something."

Sadie frowned. "But I can't cook. I'm only good for poking."

She sure got that right. "Damn it, Sadie, we'd find something for you, OK? Now, just tell me what I want to know." He pulled her closer and bent his head to kiss her, probing her mouth with his tongue, all the while rubbing her breast. He paused briefly and nuzzled her ear. "The sooner you tell me, honey, the sooner we can get on with other stuff. So, come on, exactly who uses that side door?"

It was some considerable time later that he slipped out of the bordello and headed toward Caleb Swan's place. He figured it wouldn't be too hard to persuade Caleb to open up the telegraph office and send a wire for him. The man would sell his mother for a couple of dollars. Even better, he was terrified of Fierro so Johnny could be certain that the contents of the wire wouldn't be shared with the rest of the town. He grinned; Fierro's fearsome reputation was real handy at times like this. All it took was a softly spoken hint of trouble to come if someone didn't do just as Fierro wanted, and he had people eating right out of his hand.

Caleb didn't disappoint. In fact he was real obliging after Johnny applied a touch of pressure and scared the shit out of the man. Now Johnny stood in the dusk with only one thing left to do before he headed home.

He untied Pistol and rode him toward Hausmann's home. The white clapboard house was on the edge of the town close to the church. He paused outside and looked around curiously – somebody had been putting in a lot of work on the place. The picket fence was gleaming white, and the garden, which had been overgrown and ramshackle, was now tidy with not a weed in sight. All the flower beds had trimmed edges and the scent of rose bushes was competing with the smell of new paint. It was a close run contest to tell which was the stronger smell.

Johnny pushed his hat back and leaned on his saddle horn. Yeah, someone had been working awful hard here, and he'd bet a month's wages that it wasn't the good Reverend who'd been sweating with a spade or a paintbrush. Nope, the slack-mouthed Reverend hadn't an ounce of muscle, and had real soft hands which had never done a day's work. So it kind of begged the question as to who had been working so hard there. Certainly it was somebody fit – they'd transformed the place in a short space of time. He tried hard to think of any handy man in the town who worked that hard, but try as he might he couldn't come up with a single name. Most of them preferred the bottle to a spade and did the bare minimum, taking shameless advantage of the town's widows whose yards needed tending.

He stood in his stirrups to get a better view of the side of the house and the barn out back. In the fading light he could just make out the shape of a man walking toward the rear of the barn. A tall, hefty fellow, and despite the gloom, Johnny could swear the man was fair-haired. And the man had a military look about the way he walked. Johnny gritted his teeth. The light might be bad but there was something about him which struck a chord. One thing was certain; Johnny wanted to take a closer look at him. Maybe his instincts were right, and Hausmann had put someone up to smashing up the bordello. And maybe this was the same fellow. Maybe not. But if he was the bastard who'd hit Delice then he could start saying his prayers.

He slid quickly from the saddle and looped the reins through the fence before slipping through the gate. He was level with the back of the house when the side door opened and Hausmann came out grasping a small gun in one of his pudgy hands and carrying a lantern in the other.

"Fierro, what are you doing prowling around my place at night?" Hausmann waved the gun at Johnny. "I shoot trespassers."

Johnny raised an eyebrow, noting that the man hadn't even enough sense to take the safety catch off. "That don't seem a real Christian attitude, Reverend. Do you greet everyone like this? And what about your flock if they come seeking guidance? They might come here for reassurance and comfort. A gun don't seem too friendly for a man of the cloth."

Hausmann glowered at him. "Unless you've come here seeking forgiveness and wanting to confess your sins, I don't count you as one of my flock, Fierro."

Johnny scratched his chin. "If I want to make confession, I go and see a real priest, not one with a wife, from a church I don't rightly recognize as a church. I was brought up in the true faith, you see, Reverend. So, nope, I ain't here looking for confession."

Hausmann narrowed his eyes. "Don't lecture me about the true faith. But if you're not here seeking forgiveness, then that makes you a trespasser. So why are you prowling around my house?"

Johnny widened his eyes, all innocent like. "Prowling? I don't prowl, Reverend. I was only admiring all the hard work that someone's been putting in around here. They're obviously a good worker, and I know my old man's got a lot of jobs around the place need doing, so I was just wondering who you'd hired." Johnny waved his arm vaguely around in the direction of the garden and the fence.

"Who I have working here is none of your business. I employ honest, God-fearing men but I wouldn't expect you to understand that." Hausmann waved the gun at him again. "Now, if that's all, I suggest you get off my land."

Johnny laughed softly. "You seem awful reluctant to tell

me who you got working for you. And, call me suspicious, but that does seem strange. It's almost like you're trying to cover up something. But, heck, you're a man of the cloth, now you wouldn't be trying to be dishonest, would you?"

He heard Hausmann's breath hitch. Yep, seemed like he'd hit a nerve there. "I mean, you need to be careful, Reverend, you being a stranger in these parts. There are all sorts of desperados out here in the west. You don't know who you could be hiring. Only this week our good sheriff had a man in the jail who'd been causing trouble. Yep, he went on a real rampage, anyone would think he'd been put up to it, because there didn't seem no reason for him behaving the way he did. The fellow was tall and fair with a scar on his face and arm. You seen anyone like that around, Reverend?"

Hausmann took a step back. "I told you to get off my land, Fierro. Now! Otherwise I'll have the law on you. I've come across killers like you before. And I've crossed paths with arrogant cavalrymen like your damn killer-Yankee brother, thinking they own the world. Sinners, all of them."

Johnny raised an eyebrow, surprised by Hausmann including Guy in his rant. But he wasn't going to rise to the taunt. Instead he smiled. "I'm just passing the time of day, Reverend. Only trying to be neighborly, kind of warning you about that fellow, you being new around these parts. I'd hate for you to end up employing someone like that. It could be real risky." Johnny ambled back to where he'd tied Pistol and swung himself into the saddle. "Yep, employing someone like that could be a real mistake. Maybe if you come across someone like that you should tell him to watch out."

Hausmann stepped forward. "Why? What's your meaning, Fierro?"

Johnny turned in the saddle and looked down at the man. "What do I mean? Oh, only that I'm going to kill him when I catch up with him." He tipped his hat. "Goodnight, Reverend. Sleep well."

Laughing softly, he spurred Pistol into a lope and set off toward the ranch.

All in all, he reckoned it had been a good day's work. It was bad luck that Hausmann had come out of the house when he did, but it couldn't be helped. Johnny could bide his time. But one thing was certain—the man who struck Delice was going to pay for it.

He was plotting out his next move when he arrived at the ranch. The courtyard was in darkness and there was no sound from the bunkhouse. Everyone had settled in for the night. Most of the ranch was in darkness too, except for a faint glow coming from the living room. He could make out the silhouette of his father working at his desk.

Shit. The last thing he wanted was Guthrie picking up on their fight from earlier in the day. The man never knew when to leave well alone. He carried right on riding roughshod over everybody else. Johnny shook his head. He really couldn't handle butting heads with his father this late at night. Maybe if he slipped in through the side door he could make it up the back stairs without the old man hearing him.

He led Pistol into a stall and gave him a quick rub down and a feed. Then, slipping his spurs into his pocket, he cat-footed across the courtyard to the side door. He eased the handle down gently and then grunted in annoyance. It was locked. He took the knife from his boot and inserting the blade flipped the lock, but somebody had shot the bolt across so it still wouldn't open. Damn. He'd have to go in through the kitchen which meant going up the main stairs. Still, maybe the old man would be so caught up in his paperwork that he wouldn't hear.

Keeping in the shadows he sidled around to the kitchen door. He eased the handle down slowly, and to his relief the door opened. He offered up a silent prayer of thanks that Carlita had forgotten to lock it. She forgot so often that he had to wonder if she left it unlocked deliberately, particularly on nights when she knew he'd headed into town and would be back late.

His luck held until he reached the bottom of the stairs to his room. He fell headlong over a pair of boots which had been left lying right in the middle of the darkened hallway. Shit, anyone would think they'd been put there on purpose...

He was picking himself up off the floor when his father called out. "Johnny, I've been waiting up for you. I'd like a word, please."

Mierda!

CHAPTER ELEVEN

He shut his eyes briefly and wondered about those boots lying in the middle of the hall. Was his old man that devious? Surely not. But then again, Peggy was real tidy and it seemed an unlikely place for a pair of boots.

He leaned against the doorway of the living room and eyed Guthrie cautiously. He didn't look like he was in a bad mood but it didn't take much to set the old man off. "I was turning in, can't it wait till morning?" And that probably wasn't the smartest thing to say, but hell, Guthrie always threw him for a loop. If his father hadn't been in a bad mood, chances were he would be now.

Guthrie nodded toward the liquor cabinet. "I was hoping that you'd have a nightcap with me."

Johnny ducked his head briefly. What the hell was Guthrie up to? Oddly, he didn't sound riled up, but even so, there really was no telling. "It's kind of late, Guthrie. I got an early start in the morning. I'm going to take a work crew over to the northern boundary. The river's dammed up and needs clearing out."

Guthrie raised an eyebrow. "I am surprised; you showing such great dedication to your work."

Johnny gritted his teeth and blew out a long sigh.

"Humor me." Guthrie got to his feet and limped to the cabinet. "Tequila?"

Johnny shrugged. He could tell when he was beaten. "Yeah, but only a small one, please."

He took the proffered drink and then retreated to the door post again.

"Why don't you sit down?" Guthrie stretched back in his big leather chair and waved Johnny toward the seat opposite. "Make yourself comfortable. I can hardly see you standing over there."

Yeah, like he'd believe that. The old man was as sharp as a tack and had eyes like a hawk. But he could hardly say that, so he went and perched on the arm of the couch. Guthrie grunted.

"Come and sit over here, damn it. I was hoping we could have a talk."

Johnny stared down at his Indian bead bracelets, and spun them briefly, before looking back at Guthrie. "Yeah, that's what's bothering me. I really don't want to get into another fight with you. We had a deal, Guthrie. I keep my end of deals and I kind of thought you were the sort of man who would too. My time off is my own. And it ain't up for discussion."

Guthrie sighed and sipped his whiskey, before steepling his fingers and raising them to his chin. Maybe he was praying for patience. "Did it occur to you that maybe I wanted to apologize for this morning?"

Johnny jerked his head up. "Apologize? Do you?"

Guthrie nodded. "Actually, yes, I do. So, will you come and sit down?" He gestured toward the chair.

Johnny moved across and sat facing the old man. "So? I'm sitting." He could have kicked himself. Why did he always get so prickly around Guthrie? But it was like he couldn't help himself. He flushed. "Sorry."

Guthrie raised an eyebrow, kind of like he was surprised by the apology. Hell, he probably was surprised, Johnny didn't say sorry too often.

Guthrie drew in a breath. "I wanted to talk because I wanted to apologize for what I said to you at lunchtime. I shouldn't have taken my bad temper out on you. It was uncalled for and I regret it."

Johnny narrowed his eyes. "I guess I'm an easy target."

Guthrie kind of half-nodded, like he could see the truth of that. "After I calmed down, I felt bad about it. You're right, we do have a deal and I do keep my end of bargains. To be honest, I was incensed by the nerve of Hausmann lecturing us from his pulpit. He wasn't even subtle about it. He actually named us! And then, to have Henry having a go at us outside the church added insult to injury."

Johnny stretched his legs out, leaning back in the seat. "I guess I don't know much about your religion, but I do know in mine that a priest wouldn't name names. He'd have a go at the person in private, not in public in front of everyone, and I reckon that's how it should work. I don't think much of your religion if that's what your priests do."

Guthrie pulled a face. "No, son, it's not how my church is supposed to work either. Hausmann was totally out of line." Guthrie tilted his head to one side. "You don't have much regard for my church, do you?"

Johnny shrugged. "No. I was raised Catholic and I might not be much of one—" he paused and laughed. "Hell, I ain't much of one at all. Enough priests have told me so for me to have no doubt of that. But it's still the true faith. I thought you had to turn Catholic to buy land out here back when this area was still part of Mexico. So I guess I'm puzzled as to why you abandoned the religion."

Guthrie's eyes opened a touch wider, and then he scratched his head. "Well, that's got me on the back foot." He paused and took another sip of his whiskey. "It's a hard thing to change your faith. And back home, in both England and Scotland, there was no love lost between the Papists and the Episcopalians. But I wanted this land, and if that meant adopting the Catholic faith to get it, then I was prepared to do that. I can't sit here and say I saw the light as if I had some road to Damascus conversion. It was merely a means to an end. Does that shock you?"

Johnny ducked his head, he didn't really know what to say to that. He chose his words carefully. "Guthrie, I've done a lot of bad things in my life, and I sure as hell made some bad choices. But leastways I always knew right from wrong, even if I didn't always do the right thing. So I guess that if I'm honest, I reckon lying about your beliefs is kind of like selling your soul to the devil." He sighed and shook his head slowly. "I don't know. I mean, I know I'm damned, but I'd hate to think you were too."

He stared down at the floor, awkward from talking about such things, and hating his words. But hell, it didn't pay to piss around with God.

"I think perhaps I have an image of a more forgiving God than you, Johnny. I think there's a lot more fire and brimstone about Catholicism. But, like most of the settlers out here, I've reverted to the religion of my childhood. However, Hausmann definitely doesn't fit in mine, any more than he would in yours." He tapped an envelope sitting on his desk. "And that is precisely why I've written to the bishop. I am very curious about the Reverend Hausmann and I don't think the bishop will approve of his methods."

Johnny raised an eyebrow. "You're writing to the bishop? About Hausmann? What good's that going to do?"

Guthrie shrugged. "Maybe none. But I do want to know what Hausmann is doing so far from home, and if the church keeps moving him because he puts people's backs up. Because if that's the case, they can damn well move him again. Even if it costs me money to make that happen."

Johnny paused, his glass lifted hallway to his lips. "You'll pay for that to happen? Why?"

Guthrie ghosted a smile. "I am not prepared to have a poisonous man abuse his privileged position to insult my son. He's trying to stir up hatred, and..." Guthrie furrowed his brow, like he was searching for the right words. "And let's face it, there's enough animosity toward you in this region without him making things worse."

Johnny ducked his head while he tried to figure out what to say. He was amazed to think that his father cared about him so much. "Guthrie, I can fight my own battles. I been doing that a long time, I don't need no help. It ain't that I'm not grateful for the offer, I am, but—"

His father raised his hand. "Johnny, I am very well aware that you can fight your own battles, although it grieves me that you've had to do so all these years. But the point is, you don't need to fight them alone now. You've got family. And this is what families do. Stick together."

He couldn't think of a damn thing to say. Not a word. He sat staring down at his boots, trying to figure it out. He couldn't for the life of him think why Guthrie would care, but it felt real good inside to hear the old man's words. Even so, it was tricky because he wasn't used to help. He'd done OK all these years on his own. If a man never expected anything, then he couldn't be disappointed. And he'd learned that at a young age. Never depend on anyone because they always let you down. Everyone did. Sooner or later. It was strange to think maybe things were different now. He ran his fingers through his hair and shook his head, trying to clear his thoughts. He could feel Guthrie's eyes boring into him, waiting for him to say something.

He opened his mouth and then closed it again. He didn't want to put his foot in things. Hell, he usually managed to screw things up with Guthrie and he didn't want to do that, particularly now they were getting along so much better.

"I guess I ain't used to having family." He paused, measuring each word, like he was trying to persuade a jury not to hang him. "But really, you don't need to get your bishop involved in this." He sighed softly. Might as well just spit it out and get it said. "I'm not sure I'd be too happy about having one of your priests helping me. It just don't feel right."

Guthrie nodded, kind of like he understood. "The point is that this won't only be about you. Who else is Hausmann going to decry from his pulpit? Other people could get hurt, and I know you wouldn't want that."

Damn. The old man was sneaky. He knew Johnny couldn't argue against that. Yeah, a real devious tactic. Johnny's mouth quirked. Maybe he and his old man had more in common than he'd figured. One thing was certain, Guthrie had out-maneuvered him and there wasn't a damn thing he could do about it. Trouble was though, even if the bishop did do something, it wouldn't be soon enough to save Delice. No, he'd have to carry right on with his plan there, but God only knew what the hell Guthrie would say if he got to hear about it.

"So?" Guthrie raised his glass. "Do we have an agreement?"

Johnny grinned. "Yeah, sure." He swirled the tequila around in the glass. Maybe this would be a good time to ask Guthrie about the one thing which had been niggling at him for the past few days. He took a sip and sat back in his chair, like he was all relaxed. "There is something I'd like to ask you."

Was it his imagination or did Guthrie tense up a little? But right now he needed answers and all he could hope was that Guthrie's current good mood would last a little longer.

"Oh. About what?" Guthrie's voice was level, but not relaxed.

Johnny sighed. He was going to have to tread real careful here. And that was what it always came back to; him sweating about whether he was going to piss off Guthrie. "Well, I know you had a Pinkerton report on me." He tried not to flinch as he saw Guthrie's jaw tighten.

"And that's not surprising, given as how you spent all that time trying to track me down. I mean, it's right that they gave you a report." Did that sound OK? Would it keep Guthrie calm enough to carry on with this? He bit back the desire to tell the man that most of what was in the report was crap. That wouldn't help matters any. But shit, it had hurt when Guthrie had asked him all those months ago if he'd gunned down a man in front of his wife and children. He pushed the memory away. "But what I was wondering was how much you knew about Guy's upbringing. I can understand why you had to send him away for safety, what with Indian raids going on and all. But Boston's a hell of a long ways off so I don't reckon you could have gotten to see him often. So what sort of say did you have in things? You know, during his childhood and later on."

His father didn't say a word, only stared down into his glass like he'd lost a silver dollar in it. Just when he reckoned the old man wasn't going to answer, Guthrie looked across at him. "You're right, Boston is a long way away. It was very tough. To travel there, back then, took several weeks, and was fraught with danger. But I always intended that you would both have been educated there. A child deserves the best education their family can afford, and I would have sent you both to Boston to go to the best schools. But the Indian attacks that we were having around here simply brought that event forward. I wouldn't have sent Guy until he was older. But having family there, it made sense to send him for his own safety. I regret that I wasn't able to spend more time with him, but I know it was the right decision.

"But as far as what say I had in his upbringing, his aunt and uncle consulted with me over everything through correspondence. And I was able to make a couple of visits over the years. I did the best I could."

Johnny held his gaze. "So you knew about him joining the army when the war started?"

Guthrie nodded. "Yes, of course, and I wasn't surprised. Young men are always attracted by the idea of war, or a cause.

They think it's exciting. And of course they also think they're immortal. I didn't try to talk him out of it. His uncle told me that Guy was set on the idea, and that he'd already tried to persuade Guy against it. But, as you can imagine, I was worried sick about him. But the Sinclairs have a history of serving in the army, so I consoled myself with the belief that he was carrying on an old family tradition."

"But you never asked him about it?"

Guthrie shook his head. "No, I haven't. I figured if he wanted us to know about it then he'd tell us. And I still think you should leave it alone."

Johnny eyed him curiously. Did Guthrie know more about this than he was letting on, or did he really think that they should just leave the past alone? "I find it kind of strange that you've never discussed it with him."

Guthrie tilted his head to one side. "Would you like it if I started asking you questions about your past?"

Oh boy, the old man wasn't no pushover. Johnny shrugged, still playing it cool. "But you did. My memory ain't that bad."

Guthrie nodded, but not like he really wanted to agree. "Yes, well, I decided not to ask Guy any questions, exactly like I've stopped asking you questions."

Johnny ducked his head again. Guthrie was pretty good at the fancy footwork. He reckoned they were pretty much even here. And they weren't even yelling. "Maybe you should have asked him. Something's eating away at him."

Guthrie grunted. "You never give up, do you?"

Johnny stretched his legs out and leaned back in the chair. "Nope. Never."

Guthrie shook his head. "I really think we should leave this alone, Johnny."

Johnny stayed silent for a few seconds. He'd let his father think he was going to go along with the suggestion. He watched the tension leave his father's shoulders. Then he moved in for the kill. "If you don't want me asking him questions, where's the harm in you telling me one thing."

Guthrie narrowed his eyes. "What one thing?"

"He mentioned some place called Woodstock. I was wondering exactly where it is. I don't know much about that side of the country."

His father stared down into his glass like he was looking for a gold piece now.

"It's in Virginia. In the Shenandoah Valley." Guthrie got to his feet. "I'm beat, I'm turning in. I'll see you in the morning and we'll get that letter off to the bishop. I think that's a sensible first course of action. You should get some sleep too. Like you said, you've got an early start."

Johnny rubbed his chin thoughtfully, watching his father almost run from the room. If the old man thought he'd distracted him by turning the talk back to Hausmann then he sure as hell didn't know much about his son. Because one thing was certain, while Johnny might not have spent long in the Mexican army, he sure as hell knew about diversionary tactics, and his father was full of them. But at least he now knew more about where Guy had been stationed.

Yeah, all in all, it had been a pretty successful day.

CHAPTER TWELVE

He hardly had time to draw breath over the next few days, there was that much work for the crew. He stumbled bleary-eyed from his bedroll before sun-up each morning and collapsed into it again late at night.

And he couldn't help but think that there had to be easier ways to keep from starving. The old man sure had known what he was doing when he offered Johnny a share of the ranch. A share of the work, that was for sure. Didn't catch Guthrie working flat out for eighteen hours a day. Or taking work crews to clear out rivers on the north edge.

Still, he guessed that when a man got as old as Guthrie, he probably couldn't put in the hours, poor old devil. Probably couldn't do much else either. The old man never went whoring.

"Johnny, you going to stand there staring into the distance, or do you want some grub?"

He dragged his mind back and held his plate out for Travis to fill. Johnny muttered his thanks and went and slumped onto a flat rock to eat his meal. Half-heartedly, he pushed the food around the tin plate but he felt too damn tired to eat. It was fine for Harvard – he was back at the ranch and spent half of each day doing paperwork. And much as Johnny didn't like paperwork, he could sure see the benefit of sitting down in a big, comfortable chair, and having Peggy bring him coffee and cookies.

He forked in a mouthful of beans. There was nothing wrong with them. He'd known far worse cooks than Travis, in fact the cook could make anything taste pretty good. But heavens, he was sick of beans.

He really wanted to get into town, but God only knew when he'd get the time. And the trouble was, time was moving on and he needed to put his plans into action. But he could hardly tell Guthrie he needed some time off because he had pressing business of blackmail and coercion. Coercion. He liked that word. It sounded important. He'd heard Guy use it one time. He was learning lots of new words from Guy. Guy was learning a few off him too, but mostly they were Spanish cuss words. Although occasionally he did tell Guy they meant something different to what they really meant. It was kind of fun sitting back and watch the results of that deception.

"Senor Johnny." Francisco, one of the newer hands, stood smiling in front of him, slapping dust from his hat. "We have almost done. Another hour or two should do it. Then we can all go back to the ranch. Si?"

Johnny grinned at the hopeful note in the young man's voice. Nobody liked clearing out the river. He nodded. "Si, Francisco. Y esta noche podemos tener algo mejor que los frijoles para la cena!"

Francisco's eyes lit up. They were all sick of eating beans. "Espero que sí, Senor Johnny!"

Johnny watched Francisco sprint back to rejoin the rest of the crew. He shook his head slowly. Senor Johnny. He still hadn't gotten used to being the boss. It had been different running range wars. He'd accepted command then as natural, and he'd run them exactly how he wanted to, by his rules. But this was different; he had to kind of feel his way over some things. And he was all too aware that his old man was watching him, waiting for him to slip up and make mistakes. One thing here was certain though – not all of the men liked taking orders from him. On the whole the Mexicans didn't seem to mind. But some of the gringo hands were another matter. He had sharp hearing and over the past few months he'd heard some of the muttered curses at his expense. They sure didn't like Fierro. And they didn't like him being a breed either.

But then, nobody liked a breed. Nothing new there. Even so, there were times when he felt like grinding those gringos' noses into the dirt. He might be a breed but he was the boss whether they liked it or not.

Slowly, like an old man, he hauled himself to his feet. He was getting soft – he missed his bed. But then again, he'd been working flat out for weeks now, so maybe it was understandable that he was aching. A soak in a hot tub would put him right. And boy, never had a soak seemed quite so appealing.

Francisco wasn't wrong. It took barely over an hour to finish the work. Johnny set half the men to clearing up so that they were all ready and packed by the time the last crew had finished hauling the fallen trees from the river.

Although the chuck wagon would take another day to get back to the ranch, Johnny took a small group of men, including Francisco, on ahead. He made the excuse that there was a great deal of work waiting to be done – and it sounded good enough. Trouble was, he couldn't think of a single excuse to give Guthrie for going into Cimarron. Try as he might, he couldn't see himself getting there before Saturday night when his time would finally be his to call his own. But maybe the winds of fortune would blow his way and he'd get a chance to sneak in before Saturday.

All the men were keen to get back and they pushed their horses hard, arriving at the hacienda as darkness fell. They rode whooping and hollering into the yard, making enough noise to wake the dead. Johnny grinned; the men could sure kick up a racket and hopefully it would boot Peggy into the kitchen to prepare him a late supper.

He fed Pistol and then hurried to the hacienda. Pushing open the heavy door, he was met by his father, and the mouthwatering scent of sizzling bacon.

"Peggy is getting you some supper. We heard you all ride in." Guthrie clapped him on the back. "Come on in and sit down, you've had a hard few days."

Johnny tried to stop his mouth dropping open with surprise. Maybe the old man was going soft. Still, he wasn't going to knock it, life was a hell of a lot easier when he and Guthrie weren't going at it. He followed Guthrie into the kitchen where Peggy was busy doing something with eggs – huevos rancheros if he was lucky. He leaned over her shoulder and stuck a finger in the mixture for a quick taste. He smacked his lips. "Just a touch more chili, Peggy, and it'll be perfecto. Gracias."

He slumped down at the table as she started dishing him up a heaped plateful which she set in front of him, along with a glass of her best lemonade. "I'll put the coffee on, but that might help in the short term." Grinning, she ruffled his hair, and then set about brewing the coffee.

Guthrie poured himself a glass and leaned back while Johnny forked the food in. "So, did it all go well out there? I admit, I didn't expect you back before tomorrow." Guthrie raised a questioning eyebrow before taking a swift swig of lemonade.

Johnny paused eating, with eggs balanced on his fork. "I kept the crew hard at it. Then I brought back half the men because I figured they could crack on with something else tomorrow. The rest of the crew are coming back with Travis. Didn't seem much point in us all coming in slow."

Guthrie nodded. "Good plan. There's lots of work here needs doing. Cattle broke through the fence out toward the southern mesa. It'll need re-wiring."

Johnny tried to stifle a groan. Any time fences needed wiring, it always came down to him. Mierda, but he was sick of fences and post holes. How come Harvard never had to dig post holes?

He could feel Guthrie studying him hard. Watching him. But hell, he wasn't going to fight over it. He wouldn't give the old man the satisfaction.

"But I thought I'd send Guy out to deal with that. I reckon you've done your share of hard labor this week."

Johnny almost choked on a mouthful of egg. He started coughing and Guthrie leaned over to clap him on the back. And he'd swear his father was laughing.

"I was going to ask you if you could head into Cimarron and drop some papers at the lawyer's office for me. But maybe you'd rather dig post holes? I'd hate to deprive you of something you might enjoy."

Johnny could hear the laughter now. He grinned, unable to stop the smile breaking out. "Well, it's kind of mean of me to always keep the fence posts for myself. I'm sure Guy would love to take a turn at it."

Guthrie nodded. "That's what I thought." He clambered slowly to his feet, rubbing his back. "I think I'll leave you to have your coffee in peace. I'm away to my bed. Goodnight, son."

"I won't be far behind you. I'm beat. Goodnight." Johnny watched his father limp from the room before swinging around on his chair to watch Peggy as she made coffee. "Those eggs were real good and exactly what I needed. Thanks, Peggy, I appreciate it. But I'll take my coffee with me. I'm going to bed too."

Peggy handed him a steaming mug. "Here you are." She furrowed her brow, like she wasn't sure about something, or like she was thinking what to say. "You may not believe this, but he misses you when you're not here. He would never say so to you, but he always looks out of the window more. And he's always wondering aloud about how you're getting on. And no," she held her hand up kind of to stop him saying anything, "it's not that he doesn't trust you, even though that's what you're probably thinking. He really misses you and it's very obvious. I know you all think I'm young and silly, but I can see how much he cares. Even if you can't." She leaned over and kissed him on the cheek. "Goodnight, Johnny, it's good to have you home."

He sat frozen to his seat as she clattered up the stairs. He couldn't have moved if he'd wanted to, and he sure couldn't have drunk his coffee because there was a big lump in his throat kind of blocking things. And at the back of his mind, a tiny voice was saying that maybe he was finally getting the hang of this family thing. He nodded his head slowly. Yeah, things were looking up.

He enjoyed seeing Guy ride off with the work crew in the morning.

He waited until Guy was swinging himself into the saddle, and then hurried over. "Hey, Guy, hold up."

Guy gathered up his reins before looking down at him. "Did I forget something?"

Johnny nodded, keeping his face straight. "Well, yeah. I thought I'd best explain about this." He held out the spade which he'd been hiding behind his back. "I reckoned I'd better show you which end does what. You see you put your foot on this part..." Laughing, he ducked away from the clout which Guy aimed at his head.

Guy grinned. "It'll keep! Revenge is a dish best served cold." And he swung his horse away to catch up with the crew.

Johnny shoved Guthrie's legal papers inside his jacket and headed off toward Cimarron, enjoying the warmth of the sun on his face. Not that he was going straight to Cimarron. Nope, he reckoned the time had come to start turning the screws.

Lady Luck was riding with him he reckoned, because as he rode to Henry Carter's boundary, he met the man himself inspecting a damaged gate.

Carter scowled. "What do you want, Fierro? You know that you're not welcome on my land. I've warned you before, if I catch you trespassing I'll take delight in putting a bullet in you."

Johnny leaned forward, resting his hands on the saddle pommel. "Well, seeing as I'm on public land right here, I ain't doing anything wrong. Mind you—" he paused and smiled coolly—"I'd like to see you try to shoot me. Reckon I'd get my gun clear a hell of a lot quicker than you would. You might not take delight in that."

"What do you want, Fierro? Get to the point."

Johnny raised an eyebrow. "Oh, I was just passing by. Thought I'd be neighborly and stop and see how you're doing. Seeing as how we're fellow ranchers."

Carter scoffed. "I don't see you as a fellow rancher, Fierro. You might have fooled Guthrie, but you haven't fooled me. You're a gunfighter, and that puts you at the bottom of the barrel. And I never like what I find at the bottom of barrels."

Johnny shrugged. "Meaning you're the top of the barrel?"

Carter nodded. "Yeah, you're getting the idea, Fierro."

Johnny grinned. "Well, it seems I was right then, I always thought scum rose to the top."

Carter's face turned bright red and he stepped forward, his hand hovering near his gun. Johnny held his hand up. "But hey, I'm not here to trade insults. I was wondering if you were going to the town meeting, seeing as how your wife was busy protesting against the bordello."

Carter's brow furrowed. "What the hell has that got to do with you? Although the whole town knows that you're always in that place. And not that it's any of your business, but yes, I will be going. My wife has asked me to attend and vote to close the place down. That will trim your wings a bit, Fierro."

Johnny leaned further forward, resting his elbow on the pommel. "From what I hear, it seems like it might trim yours too."

"And what the hell's that meant to mean, Fierro?"

Johnny smiled. "Oh, only that it would be a shame to close the place down. I don't think your wife would be too happy if it closed down."

Carter snorted. "I just told you she wants it closed."

Johnny sighed softly. "Yeah, but it would be a real shame because then I'd have to tell her all about your visits to the bordello, and I don't think she'd be too happy if she knew about those. No, much better to leave the place open. Then you still get to dip your pecker when you fancy, and things carry on exactly the same as they are now."

Carter paled. "I don't know what you mean, Fierro. I never go there. You've never seen me in that place."

Johnny rubbed his chin. "Oh, I know you go there, Carter. You slip right on in through that side door and sneak up the backstairs. And then you enjoy a romp in bed with your favorite girl. Clara isn't it?"

"And who told you that? That whore, Martin? You're real friendly with her, I hear. Or are you simply guessing, Fierro? You're way off the mark. And anyway, you can't prove any of this."

Johnny narrowed his eyes. "No, Miss Martin didn't tell me. But I got eyes, and I got ears. And it don't really matter if I can prove it or not. Even though you and I both know it's true. The point is, all I need to do is plant a little seed of doubt in your wife's mind, and your life won't be worth living. She'd be watching you like a hawk and keeping you on such a short leash, you wouldn't even be able to get into town for as much as a beer."

"You're trying to blackmail me, Fierro." Carter's mouth was working furiously and a nerve in his cheek was ticking.

Johnny shook his head. "Nope. I ain't trying to blackmail you, Carter." He paused and gave a cold tight smile. "I am blackmailing you. So, you listen and listen good. That meeting this week is going to be men only. And there will be a secret vote of the main committee. Of which you are a member. And you will vote to keep the bordello open."

Carter shook his head, his face pale. "You're wrong. It's going to be a public meeting, I won't be able to do as you say."

Johnny smiled. "It was going to be a public meeting, but trust me, it will be a closed meeting. There'll be a short spell for the public to air their views, and then the committee will go off to vote. In private. And you will vote to keep the bordello open. Otherwise your wife will be getting a visit from me."

Carter's mouth was opening and closing, all the color drained from his face.

Johnny tipped his hat. "So I'll be going now. Nice doing business with you, Carter." He paused and looked across at the cattle grazing the other side of the fence. "Oh, and as one rancher to another, you'd best take a look at that far steer. Looks like he's got early stages of wooden tongue. An iodine wash can help with that."

And with a brief nod, Johnny spurred Pistol off toward

Cimarron. He didn't stop grinning until he slowed Pistol down to amble into town.

He tied Pistol at the hitching rail on the main street, while he pondered his next move. He figured he'd best deal with Guthrie's papers first, and drop them off at the lawyer's office. Then he could get on with his other calls.

It took only a few minutes to lodge the papers with the lawyer; luckily the man had a client with him so Johnny had a good excuse not to linger.

He was heading toward the bordello when Stoney called out to him. "Johnny, I wanted a word if you got a minute."

Johnny grinned. "Something on your mind?"

Stoney nodded and then jerked his head indicating for Johnny to join him at the side of the boardwalk, away from the bustle of the street. "Thought you might be interested to know that Hausmann's got that joker working for him. The one I had in my jail."

Johnny tensed. "The man who hit Delice?" Damn it. He'd known it was that son of a bitch he'd caught sight of at Hausmann's.

Stoney nodded, his eyes narrowed. "Figured you'd find out from somewhere and I wanted to see you first so you could hear it from me. So listen here, Johnny, I'm warning you not to stir up trouble with that fellow. You were real agitated about him the other day, but he spent time in my jail, and that's an end of it. Whether you like it or not. Let it go, Johnny."

"Is that an order?" Johnny kept his voice real cool.

"Yeah. That's an order. As long as he ain't causing any trouble, it's over. From what I hear he's some relative of that old devil Hausmann and he's working there fixing the place up. So, it's over. You leave him alone. Don't reckon I can make it plainer than that."

"I don't like taking orders from any man, Stoney."

"Well, you better damn well start, because otherwise I'll throw you in jail. And believe me, that's a promise. I'm the law around here and you'd best not forget it. The fellow did two days in my jail. I don't like him, but he ain't doing anything wrong. So it ends here, Johnny."

Johnny shrugged, like he wasn't interested. "If you say so." Except the bastard wouldn't be working for Hausmann for much longer. Wouldn't be working for anyone.

Stoney glared. "Yeah, I do say so. And don't you forget it."

"Fine. If that's all, Stoney, I got some errands to run. Catch up with you later." With a brief nod, Johnny turned and strode on up the street, unable to believe his good fortune. At least now he knew that the man at Hausmann's was the one who hit Delice. The bastard was going to pay for that.

He came to an abrupt stop as he reached the bordello. Two men sat outside. One held a scattergun across his knees and the other was spinning the chambers on his Colt.

CHAPTER THIRTEEN

Johnny glared at them. "What the hell are you two doing sitting out here? When I wired you, I made it plain you're supposed to be inside the damn building, not sitting out here sunning yourselves. I ain't paying good money for you to sit around on your butts."

The bigger, uglier one, with a nose which had received one too many punches, put his scattergun down and shuffled to his feet. "We came as soon as we got the wire, Johnny." He looked kind of hopeful, like he figured his speedy arrival would make up for the fact he wasn't doing the job he was being paid to do.

The smaller one shoved the Colt back in his holster as he scrambled to his feet. "Yeah, Johnny, we came straight over from Elizabethtown, just like Bob said."

Mierda! Seemed if he wanted a job done right he had to do it himself. "I asked you to come over and go inside the bordello to keep an eye on things, not sit outside it." Johnny spoke slowly, emphasizing the words because maybe they were too dim-witted to understand otherwise.

Bob flushed and chewed on his lip. "Yeah, well, that's what we tried to do, Johnny. Honest. Clem here will tell you the same."

Clem nodded enthusiastically, obviously keen to back up his pal. "Yeah. We did try to do what you asked, Johnny, honest."

Bob, who was slow witted at the best of times, even if he was real handy with his fists and a rifle, nodded toward Clem, kind of acknowledging his friend's support. "Yeah, we come straight over when we got the wire, and we did everything you said. But that woman! Phew! I mean, shit, Johnny, she's one hard-nosed bitch."

Johnny glared and opened his mouth to say something but Clem butted in. "And that's putting it politely. We went in and ordered drinks, and we sat around some. Like we weren't in any hurry to do anything. But that woman was real nosey about what we were doing there. So we went and had ourselves a bit of a poke with a couple of the girls, so it would look like we was simply ordinary customers."

Bob grinned and nodded as he elbowed Clem in the ribs. "Yeah, we had ourselves two real pretty girls. Mine had a big dimple in her chin and real big—" He started to make exaggerated gestures at his chest.

Johnny grunted in irritation. "Just get on with telling me what happened. Never mind which girls you poked."

Bob sighed and looked sort of put out. "Only trying to explain, Johnny. And I thought you might be interested in hearing how pretty they is."

Clem nodded. "He's right, Johnny. You're always looking for girls—"

"Stop! Get on with the damn story." Johnny spoke with gritted teeth. Dios. Clem and Bob were honest and loyal, but sometime he wondered if they had a brain between the pair of them.

Bob sniffed. "I'm getting there. No need to get your hackles up. Well, then the old hag threw us out."

Johnny stared at him blankly. "Well, something must have happened between you having your poke and being thrown out. And she ain't an old hag! Hell, Bob, tell me what happened in between those two events."

Bob scratched his head like he didn't understand. Johnny turned toward Clem. He was marginally brighter, so maybe he'd shed some light on it. "Clem? Can you tell me what happened?"

Clem pushed his hat back and rubbed his chin. "Well, yep. You're right, something did happen. You see, we had our pokes. Bob had his dimpled one, and I had me a redhead with lots of freckles. She had freckles in all sorts of places. You wouldn't believe the places she had freckles. I like freckles." He paused, a faraway look in his eyes like he was thinking about girls with freckles. "Have to say, Johnny, the girls here are a sight prettier than most whores."

Johnny ground his teeth. "Never mind the girls, or the poking, or the dimples, or the freckles. Just tell me what happened – outside of the bedrooms."

"I'm a-getting there, Johnny." Clem sighed. "Well, me and Bob came downstairs and we bought our girls a drink and then we sat in the corner and got out some cards. Figured it was as good a way to pass the time as any. But after we'd been there a while, the old hag said she wasn't running a saloon or a gambling house and if we wanted to drink or play poker we should go to the saloon." Clem paused to scratch his belly. "So we told her we was there to help her. That we'd heard there'd been some trouble in there and we figured we could help out."

"That's right." Bob nodded. "We said we were real handy to have around as protection. But she wanted to know who'd sent us."

Clem butted in. "Well, we figured you didn't want her to know as it was you who'd hired us, so we said that we'd heard some miners talking about the trouble and we decided to come over to keep an eye on things."

Johnny raised an eyebrow. He hadn't credited them with being sharp enough to consider that.

"And that's when she got all bossy." Bob shook his head. "She's a real old cow. She got all sharp and said if we'd wanted work we'd have asked straight out. Then she started on about how it was obvious someone was paying us either to cause trouble or stop trouble." Bob paused, his brow furrowed like he was thinking real hard. "And she used some long words too that I couldn't figure at all. I mean, really, really long words. But we told her that we were only there to offer the place some protection and that's when she threw us out. She seemed to figure that you had a hand in us being there. And she said to tell you to... Well, she wasn't real polite..." Bob trailed off and flushed again.

Clem leaned forward. "Anyway, we figured if we couldn't sit inside, we'd sit outside and guard it instead. That way, if there was any trouble we could rush inside and break it up." Clem sounded kind of proud, like that thought had been a stroke of genius. "But then, she come out and wouldn't even let us sit leaning against the wall. She drew a line with a bit of chalk which she said marked her boundary and that we'd better not step over it."

"Yep. She was real fussy about that damn line." Bob sighed. "Women! They're all real tricky. But I reckon she's about the trickiest woman I ever done met. And bossy. And damn ugly."

Johnny rolled his eyes and held his hand up to stop them carrying on. "OK! Enough. Leave this to me. I'll go talk to her. And she ain't ugly. She's a friend of mine."

Clem snorted. "A friend! The way she was carrying on about you, I doubt she reckons you're friends. You should have heard the things she—"

Johnny narrowed his eyes. "Enough. I said I'll go talk to her. You two just," he paused, trying desperately to think of something the two idiots could do. "Just sit there and clean your guns or something."

He stood with head bowed trying to figure out how to deal with things. He should have known better. Sending those two to the bordello had not been one of his brightest ideas. But the two of them were as honest as the day was long, and there was a lot to be said for that. And when it came to taking care of potential trouble makers, Bob and Clem were pretty much as good as it got. He glanced across at them. They were both standing watching him, kind of eager like a pair of old, willing, hunting dogs. Hell, this wasn't their fault. He should have known that Delice would get suspicious of anyone sitting around in the bordello and not being in a hurry to go anywhere. He grinned at them. "Go on. Get back to playing with your guns. I'll go talk to her."

It was quiet in the bordello. It was too early in the day for any customers but the girls brightened up when they saw him and came rushing over in a cloud of scent, all feathers and ruffles. Sadie pushed to the front of them and stretched up to whisper in his ear. "Madam's mad as hell with you. Might be best if you made yourself scarce."

Even as Sadie spoke, Delice came out of her office and glared at him. "I want a word with you, Johnny. Now."

Sadie squeezed his arm as he pushed through the throng of girls and followed Delice into her office. He whipped his hat off so at least she couldn't criticize his manners. There was no point in pissing her off any more than she already was. She leaned against the wall and folded her arms, her lips compressed in a tight line.

He'd seen friendlier looking bears.

He tried his widest smile. The one that always charmed the girls. "Lovely day, Delice." He didn't get any further.

"Don't you 'lovely day' me!" Her voice was like a snake hissing. "How dare you poke your nose into my affairs. How dare you interfere in my business. My God, but you've got one hell of a nerve. I do not need your help. I do not need any man's help or interference. I run a successful business and I run it damn well – better than any man could run it. And if I feel the need to hire men to protect the place, I am more than capable of doing so myself. I hire and fire my own staff. And believe me, if I was hiring some bouncers, I would hire men with brains. Not that pair of half-wits you sent me."

He swiped his leg with his hat and then tossed it onto the chair. "That ain't fair. Bob and Clem are real good at taking care of trouble. And they're honest. Damn it, Delice, you need someone around to keep an eye on things. And I know a damn sight more about the sort of men you need for that than you do. Why the hell can't you accept that I know what I'm doing?"

Her eyes flashed. "Know what you're doing? Know what you're doing! The only thing you're doing is drawing attention to the place with your two idiots sitting outside nursing their guns."

"They wouldn't be sitting outside if you'd let them do their job and come inside." He snapped the words out. Dios but she was awkward at times. Probably one of those damn women who figured they should have a vote.

"I don't need their help. I don't need anyone's help." She picked up some papers off the desk and slammed them into an open drawer which she shut with a bang. Johnny winced. He had the feeling she wished she was banging his head into something.

Maybe he should try a different approach. "You needed some help the night that fellow came in and smashed the place up. You didn't do so good at looking after yourself then. And you didn't look after the girls neither. You all came out of that roughed up. And I don't want to see you all getting hurt."

"You mean you don't want to see your precious Sadie bruised?" She stopped real sudden and took a deep breath. "Well, I've got news for you, Johnny. Occasionally things like this happen in bordellos. Hell, in some bordellos it's a regular occurrence. And after all, what does it matter – we're only whores! But I run this place well and I keep everything under control. What happened the other day was a very rare event. But if you think I'm going to pay men to sit around the place playing cards on the off chance that something like that will happen again, you have another think coming. I am not running a charity."

Johnny folded his arms and leaned against the door. "He's still in town. And if he comes back here you can't handle it. So, you let my boys stay put until I deal with him."

She opened her mouth, but didn't say anything for a heartbeat. "What do you mean, he's still in town? Who?"

Johnny tilted his head to one side and took his time replying. Let her stew on it for a second. "You know damn well who I mean. The man who smashed the place up. From what I hear, he's some relative of the Reverend. He's working for Hausmann at the moment. I don't know for sure whether Hausmann put him up to causing trouble in here, but I'd bet good money that he did. Anyway, I'm going to deal with him."

She sucked in a breath. "What do you mean – you're going to deal with him?" He could hear the fear in her voice.

He shrugged. "You don't need to worry about that. But I will deal with him." He ducked his head briefly before looking back at her. "So, as long as he's still around, you let Clem and Bob hang around too. It ain't costing you nothing. I'm paying them."

Seemed that wasn't the right thing to say because her eyes narrowed and went all flashy. "I do not need your charity. If I wish to hire people I will pay their wages myself."

Johnny ran his fingers through his hair. Damn but she drove him crazy at times. "Fine. You pay them. But let them stick around for a few days. And then, later, maybe we can discuss you getting someone in permanent."

"That won't be necessary." She looked away from him and her voice was cool.

He eyed her curiously. "Why not? Cimarron's a rough town, Delice. It's been getting rougher since Maxwell left. It's growing fast with new people coming in from other territories, and they ain't all law abiding citizens. And apart from that, with all the fighting over Maxwell's land and the leases, I reckon we'll see range wars before too long."

"It won't be necessary because I have decided that my girls and I are relocating to Santa Fe. I am travelling there next week to view suitable premises."

He stared at her. Couldn't think of a damn thing to say. He'd never believed that she was serious when she'd talked about it. Shit. No! No, she couldn't mean it. Could she? "But, but..." He shook his head and tried to get his words into some sort of order. "Look, why don't you wait until after the town meeting. I'm sure you'll feel differently then. I don't reckon they'll close you down. And moving would be real troublesome." He paused. "And like I said the other day, it would be expensive. Real expensive. Only the other day, my old man was saying how prices have risen in Santa Fe, and it's gotten awful pricey. And it ain't like it's a peaceful place. And it's not friendly like Cimarron." The words almost stuck in his throat. There was always trouble in Cimarron these days, and that sure wasn't making it friendly! Judging by her raised eyebrow she wasn't buying into that line. He couldn't blame her for that. Especially immediately after his comments about range wars.

"My mind is made up, I am going to relocate to Santa Fe. But for the time being, I will employ your idiots, but only because it would be too time consuming to find someone else. It might be as well as I shall be away from here for a few days when I visit the town to look at property. I hate to disillusion you, but I think that the town meeting will vote to close this place down."

"I wouldn't bet on it." He muttered the words, not really

expecting her to hear. But hell she had sharp hearing.

"What do you mean? What have you heard?" Her eyes were narrowed, and he'd swear that if she'd been a dog her nose would have been twitching, trying to sniff out what he was getting at.

He shrugged, trying to buy some time while he thought of a reason. "Well, the bordello brings people into town, people spend money. It's good for business. And the mayor likes people spending money in his town." He smiled, pleased with himself.

She made one of her pffftt noises. "So suddenly you're an expert on economics. Maybe I should call you Adam Smith."

He stared at her blankly. "Adam who?"

"Never mind Adam Smith, why do I get the feeling you know something?" Her eyes hardened and seemed to bore into him as she looked him up and down, like she thought she might find the answer written on him. "I don't trust you an inch. Stay out of my business, Johnny. And don't go interfering in town business either." She paused, looking at him intently. "And tell those two idiots of yours, if they're going to work here for a few days, to keep their hands off the girls. Free gropes don't come with the job."

Johnny grabbed his hat from the chair. "I'll tell them. You don't need to worry yourself about that." He knew he sounded snappy, but hell, she was pissing him off. "But they're good men and they'll look after the place. Better than your Adam Smith would." Who the hell was Adam Smith anyhow? A friend of

Delice? And how good a friend?

She rolled her eyes. "Go away, Johnny. Send your idiot friends in to see me. And don't you dare meddle in my affairs again. I won't be so nice about it next time."

"Nice! Madre de Dios." If that was her idea of being nice... He stomped out, and went to talk to Clem and Bob.

He outlined briefly what would be expected of them. "She'll be paying you. But for God's sake, please don't piss her off. And don't go poking any of the girls. You got that? Keep your dicks in your pants. That's an order."

Clem and Bob exchanged glances before nodding reluctantly. Clem sighed. "I really liked my redhead. And Bob was real taken with his girl with the big—"

"Sadie." Bob beamed. "That was her name. Yeah, Johnny, she had real big—"

Johnny held a hand up. "Enough. Go and see Miss Martin. Now!"

Biting back a grin, he watched the two of them shuffle into the bordello. Maybe Delice had a point – they weren't the sharpest knives in the drawer, but leastways nobody would be beating up on her with those two around.

He set his hat forward to shield his eyes from the sun and scanned the bustling street. There were a few calls that he'd need to make, but maybe his first visit should be to the mayor. He grinned. Yep. Definitely the mayor first – he was looking forward to that.

CHAPTER FOURTEEN

He ambled along the boardwalk of the main street, dodging people who seemed to have nothing better to do than stand staring in shop windows.

He hadn't been wrong when he told Delice that Cimarron was a growing town. He'd swear there were more shops each time he visited. But then, there hadn't been that many to start with, so maybe there was a call for more. Still, for the life of him he couldn't imagine why people wanted to stand and stare at them. If all the shops had been gunsmiths, well, leastways there'd be something interesting to look at.

But the mayor's store was the biggest in town. Johnny paused in front of its gleaming windows. There wasn't a mark on the shiny green paintwork, and all sorts of goods were displayed in the windows to tempt customers in. Johnny shook his head – he'd bet a month's wages that if any other shop grew as large, the mayor would build a bigger one.

A bell tinkled as he pushed the door open and the staff, lined up behind the counter, all beamed welcoming smiles, kind of like they were ordered to do that. Mrs. Tandy' smile faded real fast. She nodded to him. "Mr. Sinclair, how may we be of service?"

Johnny swept his hat off, suppressing a smile because from the tone of her voice it was damned obvious that she would rather serve anyone other than him.

"Mrs. Tandy, ladies." He smiled at the staff, still standing like they were on a parade ground. He glanced around the store, nodding slowly like he approved of it all. "I must say, Mrs. Tandy, you got a real nice store here. Yep, a real fine store. I'll bet it's the best shop in town."

She blushed at the compliment, the scarlet clashing with the mesh of purple veins which covered her plump face.

"I bet Mayor Tandy is real proud to have a wife like you, someone who knows how to run a successful business. That's a real asset to a man."

Her face cracked into a smile. "Why, Mr. Sinclair, that's too kind of you. We do try to cater to the more discerning customer."

She said the words slowly, like she'd learned them, but maybe wasn't too sure what they meant. In which case that made two of them. He made a slight bow. "Well, Ma'am, I think you've got that exactly right." He turned slowly, looking at all the shelves and counters. "Yep, exactly right. There are so many different things here for folks to choose from. I have to say the mayor is a very lucky man."

Mrs. Tandy giggled like some young girl and fanned her face with her hand. "Mr. Sinclair, it seems that contrary to what I might have expected, you are a very discerning customer. I'm delighted that you're impressed by our emporium. It was only this week that my husband and I were discussing the possibility of expanding and opening another branch in Elizabethtown. But forgive me," she fluttered her hands. "Here I am chattering on. Now, what can we tempt you with today?" She wiggled her eyebrows, like she was trying to flirt with him and waved her hand in the direction of the shelves where all sorts of goods were displayed, from scarves and handkerchiefs to medicines claiming to cure all ills. "Maybe something pretty for Miss Peggy? Or we do have some very fine and unusual pipe tobacco. I think your esteemed father smokes a pipe, does he not?"

Johnny bit back a smile. "He does indeed, Mrs. Tandy. And I'd like a couple of ounces of whichever tobacco you'd recommend. And, one of those pretty hair slides would be nice for Peggy. She works real hard looking after us. But you'd know how hard women have to work to make a home comfortable." He turned on the full smile now.

"How nice to meet a young man who appreciates what hard work running a home is. So many men," her eyes hardened a touch, and she sniffed like she was thinking of someone real close to her own home. "So many men are not appreciative of women's work."

Johnny tried to look sympathetic. "Is that so, Mrs. Tandy? Well, any men who don't appreciate how hard women have to work must be really dumb. I mean all that washing and cooking and cleaning, all to make a nice home for your menfolk." He shook his head. "Yep, you ladies never stop working. And how you can fit in working here as well, I think that's really something." He gave her another huge smile, trying to block out the thought of what his family would say if they could hear him at the moment. Peggy would probably punch him on the nose. She was always telling them that they didn't appreciate her hard work.

Johnny fished out some money to pay for the tobacco and hair slide, and glanced around the shop. "Now, Mrs. Tandy, is your lucky husband around? I wanted a quick word with him if he's here."

At the mention of her husband, Mrs. Tandy's mouth turned down at the corners and she sniffed again loudly. "He's in the office through the backyard. Do go through, Mr. Sinclair, and I do hope we'll be seeing you in here again soon."

Johnny tipped his hat. "Now I've seen inside here, Mrs. Tandy, wild horses won't keep me away."

He strolled through to the mayor's office which was out behind the main store in the darkest corner of the yard. Johnny grinned; it seemed Tandy didn't want anyone keeping too close an eye on his comings and goings. Particularly his comings...

The mayor was poring over a pile of ledger books, sweat trickling down the side of his face as he ticked off figures. A flash of annoyance showed on his pudgy face when he saw who was interrupting his work. "What do you want, Sinclair?"

Johnny glanced around the room and then used his hat to dust off a chair before sitting down and stretching his legs out. "Mr. Mayor." He nodded at Tandy. "What do I want? I wanted a few words with you, I won't take up much of your time."

Tandy mopped his brow with a big handkerchief. "I'm a busy man, Sinclair, so make it quick."

Johnny smiled. Oh boy, he was going to enjoy letting the air out of this puffed-up windbag. "I thought maybe we'd better have a word about the town meeting, seeing as you're organizing it."

A small furrow appeared on Tandy's damp forehead. "I don't see that we need to talk about that. People can have their say and then they'll vote." His mouth quirked, like he found something amusing. "And the people will vote to shut the bordello down. That'll spoil your fun, Sinclair."

Johnny nodded slowly, shifting in his seat and crossing his feet and jingling his spurs. He didn't say anything. That would make Tandy sweat even more.

Tandy mopped his neck. "Well? I thought you wanted to say something. I'm a busy man, so if that's all, I'll thank you leave me to my work."

Johnny raised an eyebrow. "Well, I don't think the town

should lose the bordello. I mean, you're a businessman, Mayor. You know the bordello brings customers to town. And those people spend money here. Everybody benefits from the bordello being here."

Tandy shrugged. "That sort of person doesn't spend money in my shop. And it seems that feelings are running very high since that trouble in the bordello the other day. People are frightened the violence will spread to other places. So, in the light of that, I feel the people should have the right to vote on it."

"*That sort of person?*" Johnny leaned forward. "Sorry, Mayor, I don't quite understand."

Tandy grunted. "The sort of people who frequent the bordello, they are not the sort of people who come in my store."

"Ah!" Johnny turned the smile full on. "I see. And, um, the question of the people voting? That wouldn't have anything to do with the fact that your term of office is coming to an end and you'll be looking for re-election soon?"

Tandy flushed an unpleasant shade of red. "That has nothing to do with it. As I just said, I believe that people should vote as feelings are running high."

Johnny laughed softly. "Of course you do. I understand that." He paused and continued to smile at Tandy who shifted in his chair like he'd sat on a burr.

Tandy glared. "So, is that all, Sinclair?"

Johnny shook his head slowly. "Well, no, I guess it ain't quite all." He ducked his head briefly and then looked back at

Tandy, who was mopping his neck again. "You see, there's the little matter of the people who frequent the bordello. It's providing a service for them, wouldn't you agree?"

Tandy sighed loudly, like he was getting real irritated by things. "I really don't see that there is much point in discussing this, Sinclair. I think the town's people feel strongly about it, and therefore they should vote on it."

"Because you care about..." Johnny paused, like he was searching for the right word. "Democracy. That's it. Because you care about democracy."

Tandy nodded, a smug smile spreading across his face. "That is it exactly. I care about democracy. Now, Sinclair, if that's all, perhaps you could leave me to my work."

Johnny scratched his cheek and furrowed his brow, like he was thinking hard. "Trouble is, Mr. Mayor—"

Tandy sat back with another loud sigh, and crossed his arms. "Yes, what now?"

"Well, all those people who use the services of the bordello."

"People like you?" Tandy sounded real snappy.

Johnny nodded. "Yeah, people like me, and all the other people. We'd miss the service, wouldn't we?"

Tandy glared. "You mean gunfighters and saddle tramps?"

Johnny raised an eyebrow and then ghosted the smile. "Well, yeah. Gunfighters, saddle tramps, and storekeepers."

Tandy narrowed his eyes. "I really wouldn't know what

sort of people use the bordello."

Johnny shrugged. "Oh, you'd be surprised, Mr. Mayor, at the people who go there." Johnny wriggled to get himself more comfortable in the chair. "All sorts of people. Ranch hands, bank clerks, storekeepers, hell, even the odd politician uses the bordello." Johnny paused. "A very odd politician. The fellow likes to pretend he's a rooster and have some of the girls scratching around pretending to be hens." Johnny turned the smile full on, even as Tandy turned a real interesting shade of red. "Now ain't that something? I mean what sort of man wants to pretend he's a cockerel? I wonder where a fellow like that would go for his fun if the town closes down the bordello. I guess he'd have to travel to Elizabethtown."

Tandy opened his mouth and shut it again.

Johnny grinned. "You see, you're lost for words. You had no idea that the bordello supplied such a range of services did you? And, I guess a fellow like that couldn't ask his wife to perform the service. I wonder what his wife would say if she knew about her old rooster of a husband holding some feathers and strutting around a bunch of naked girls. What do you think she'd say? Speaking of wives, I was talking to your good lady wife earlier. She mentioned that you were thinking of opening a store up in Elizabethtown."

Tandy turned from red to an unhealthy grey. "What d'you want, Fierro?" His voice was barely a croak.

"Fierro?" Johnny raised an eyebrow. "Hell, no, Mr. Mayor,

I'm here as a concerned citizen. I just wouldn't like to see people like that lose their place of... relaxation, shall we say? Someone has to speak up for them. Maybe I should speak up at that meeting on Tuesday. It would show that I'm really settling in here and becoming a good citizen worrying about my fellow man. I guess we could even say it's my civic duty to speak up. What do you think? Do you think I should draw everyone's attention to his situation? Of course, people might want to know who he is. What would you do in my position?" He leaned forward and spoke softly. "Well, Tandy."

"Tell me what you want." Tandy voice was barely a whisper.

Johnny sat back and crossed his legs, his spurs jangling. "Well, I been thinking about that. And you know, I reckon that if you let people all have their say, well, the men that is, we don't want women bringing emotions into this, do we?" He smiled broadly. "I reckon women might be best left out of this. They don't seem to understand that men have needs that need seeing to. Just like that fellow who wants to be in charge of the henhouse has needs that I guess he wouldn't want his wife to know about. So, let all the men have their say, seeing as how we care about democracy, and then close the meeting to the public, and you and your fellow members of the town council, have a secret vote. Hell, you can't get more democratic than a secret vote." Johnny leaned forward again. "What do you think? Seems democratic to me. I'm a big fan of democracy. It's hypocrisy I hate. I'm sure you agree."

Tandy nodded weakly, mopping his face repeatedly. "What if the committee votes to close it down? What would happen then?"

Johnny laughed softly. "Oh they won't vote to close it down. Trust me."

He stood and strolled to the door. "So, you set up the meeting the way I suggested. And make sure you vote the right way. That's all you got to do, and I reckon we'll get the result we both want. Now, that'll give you something to crow about." Johnny tipped his hat. "Nice doing business with you, Mr. Mayor."

He ambled back to the main street, unable to stop from grinning. He only needed to see four more people, then he'd collect the mail and head back to the ranch.

He dealt with the four men easily. It seemed they were only too eager to find a way to keep the bordello open. And, he'd be prepared to bet that pretty much all the men in the town would like it kept open. Apart from Hausmann. One thing was certain, there hadn't been any men in the protest outside the building that day, only women. What these women didn't seem to figure out was if they let their husbands have a bit of fun with them, their men-folk wouldn't need to go the bordello.

He was strolling back to where he'd left Pistol hitched, when he bumped into Stoney again. He sighed softly. Was Stoney going to start in on him again about the man who smashed up the bordello? He smiled in a friendly fashion, hoping to take Stoney's mind off any idea of issuing more warnings. But the look on Stoney's face suggested that his temper hadn't improved any.

Johnny moved to walk past him but Stoney stepped into his path. "You been in town a long time, Johnny. What you been doing?"

Johnny's jaw clenched. Since when was what he did Stoney's business? Damn it, but the job of sheriff seemed to have gone to Stoney's head. He bit back a sharp retort even as he realized that Stoney was actually damn good at his job. The man was smart enough to know that Johnny was unlikely to let things rest. He forced a smile. "Oh, I had some errands to run for Guthrie, and then I got waylaid talking to folk I hadn't seen of late. And I had to collect the mail." He waved a handful of letters at Stoney. "Almost forgot it. Guthrie would have had my hide if I'd gone home without it."

Stoney narrowed his eyes, cocking his head to one side, like he didn't believe a word of it.

Johnny bit back a sigh. He'd have to try some other way of distracting Stoney. "Actually it's kind of lucky I ran into you, there was something I wanted to ask you, Stoney. You ever heard of a man from around these parts called Adam Smith?"

The ploy worked. Stoney ducked his head, scratching at the back of his neck while he seemed to think on it. He shot Johnny a quick glance and raised an eyebrow. "Adam Smith?"

Johnny nodded. "Yeah. That was the name but it didn't ring

any bells with me. I wondered if maybe you knew him."

Stoney shook his head slowly. "Adam Smith? Nope, can't say as I recall hearing the name. Why do you ask?"

Johnny smiled, real easy and relaxed. "It's somebody Delice mentioned to me and I wondered who he was, that's all. Oh, and talking of Delice, she's got a couple of bouncers working for her now, so we don't need to worry any more about the bordello. You said she should get some protection in, and that's exactly what she's done. You'll be able to reassure people that there won't be any more trouble there. But I should be getting back. Guthrie gets mad as hell if his mail is late." He dodged around Stoney toward the hitching rail.

"Johnny." It was the tone in Stoney's voice that stopped him and caused him to look back.

"I meant what I said earlier. Don't go trying anything with the fellow at Hausmann's. He's served his punishment. It's over."

Johnny swung himself up into the saddle, and gathered up the reins before tipping his hat to Stoney. "Fine, whatever you say, Stoney." And with just the lightest touch of his spurs to Pistol's sides he headed out of town toward the ranch.

CHAPTER FIFTEEN

Guy.

Johnny pushed his hat back and slowed Pistol to an easy walk.

Guy — what the hell was he going to do about Guy?

All his plotting over the town meeting was stopping him getting to the root of what was eating Guy. He'd been kind of hoping that Guy would get back to his usual self, but it sure didn't look like that was going to happen any time soon.

And although they did have the occasional easy moment, like funning with Guy over the spade, Guy stepped wary around him now. Maybe Guy guessed that Johnny was unlikely to let matters rest. Leastways, now he'd rigged the mayor's meeting, he could concentrate on matters closer to home. But the trouble was he hadn't a clue how to find out about what happened in the war.

He figured maybe Guthrie knew something about it but his mouth was shut as tight as an old spinster's legs.

He suspected Delice knew a thing or two about the war as well; she seemed to read books and newspapers all the time. But if she did, he couldn't see her telling him anything, particularly in her current bad mood. And what the hell was that all about? She'd been grumpy for a while now and he couldn't figure what he'd done to piss her off. And he was certain it hadn't anything to do with him getting Bob and Clem in to keep an eye on things, although that hadn't helped. No, she'd been off her stride before that happened.

Maybe her mood would improve once the town council voted to let the bordello stay in business. Always provided she didn't take off for Santa Fe in the meantime. He grunted in irritation, loud enough to make Pistol skitter sideways. What the hell did she want to go to Santa Fe for? Women. He'd never figure them. Maybe she was simply being— He scratched his ear, flicking a fly away. Tricky. Yeah, maybe she was just being tricky. Women were tricky at times.

Even so, it was odd. Delice wasn't the same as other women and didn't seem the type of person to be difficult for the sake of it. He shook his head. One thing was certain – he wished she'd go back to being her usual self. He missed things being the way they were. In the past they'd gotten along so easy and now he felt out of sorts. Despite all his fun and games at the expense of

Carter and Tandy, all he really wanted was for him and Delice to get back to normal.

But if she wasn't going to tell him nothing about the war, and Guthrie wasn't going to say squat, how the hell did he find out about it? Were there records kept somewhere of what had happened? Yeah, there had to be records somewhere. Hell, somebody had probably written a book about the war. It seemed that people wrote books on all sorts of things. But even if there wasn't a book, there had to be some sort of record. And if so, how did he find out where? And shit! He couldn't even begin to imagine himself trying to read through the records. He wasn't too good at reading. Well, not quickly anyways. The only book he'd ever read was Ivanhoe, which the old man had loaned him when he was laid up sick one time. And it had taken him ages to finish that.

Maybe he should go to Santa Fe. There was a library there. He remembered that Guy had gone on and on about it. And on and on. He wished now that he'd paid more heed to Guy but he'd gone into a day dream instead – it had seemed better than listening to Guy droning on about damn books.

But leastways it was a plan. Go to the Santa Fe library and maybe he'd find someone to help him look for what he needed. He'd turn on the charm and get somebody who worked there to help him. Then they could do all the reading and tell him what he wanted to know.

He urged Pistol into a lope, happier now that he had some sort of a plan. He'd get the town meeting over and then go to Santa

Fe. Though how the hell he'd explain that to the old man, he couldn't even begin to imagine. Still, he'd come up with some sort of excuse.

He rode into the yard at the ranch and tethered Pistol to the rail outside the house. He'd need to keep Guthrie in a good mood if he was going to get away with a trip to Santa Fe. Best he took in the mail right off – that would keep Guthrie happy. Even so, sometimes he got real tired of worrying about how to keep the old man in a good temper. It felt like he spent his life walking on eggshells. Sighing softly, he put on his best smile and headed in search of his father.

Guthrie was in his study going over the accounts. But luckily he was in a good mood because he looked up with a smile as though he was pleased to see his gun-hawk son. "You've been a while. Did you get everything done in town?"

Johnny grinned, wondering what his father would say if he knew exactly what Johnny had been up to. "Yep, all done. I gave the papers to the lawyer. And then I went and collected the mail."

Guthrie's smile broadened. "And a newspaper?"

Johnny nodded. "Yeah, I even remembered the newspaper." He tossed the paper and mail onto the desk before sinking into a chair and stretching his legs out.

Guthrie scanned the letters, before grunting and selecting one to open. "Well that's a surprise, the bishop has been very speedy in replying to my missive. Let's see what he has to say about the Hausmanns."

Johnny frowned as Guthrie opened the letter carefully, using a knife that he kept especially for that purpose. God only knew why. Why couldn't he just rip it open like other folk? Who the hell kept a knife just to open letters? Although Guy opened his the same way. Maybe it was something they taught people at fancy schools.

Guthrie scanned the letter, frown lines showing deep between his eyes. He glanced across at Johnny. "It's exactly as I suspected. The Hausmanns have been moved repeatedly by the church. But there were numerous complaints about him in each parish. It was hoped that a fresh start, so far from the east, would be good for him. They've given him some leeway because he lost his only child, a son, in the war."

Johnny's head jerked up. "In the war? Does it give any details?"

Guthrie eyed him, quirking an eyebrow. "You mean is there a link with Guy?"

Johnny shrugged and grinned. "That easy to read, am I?"

Guthrie shrugged. "Let's just say that I've been watching you these past few days and it's eating away at you. Considering how many thousands of young men fought in the war, and how widespread the campaigns were, it's highly unlikely that Hausmann's son should ever have come into contact with Guy. And this letter won't enlighten you a great deal. Apparently the Hausmanns' son fought for the Confederates. But the bishop doesn't give any details about it, he only writes that the boy died.

And believe me, an awful lot of young men died in battles, and also in the prison camps where disease was rife. But of course it was a tremendous blow to the boy's family. According to Henry, the bishop, although the Hausmanns were very keen on their moral crusades before the war, since their son died they have gotten far worse. And then Hausmann's brother died too, although Henry doesn't go into details about that. He describes it as a delicate matter. Anyway, they've upset a great many people. From what Henry says, it seems that their crusades gave the Hausmanns something to focus on and took their minds off their grief."

Johnny ducked his head. He had to agree with Guthrie that almost certainly Guy would never have come into contact with the Hausmann's son. But at least he now knew that the boy had been on the opposite side to Guy in the war. And presumably the fellow working at the house had been in the confederate army too. If Stoney hadn't been keeping such a close eye on Johnny's movements in town, he'd have gone poking around the Hausmanns' place. Stoney was getting far too nosey for his own good. Still, maybe he'd get a chance to sneak around there on the day of the town meeting. The town would be busy and he could maybe slip in unnoticed. Hausmann was bound to go to the meeting to have his say.

He looked back at Guthrie. "When Guy met the Hausmanns how did they behave? I mean I wasn't there when they were introduced but nothing happened that made you suspicious, did it?

"Suspicious!" Guthrie laughed. "What on earth was I supposed to be suspicious about? Sorry, son, but it's you who has the suspicious mind." Guthrie stood to look out of the window before walking around and perching on the corner of his desk. "What on earth is bothering you?" He tilted his head looking at Johnny with a raised eyebrow. "Is there something you're not telling me?"

Johnny shrugged, he might as well be honest. Or partly honest, at any rate. He sure wasn't going to mention the bordello – that was always a red rag to a bull with his father. And he certainly wasn't going to tell Guthrie that he was intending to kill the man. "Stoney had a fellow locked in the jail for smashing up a place in town. It turns out that he's some relative of the Reverend. I reckon Hausmann put him up to it. And I saw Hausmann in town a few days ago and he made some real nasty comments about Guy being in the Union army. He's obviously got a real grudge about that. I reckon the man's loco and there's no knowing what he might do. So I'm kind of worried that maybe he'll send the fellow after Guy next."

Guthrie hissed in a breath and started pacing the floor. "You think he'd do that? No. No! I really can't imagine why he should. I think he's merely a pompous and unpleasant man, who likes to try to bully people. I think it would be ridiculously far-fetched to think of him sending someone to mete out some form of punishment to Guy, for a war that was over years ago. No!"

Guthrie shook his head hard. "No, Johnny, I'm sorry but I think you have an over-active imagination. The idea's preposterous."

Johnny gritted his teeth. He should have seen this reaction coming. And, to be fair, Guthrie had a good point – it did sound far-fetched. But hell, he hadn't survived this long without damn good instincts. And his instincts were screaming that there was something wrong.

"What's preposterous?" Guy stood in the doorway covered in dust. His shirt was drenched in sweat and a big rip in the sleeve kind of suggested he'd had a fight with the fence wire and come off worse.

"Ask your brother, maybe he'll explain himself to you better than he did to me." Guthrie waved his hand in Johnny's direction.

Guy raised an eyebrow and turned toward Johnny. "Would you care to enlighten me?"

Enlighten? Johnny rolled his eyes. Why couldn't Guy just talk like other folk? Johnny went and poured Guy a large measure of malt.

"The news is that bad, is it?" Guy grinned as he held his hand out for the drink.

Johnny sighed. He hadn't figured on Guy getting back so soon. "I was just telling Guthrie that Hausmann's got some relative of his working for him. It's a fellow who Stoney had behind bars a few days back. I reckon Hausmann got the man to smash up a place in town. And then I saw Hausmann in town and he was calling you a Yankee killer. I'm worried he might send this fellow after you next. He seems real worked up about the war. He had a son who died, he was in the Confederate army."

Guy's mouth tightened a touch and a nerve in his temple started pulsing. He turned an icy stare toward Johnny. Cold enough to freeze a damn ocean. "The war was over years ago! Why on earth would Hausmann send someone after me? And how on earth do you know about his son? Father's right – it is preposterous."

Guthrie stomped across the room to pour himself a drink; the nerve in his temple was pulsing now. Shit, the old man and Guy were a matched pair.

Guthrie turned toward Guy. "Guy, I'm glad that you agree with me. But at least the business about Hausmann's son is true. I received a letter from the bishop today in response to my inquiries about our new Reverend. The information came from him."

Guy threw up his hands with a loud sigh. "Thousands of soldiers died in the war – on both sides. And most families lost someone they loved in the war. I can't imagine that Hausmann holds me personally responsible for his son's death. And over the past few years of his ministry, he must have met hundreds of soldiers. The whole thing is ludicrous. I would have thought you, Johnny, had more important matters to occupy your mind than dreaming up such far-fetched and half-baked theories. We do have a ranch to run."

Johnny flinched. It seemed that Guy had left his normal level-headedness back at the fence line; he sure wasn't being too careful to choose his words now.

"I guess that what's concerning me, Harvard, is that the man working for Hausmann has already proved he's violent, and that, combined with things that Hausmann said to me, worries me."

Guy snorted. "I think you are letting this obsession you have with my military service distort your view of reality. Presumably Hausmann is employing the man because he's a relation, and maybe Hausmann is also employing him out of a sense of Christian charity."

"Christian charity! Damn it, Harvard, Hausmann don't know the meaning of that." Johnny gestured toward the letter which Guthrie was scanning again. "Even your bishop says they kept moving Hausmann because of the number of complaints about him."

Guthrie looked up at him. "I think Guy is right and you're reading too much into this." He glanced at Guy. "It is a little far-fetched. As you say, the man is a relative of Hausmann's, so it's natural that the Reverend would give him work. And Johnny has no evidence whatsoever to have such a notion apart from his supposed instincts."

The tone of the old man's voice was cool. Johnny wrapped his arms around himself. Yeah, trust Guthrie to instantly take Guy's side – nothing ever changed. Would there ever come a time when he backed Johnny over Guy? Somehow he doubted it.

Guthrie tossed the letter back on his desk. "Anyway, as Guy said, we have a ranch to run and we need to finalize the annual accounts. And in case you've forgotten, you are a partner in this enterprise and that means pulling your weight with paperwork too, not just riding herd."

Johnny shrugged. "Fine, whatever you say." He hesitated, but only briefly. He'd done with walking on egg shells. "So that's your final word? You've given your orders."

Guthrie swung around in his chair, his lips compressed and the pulse in his temple more pronounced. "Don't take that tone with me, boy."

Johnny laughed humorlessly. "Fine, but if Guy ends up with a bullet in his back, then we'll know that I was right."

CHAPTER SIXTEEN

The next couple of days were hell. Guthrie kept them all working hard at the accounts, insisting on double and treble checking all the figures. They didn't hardly even get outside of the hacienda because they had their noses stuck in the damn books. And boy, was he sick of figures and books and accounts! It was getting so he'd welcome the chance to dig fence holes.

And Guy was acting real sour, like he'd swallowed a bottle of vinegar. Hell, he was acting like he was afraid he'd catch something if he came too close to Fierro. But damn it, he should be grateful that Johnny cared enough to watch his back.

Cared enough... And there was the crux of it. Guy had cared enough to stand by Johnny's side all through the trial in Utah. He'd stuck by him despite everything that he'd heard in court. So if he could stick by Johnny through all of that, why didn't he trust Johnny enough to open up a bit and say what was eating him?

Johnny aimed a savage kick at one of Peggy's empty plant pots. He flinched as it shattered, sending shards flying across the path.

Guy couldn't have done anything to be ashamed of, could he? Guy wasn't like Fierro. He was a good man. That much was obvious.

Johnny kicked the broken bits of pot into the flower bed and scuffed the soil up with his toe. Maybe Peggy wouldn't notice. He sighed. She probably would though. She tended her plants like they were babies and seemed to know exactly how many plant pots she had – each one apparently had a special purpose.

Seemed he was ticking everyone off right now. Guthrie was mad at him. Guy was mad at him. Peggy would be mad at him, and Delice was being downright strange – and mad at him.

He sank onto the stone seat by Peggy's rose garden, watching a bee bumbling around collecting nectar from the lavender hedge which ran around the flower bed. Maybe he should never have accepted the damn partnership deal. Maybe he should have stayed working around the border as a gunfighter. At times like this he felt like walking out and never coming back. He shook his head slowly. No, if he was honest, he knew that if he walked away he'd miss this life. He'd miss the ranch. He'd miss the land. And damn it, but he'd miss his family and friends too. He sighed. Miss them – that was rich. Right now he was sick of his family.

And friends. They drove him loco at times. If only he was better at this family thing, but it remained a mystery. Sometimes, like the other night when Peggy had said that his father missed him and worried about him, he'd thought maybe he was getting the hang of it, but he was kidding himself. He never knew what they expected from him, but he knew he screwed up regularly. And normally he could go and talk to Delice about things, but there was no chance of that with her in her current mood.

Johnny ground his teeth and kicked at the soil again. He wanted to meet Hausmann's nephew, or whoever the fellow was. He was going to pay for what he did to the girls at the bordello and, more importantly, he was going to pay for striking Delice. Johnny bit his lip, trying to blot out the memory of the bruise on Delice's face. The west might be wild, but most men treated women right. It was the unwritten law of the west. Men could do, and did do, dreadful things to each other, but they didn't hurt women. And there wasn't no man alive going to knock his Delice around and get away with it.

A scrunch of gravel made him glance up. Guy stood outside the door of the hacienda but catching Johnny's eye turned as if to go back inside. Johnny quelled a flash of irritation. "I ain't got anything catching. There's room for two out here." He waved his hand toward the other stone bench. "I needed some air. It feels like we been cooped up for years poring over them books."

Guy made a slight inclination of his head, but didn't speak. He walked slowly to the bench and sat stiffly, kind of balancing on the edge while he stared at the distant view. Stared at anything other than his brother it seemed.

"Never figured there was so much paperwork involved in running a ranch." Johnny tried to keep his tone relaxed, hoping maybe that Guy would unbend a touch. "I thought it was all punching cattle, rounding up strays, and driving them to stockyards. But here I am trying to balance books and worrying about how much damned alfalfa we need to plant." He paused, trying to toe in a bit more soil to cover the fragments of Peggy's pot. "Is it what you expected? I mean, did you figure working on the ranch would be like this?"

Guy shot him a quick glance, a small furrow showing between his eyes, like maybe he was puzzled by Johnny's relaxed tone. "I do remember, on my first morning here after coming home, lying in bed thinking that the ranch hands would do the actual hard work. And I remember very clearly hoping that I wouldn't ever have to deliver a calf." Guy's mouth quirked. "I was very quickly disillusioned of those romantic ideas. I think that hauling cows out of a gully and getting beat up and muddy soon straightened me out!"

Johnny grinned. Now he needed to keep up the banter; it was good to see Guy smile. "And the rain. Herding cows in driving rain and wind. God, but I hate the rain. And fence posts. I really hate digging post holes."

Guy's mouth quirked again. "I rather had got that impression. And to be honest you do seem to have done more than your fair share of that."

Johnny laughed. "Reckon the old man thinks that's what I'm best at, and you're better with the books."

Guy shrugged. "I think he thought that at first, but he soon realized that you're just as good with figures as I am, it's just that you raise more objections to doing it." Guy laughed suddenly. "And he soon cottoned on to the fact that you were making ink spots deliberately in an effort to avoid being asked to perform that particular chore."

Johnny scuffed in a little more soil with the toe of his boot. "Yeah, he didn't fall for that one, did he?"

"Just as Peggy won't be fooled by you trying to cover up a broken pot." Guy shook his head. "You might as well come clean and tell her that you broke it. And then buy her a new one."

"She'll never miss it." Johnny sounded more confident than he felt. Peggy noticed everything. "Anyway, are you coming into Cimarron for the public meeting?"

Guy jerked his head around and gave Johnny a sharp look. "Cimarron?"

Johnny nodded. "Yeah. Have you forgotten about the meeting where they're going to decide if the bordello can stay open?"

Guy narrowed his eyes and gave Johnny the sort of look which said he didn't trust him at all. "The public meeting? Is that today?"

"Yeah. I thought you might like to come into town with me."

Guy shook his head. "No." He sounded kind of distant, like he'd moved back out of reach again. "And anyway, Father doesn't want us to go to the meeting. He said it's the town's business to decide, and we should stay out of it."

"What?" Johnny leaned forward, his shoulders suddenly tense. "When the hell did he say that?"

"Earlier today. He said there was a pile of work for us both and we were to stay out of it."

Johnny shook his head slowly. "Or he doesn't want you going into town right now because of you getting into a fight with Hausmann or his relative."

Guy's mouth tightened as he rose swiftly to his feet, looking like he was heading back to the house. "It was only a matter of time before you came back to that, wasn't it? You just won't leave it alone, damn you. You're obsessed with it. There's no reason why they should be interested in me."

Johnny sighed heavily. "Guy, before you go charging off again, can I say something?"

Guy glared. "Well?"

Johnny shrugged. "You know, you stood by me all through that business in Utah. It seemed that whatever you heard, whatever the court said, you still backed me up regardless. You never once failed me. And you got no idea exactly how much that meant to me. It kept me going, if I'm honest. And when you walked into the court, when I reckoned you'd headed back to the ranch, well, I felt taller. I felt like I mattered and that I could cope with whatever the lawyers were going to throw at me. Then later on, when we were talking in the cell, you said something to me about facing things together, being on the same side.

"Well, I guess that's what I'm saying here, too. I'm on your side, Guy. I ain't your enemy. And I know you're going through hell over something to do with the war, and somehow I don't think it's to do with the battles you were in. It's like you're feeling guilty about something. But I know you, Guy, you're a good man. And whatever it is, it can't be that bad, because I know you'd never do anything that wasn't..." Johnny paused, struggling to find the right word. "Wasn't honorable."

Guy flushed and turned away staring out over the ranch to the distant mountains, hazy in bright sunlight.

"Ever since we arrived here, you been pushing me for all sorts of information about my past, but you ain't said anything about yours. And I know I ain't much of a deal as a brother, and that I don't deserve all the backing you've given me. But you got no idea how much your backing me has meant, and I want to do the same for you. So, I just wish you'd level with me, Guy, and then maybe we can sort out whatever's eating at you. I hate seeing you so down. And I hate the fact that we ain't getting along too well right now."

It was one of the longest speeches he could ever remember making. He never had been much for talking, but maybe Guy would realize how much he meant to Johnny. And that was pretty amazing in itself. Nobody had ever gotten under his skin the way Guy had.

Guy stood with his back to him, still staring into the distance. Was he going to say anything? Anything at all?

After what felt like an age, Guy sighed softly, and his shoulders slumped. "Honorable?" He sure didn't sound like he agreed with that word. But it was the right word, Johnny felt sure it was the right word.

Guy turned now toward him. "I'm sorry, Johnny, I really am, but this isn't something I want to talk about. Some things are better left alone. They should be left in the past. And I feel that's for the best, and we should leave things be."

"Except when it's my past?" Johnny couldn't resist the dig. "Everyone seems real interested in my past. Feels like there's one rule for most people but a totally different one for me." He flushed. He knew it sounded petty but damn it, it wasn't fair. But hell, when had life ever been fair?

Guy smiled briefly. "I guess it must seem that way. I'm sorry."

Johnny shrugged. "I will find out, Guy. We will have this out at some point, whether you like it or not. And I'll be watching your back because something tells me that Hausmann's relative is trouble. And don't bother getting mad at me, it won't make no difference. Ain't nobody going to hurt my family."

Guy raised an eyebrow. "I appreciate the sentiment, but leave my past alone, Johnny. It's dead and gone. And now I suggest we get back to the books."

"I'm going into Cimarron for that meeting." Johnny narrowed his eyes. "Whether the old man likes it or not."

"For God's sake, it's only a meeting about the bordello. Surely that's not worth falling out over with Father? You seem to take delight in doing things that nobody wants you to do. Like poking into my past." Guy glared at him.

"I don't like bullies. And those folks are trying to bully Delice, just because the sour-faced Hausmanns don't approve of the bordello. And I ain't going to stand by and do nothing."

Guy snorted. "It might be news to you, Johnny, but very few people approve of bordellos. They are not considered to be attractive amenities for civilized communities."

Johnny grunted in irritation. "Civilized? There's enough men who use them, even when they don't want nobody to know. Hypocrites. I hate hypocrites. And bullies."

"I can't say that I see Delice as being the type of person who would allow herself to be bullied." Guy sounded kind of superior. "I really think you should let the town deal with its own affairs. And if the bordello closes, so be it. You'll simply have to avail yourself of the saloon girls. It's hardly a major catastrophe."

"Delice is a friend, Guy. And nobody hurts my friends and gets away with it. So I'm going to make sure the bordello stays open. And when I've done that I'm going to find the fellow who smashed the place up and I'm going to kill him. I don't stand by and let men make war on women."

Guy hissed in a breath. "For God's sake, Johnny, leave it all alone. You're going to end up at war with Father or with your neck in a noose at this rate. And the bordello isn't worth it."

Johnny shrugged. "Maybe not to you, but it is to me. And now I'm going to town, whether the old man likes it or not. Nobody tells me what I can or can't do. Including him."

Shrugging off Guy's restraining hand, Johnny stalked to the barn to saddle Pistol. Then, mounting swiftly, he spurred the horse away from the ranch and headed to town.

CHAPTER SEVENTEEN

So many people.

Too many damn people. He didn't know so many folks lived around Cimarron. Johnny reined in Pistol and watched them crowding down toward the small schoolhouse.

He checked the time on his pocket-watch. Hopefully he had time for a quick scout around the Hausmanns' place before the meeting. He wanted an opportunity to meet the Reverend's nephew so he could size him up. He needed to know if he was the sort of man he could push to draw on him. Because although he intended to kill the fellow at some stage, he had no intention of hanging for it.

So, he'd deal with that first. Then he'd go and remind Tandy, Carter, and the rest, that he was keeping an eye on them.

He left Pistol tethered near the saloon and slipped along the road leading to the Hausmanns' house.

He eased the gate open and cat-footed around the side of the house toward the barn. Even as he did so, a tall, fair-haired man, carrying a hay fork, walked out. He stopped dead when he saw Johnny. "If you're looking for the Reverend, he's gone to the meeting at the schoolhouse." A vivid red scar covered a part of his face, which puckered when he spoke, and his eyes were curiously blank.

Johnny smiled thinly. "Nope. I was looking for you. I'm surprised the Reverend didn't tell you to expect me."

He didn't blink. "Sinclair?"

Johnny nodded. "Yeah, Sinclair. Or Fierro. I answer to both."

"He told me." The man still didn't blink.

"Did he tell you I'm going to kill you?"

The man twisted his mouth into a sneer. "For beating up on a few whores? Whores carry disease. They kill men."

"They're my friends," Johnny said. "And you hurt them."

"Well, the town will get rid of them now. And there's nothing you can do about it."

"Hey, Johnny, I thought you'd be going to the meeting." Stoney's voice boomed across from the gate.

Johnny closed his eyes briefly before turning to face the sheriff, who had a real unfriendly look on his face. Johnny rolled his eyes. "I am."

Stoney raised an eyebrow. "Is that so? Well, in that case, you're in the wrong part of town. The meeting's in the schoolhouse. Back there." He jerked his thumb back toward the main street.

Johnny glanced once more at Hausmann's nephew, and leaned in toward him, speaking softly. "You're not wearing a gun today. Next time we meet you'd better be."

He turned and walked slowly back to Stoney.

"Maybe I'd best show you the way." Stoney glared at him. "I saw you heading in this direction and I figured you were going snooping. Or maybe had something else in mind." The tone of the sheriff's voice suggested that was exactly what he knew Johnny was up to.

Johnny stepped toward him, narrowing his eyes and speaking real soft. "Back off, Stoney. Don't push me. You ain't my keeper and I sure as hell don't need you watching my every move. Believe me; you really don't want to piss me off."

Stoney swallowed hard but didn't step back. "I might not be your keeper, but I am the law around here and you'd best remember that. You think I don't know that you're after Hausmann's nephew?"

"The law? Maybe you'd best remember who got you the job and who pays your wages, Stoney." He knew it was a cheap shot. And judging from the look on Stoney's face, he thought so too. But damn it, he should keep his nose out of Fierro's business.

Stoney's jaw tightened and he stepped forward, coming too close now. "That's low, and you damn well know that your pa offered me this job before he knew you'd vouch for me. And I done a good enough job that the town would pay me now if Sinclair stops paying my wages. So don't threaten me, Johnny. I know that you're looking for a fight with that fellow, and that you won't leave it alone. I know you too well."

Johnny raised an eyebrow. "No, Stoney. You don't know me at all. You got no idea what I'm capable of. You only know what I want you to know. So, like I said, back off."

Stoney shook his head. "I can't do that, Johnny. I'm paid to keep law and order in this town, and that's damn well what I'll do."

"Law and order!" Johnny laughed at that, but he sure didn't think it funny. "Where was your law and order when he hit Delice, when he smashed up the bordello? Seems to me that maybe you ain't too good at your job, Stoney. Or is it only so-called respectable folk you look out for? Think you're above looking after a bunch of women in a bordello, is that it?"

Stoney stepped forward, his fists clenched, and for a second Johnny thought the man was going to hit him.

"I don't know what's gotten into you lately, Johnny. And you know damn well that I won't have one rule for some people and a different rule for others. But I can't be in two places at once. And when I heard what was happening at the bordello I went straight down there and took the fellow into the jail."

"The jail!" Johnny shook his head. "That ain't no punishment and you know it! I bet if he'd smashed up one of the shops in town, he'd have been hauled in front of a judge. Then he'd have spent a damn sight longer behind bars than a couple of nights." Johnny ground his teeth. And wasn't that the damn truth? It was always one rule for the haves and another for the have-nots. And nobody gave a damn if a few whores got knocked around.

Stoney stared at him, long and hard. "What the hell's eating you? You been acting loco of late. God almighty, Johnny, you're going to end up with your neck in a noose, the way you're carrying on. I don't make the damn laws; I simply try to enforce them and do the best job I can. And somehow, I don't reckon you'll do me any harm, whatever you might say. You owe me, and you don't hurt the people you owe. I figured out that much about you."

Stoney sounded real pleased with himself over his final words. When did Stoney get so damn smart? Johnny shrugged. "Maybe you're right over that, Stoney. Normally I wouldn't hurt anyone I owed." Johnny ghosted a cold smile. "But in your case I might make an exception."

He saw the concern flicker in Stoney's eyes. Good. Stoney wasn't as sure of himself as he was making out. But the look was gone almost as quickly as it came. Stoney glared at him and then pointed back toward the schoolhouse. "So, Fierro, that's where the meeting is. Coming?"

Johnny raised an eyebrow. "It's why I came to town. I wouldn't miss it for the world."

Stoney narrowed his eyes and shot him a sharp look. "Just as long as we understand each other, Fierro." Stoney scratched his chin thoughtfully. "But this meeting, it's got me puzzled. What I can't figure out is why that old windbag of a mayor has suddenly decided there should be a secret vote. And that the only people allowed to vote are his committee. He sure changed his tune all of a sudden."

Johnny turned and started walking back toward the main town. "It's what politicians do, ain't it? They change their minds as often as the wind changes. And they always go whichever way the wind's blowing."

Stoney grunted. "Ain't got no time for any damn politicians. I don't trust none of them. And as for Tandy, well, it strikes me as odd that he suddenly changed his mind over letting folks vote on it."

Johnny bit back a smile. "He's no different from any other politician – he likes a little bit of power, Stoney. He wants to be the rooster in charge of the hen house."

Stoney snorted. "Rooster? Puts me in mind of a jackass, not a damn rooster."

Johnny paused at the door, stepping aside to let two elderly ladies into the crowded room. "So, you coming, Stoney?" Johnny swept his arm back to wave the sheriff in.

Stoney paused briefly. "Oh, yeah, Johnny, I'm coming in." He leaned forward to speak softly, so as only Johnny could hear. "I'm coming in, because it's the only way I can keep an eye on you. I'll be watching you, Johnny. Every move you make, I'll be there. Don't that make you feel nice and safe?"

Johnny raised an eyebrow. "Sounds like an unhealthy way

to live, Stoney. A man could wind up dead acting like that." He turned on his heel and stalked into the room.

It was stiflingly hot, and full of sweaty people. God but he hated crowds. His hand hovered near his gun – same as always in crowded places. Tandy was talking to a group of local do-gooders, his voice loud and full of self-importance.

"I felt that it was important that everyone should have their say, but in the interests of democracy, a secret vote seems the best way of dealing with this unfortunate matter. Several businessmen have spoken to me in private to air their views, and they've entrusted me to pay due consideration to their opinions when it comes to a vote."

"Mr. Mayor." Johnny beamed at the man. "Good to hear that you care so much about democracy. Real refreshing to find a politician who wants to hear everyone's views." Johnny clapped Tandy on the back and nodded approvingly to the group standing watching. "Yep, Mr. Tandy is a rare sort of politician. Ain't we lucky to have such a good mayor? He does a fine job of running the town." Johnny nodded again. "Yep. Mayor Tandy really is the top rooster in this town."

Tandy paled, and a nerve started twitching in his cheek.

Johnny grinned at him. "Well, I'd best leave you to it, Mr. Mayor, seeing as how you're talking to these fine folks. I'll go have a word with Henry Carter. I see he's over there with his wife. Ladies." He tipped his hat and headed toward the far end of the room where Carter stood listening to his wife who seemed to have an awful lot to say for herself.

Johnny paused briefly, listening to the woman's shrill voice. Mierda, no wonder Carter needed the girls at the bordello. A smile came to his lips. Hell, he was doing Carter a favor. He could hardly call it blackmail or coercion – more like an act of mercy. Yeah, he was doing the whole town a favor. All the men would be happy if the bordello stayed open, and it would give all these sour women a break from their men-folk. Really, he deserved a medal for his action.

"Mrs. Carter." Johnny tipped his hat to the hatchet-faced woman, as her husband glowered at him. And there looked to be a nerve twitching in his face too. "I'm sorry to interrupt, but I needed a quick word with your husband." Johnny turned toward him. "I wanted to check how that touch of wooden tongue was doing. Remember, when we spoke the other day? We had a chat all about wooden tongue and things."

Carter narrowed his eyes. He seemed to have trouble answering for a second – maybe it was the clenched teeth. "I haven't forgotten our conversation." The man took a deep breath, like he was trying to pull himself together. "And I treated the wooden tongue, thank you."

Johnny smiled. "Well, I'm glad you remember our talk. And pleased to hear you treated the wooden tongue. You got to watch things like that." He tipped his hat again. "Mrs. Carter."

He moved through the room, stopping briefly to talk with the other members of Tandy's committee. Kind of to remind them that he was around. He could see the good Reverend holding forth, surrounded by a group of people. They looked like a flock of sheep, all slack-jawed, hanging on the man's every word and not enough brains between them to think for themselves. Why couldn't they see the man for the piece of shit that he was? Johnny stood watching them until Hausmann noticed him. His piggy-eyes widened and he stopped talking mid-stream. Johnny shot him a full smile and made a small, mocking bow, kind of acknowledging the man's presence. It sure took the wind out of Hausmann for a few seconds, but not long enough. Off he went again, and now he was pointing Johnny out to his audience. Even from where Johnny stood, he could hear Hausmann's voice.

"And there's a sinner in our midst. Guthrie Sinclair's son has no shame whatsoever. His murderous past is bad enough, but he compounds his sins by going whoring, and his weak-willed father is powerless to stop him. That sinner, standing there before you, is yet another reason to see that den of iniquity closed down."

The people all turned as one and stared across at Johnny, following the pointing of Hausmann's accusing finger. Johnny grinned widely and made another small bow. He tipped his hat before turning away to see what Tandy was up to.

The tub of lard, puffing and wheezing, was pushing through to the front of the room and stepping onto a wooden box so that everyone could see him. As Tandy called the room to order, Johnny leaned against the wall at the side of the room, where he had a real good view of everyone. And everyone had a real good view of him.

Tandy droned on about how there were all sorts of views about the bordello and that it was his civic duty to listen to everyone. Dios but the man could talk. And talk. Didn't he need to draw breath like other people?

Then Tandy started telling everyone that it had been pointed out to him by a variety of "businessmen" that the bordello brought lots of people into the town who spent money in other shops and how the bordello could be seen as being good for the town.

All of the women in the room started hollering at that, red-faced and all talking at once until Tandy banged a little hammer to try and bring some order back. Johnny grinned, leaning back with one knee bent and his foot against the wall. It was the best entertainment he'd had in a long time. Such a lot of fuss over something as harmless as a bordello. He shook his head. He'd never figure folks. Seemed to him that most of them were only happy when they were trying to spoil other people's fun. Yep. Most folks were shit, and there were an awful lot of them at the meeting.

Hausmann forced his way through the throng, calling out for the "right" to address the meeting. Johnny's mouth quirked. Tandy didn't like that. He hated anyone trying to steal his thunder and boy, did it show on the mayor's pudgy face.

Tandy banged his hammer again. "We will give lots of men the chance to air their views. But due to time constraints, only one minute per person will be allowed. We'll pursue that until such time as we feel that no useful purpose can be served by continuing. If things get repetitious we will call a halt and the committee will retire to vote."

Hausmann pushed forward, trying to step onto the mayor's little box. "I feel that as guardian of the town's morals and being God's representative, it would be most appropriate if I speak first."

Tandy pursed his lips and puffed his cheeks out, but he gave way. Johnny ducked his head, trying not to laugh. Dios, but Hausmann sure knew how to make enemies. He was so full of himself and his own importance. The only wonder was why on earth anybody bothered to give him the time of day. Trouble was, it was always the way with religious men. Like the priests in Mexico – people treated them like they were God, not just ordinary men.

Hausmann, his face red and puffy, cleared his throat. He held up a hand and made the sign of the cross before scowling around at everyone in the room. "We are gathered here today, as one people, united in our opposition to the den of iniquity which thrives in our midst. And, as a man of God, I must tell you that it is your solemn duty to rid this society of that sinful blot which sullies the name of this small town. We must destroy that house of harlots. Cimarron can never thrive while that whorehouse prospers. If you allow it to remain, God will ensure that this town, this Gomorrah, this ruined heap, will be destroyed, just as he did smite down Sodom and Gomorrah. Are there ten righteous men here who will stand up and fight for the Lord? Because if that whorehouse is allowed to stand, God will bring down the most dreadful vengeance on you all and on your children. There will be disease and destruction beyond your wildest imaginings as the Lord takes his vengeance on you—"

Tandy banged his hammer. "Well, thank you, Reverend Hausmann—"

"I have not finished!" roared Hausmann.

Tandy narrowed his eyes. "I'm sorry, Reverend, but I do believe you've had your one minute. Mr. Baker, I believe you wished to speak." Tandy wiped his face with a large handkerchief and waved the next speaker on while Hausmann puffed and complained to all around that he had only just started saying what needed to be said.

Johnny caught sight of Stoney watching the proceedings from the back of the room, shaking his head and muttering to himself. Or at least Johnny presumed he was talking to himself, nobody close to him seemed to be paying him any heed.

Johnny sighed, looking around at the sea of angry faces. What was wrong with people that they had to behave like this? He'd never had a good opinion of folks in general, and from where he stood now, he reckoned he hadn't been wrong. The world was full of small-minded people, but he'd bet a month's wages that for every speaker voicing dissent about the bordello, there were a couple of men who enjoyed the benefits, even if they hadn't got the guts to stand up and say so.

Eventually Tandy and his cronies all shuffled off to vote in secret, while everyone stood around waiting for the decision.

Stoney pushed through the crowd to stand by Johnny. "Well, what d'you make of that show?"

Johnny looked around the room, shaking his head slowly. "Reckon my horse got more sense than all of this lot put together. Why can't they leave folks be? But I always reckoned that most people are shit. They're probably the same the world over. And I sure ain't seen anything here to make me change my mind."

Stoney swatted a fly away from his neck. "Reckon you and I think alike on this then. If Tandy hadn't put a stop to Hausmann's ranting, I was going to arrest the puffed up windbag. I figured he was building up to getting a lynching party ready. And all over a bunch of harmless whores."

Johnny pulled a face. "I don't reckon he'd get much support from the men. And I don't think this bunch of women would be much of a match for Delice's girls. It would turn into a cat fight and I know who I'd put my money on. Sadie, for one, packs quite a punch. And have you seen the nails on her?"

He saw a hint of a smile pull at Stoney's mouth. Seemed the sheriff had calmed down from his rant at Johnny earlier. Dios. Wasn't enough that he had Guy and Delice to worry about; now he had to worry about keeping Stoney happy too. It would be much easier to shoot the lot of them, ride out and head on back for the border. Yeah, like he'd ever do that!

Stoney nudged him. "Here comes Tandy. A dollar on them

closing it down."

Johnny glanced at him. "A dollar? Skinflint. Make it five and you got a bet."

"I ain't a skinflint! And to prove it, Fierro, how about ten dollars then?"

Johnny ducked his head. Oh boy, he was going to enjoy this. "OK, Stoney. Ten dollars. Come on, let's see the color of your money. Not that I don't trust you or nothing."

Stoney dug in his pocket and pulled out a ten dollar bill and waved it at Johnny. "See. Let's see yours."

"Ssssh." Johnny elbowed Stoney in the ribs.

Tandy stepped up onto the box. "For a variety of reasons, but particularly because of the financial implications for this growing town, the committee has voted to allow the bordello to remain open and not to introduce a town ordinance banning it."

Johnny grabbed the note out of Stoney's hand even as uproar erupted with everyone talking at once, with Hausmann's voice the loudest. "Thanks, Stoney. Easiest ten dollars I ever made." Johnny glanced around the room. "And I reckon you'd best calm this lot down and make sure they all disperse real peaceful. Ain't that what a lawman's supposed to do? But now I'm off to tell Delice the good news."

With a broad grin Johnny pushed through the throng and back into the fresh air. He sucked in a couple of good breaths to clear his head of the stench of people before hurrying down to the bordello.

He pushed open the heavy door, and wasn't surprised to see that there were no customers – he'd bet that they were all down at the schoolhouse thanking their lucky stars that the bordello had been saved.

Clem and Bob were playing cards. A couple of the girls perched next to them offering advice and plenty of distraction, while bickering over who had the best hand. It didn't look like Clem or Bob minded the girls' attentions.

Sadie came rushing over to fling her arms around him, her breasts almost spilling out over the top of her dress. "Johnny. Oh my, just the sight of you does a body good. I didn't expect you in at this time of day." She leaned in closer, dropping her hand down to massage his cock through his pants while she nibbled on his ear.

Gently he squirmed out of her embrace. "Not at the moment, honey. I was looking for Delice. I got good news for her."

Sadie stumbled back and stared at him, her mouth slightly open. "But didn't you know? Madam ain't here. She went to Santa Fe to buy a new place; she's there now seeing the lawyers. And us girls, we're all packing. We're leaving Cimarron."

CHAPTER EIGHTEEN

He could hardly take in her words. He felt like he'd been gut shot as the world slowed down around him. He could see her mouth opening and closing but he hadn't got a clue what she was saying. And the background noises all faded out – nothing was real.

He closed his eyes briefly. Shit. She'd really meant it. But how could Delice do this?

How could she just up and leave? Hell, they were friends. Weren't they?

Friends didn't do this to each other.

What the hell had gotten into her?

"Johnny. Are you listening to me? Johnny!"

He tried to drag his attention back to Sadie, who stood with her hands on her hips looking pissed with him.

"I said, if you'd a-been-a-listening, we got to use what time we have, Johnny. Me and the girls won't be around for much longer." She pushed up against him, and started fumbling with his belt.

But he swiped her hand away. "Not now, damn it, Sadie. What do you mean she's in Santa Fe? Is she already there? When did she leave?"

Sadie's mouth puckered up. "Ain't no call to be so bad-tempered, Johnny." She pursed up her lips and then gave him a sideways sort of smile. The sort that normally perked up his pecker. But right now it only irritated him.

"Come on upstairs with me, Johnny. You and me..." She reached out her hand to rub at his dick even as he pulled away.

"I asked you a question, Sadie. When did she go? Where does she stay when she visits?"

Sadie glared. "She caught the stage the day before yesterday. She'd have gotten there yesterday. And I don't know where she stays. Why do you want to know? Come on, Johnny, me and you got to—"

He didn't wait to hear what Sadie was saying. Instead he shot out of the building back to where Pistol was tethered on the main street. Groups of people were standing around talking about the mayor's decision, but he pushed past them, ignoring the stares and snatches of comments. He needed to get to Santa Fe and fast.

He hesitated as he lifted his foot to step into the saddle. Was this the best way to get to Santa Fe? There wouldn't be another stage until tomorrow and then it would be slow and uncomfortable. No. It would be much quicker to ride, even though it would be hard on Pistol. Still, the horse needed to earn his keep. Not much point in having a fast horse if all he did was ride around the ranch.

The ranch.

Oh hell.

Guthrie.

Shit, shit, shit.

Johnny stepped back onto the boardwalk, chewing on his lip. Guthrie would go loco if he just took off to Santa Fe without a word. But then if Johnny asked for time off, there was no way his father would agree when they were so busy. And hell, even if he did ask, what could he say? That he had to try and stop the local madam from shutting up shop and relocating? Johnny flinched at the thought of the old man's reaction to that. No, Guthrie wouldn't understand at all. Didn't understand about anything other than his beloved ranch.

Shit.

But hell, there was life outside of Sinclair Ranch. More to life than all that land and cows that the old man loved so much. Sometimes a man had to do what he knew to be right. Like looking out for friends and stopping them from making dumb mistakes. Because it would be a mistake if Delice moved to Santa Fe. She'd gotten everything she needed in Cimarron – a good business and friends. Friends like him and Ben.

Friends. Who the hell was that fellow Adam Smith she'd mentioned? Was he the reason she was moving to Santa Fe?

Johnny kicked at the boardwalk trying to remember what she'd said about the fellow. But she hadn't said much about him at all. She'd changed the subject. Well, whoever he was, he hadn't been around to check on her after the bordello was smashed up, so he wasn't much of a friend. But women were kind of dumb and maybe Delice thought the fellow was a good friend. Johnny directed a more savage kick at the boardwalk. Damn it, Delice was making a huge mistake and it was up to him to go and talk her out of this dumb idea. And if Guthrie didn't like it he could go to hell.

Even so... Maybe he should leave a note. But what could he say in a note? He'd still have to give a reason for going. So no, there was no point in leaving one. Maybe it would be best to simply send a message. Yeah, that would be best. A message could be very short with no explanation for his action. After all, it wasn't like he wasn't planning on coming back. He'd only be away for a few days. Guthrie had gotten by all those years without him, so he could survive a few more days without his gun-hawk son.

He hurried over to the livery stable. He could get the young lad, Antonio, to take a message to the ranch. But he'd make sure that Antonio didn't go until later in the day – late enough that the old man couldn't send Guy out after him to drag him back. He needed to be well on his way before they knew what he was up to. Guthrie would be mad as hell, but he'd deal with his father's rage later.

After issuing firm instructions to Antonio, and buying some jerky and coffee, he headed out toward Santa Fe. He pushed Pistol hard, wanting to get as many miles as he could under his belt before nightfall. Leastways there'd be a full moon. He could ride through the night and just take a couple of hours break to rest Pistol. Although their progress would be slow at night, it was better than no progress at all.

Normally he'd have enjoyed the night ride. The moon lit the route almost like daylight and only a gentle breeze stirred the leaves on the trees. He heard the occasional call of a coyote, and the odd squeak and rustle as some small creature met its end as a meal for a solitary owl gliding on silent wings. But for now, all he could think about was that he find Delice before she did anything damn stupid – like buying a new place. It had to be that fellow Adam Smith's fault – there couldn't be any other reason for her moving to Santa Fe. After all, the man wasn't from Cimarron, Stoney would have heard of him if he had been. He'd asked Alonso too. He'd been Guthrie's foreman for years but even he hadn't recognized the name either. So, it followed that the man must be in Santa Fe.

Johnny ground his teeth. Damn it but women were tricky. Delice should be content with the good friends she had in Cimarron and not go haring off around the countryside causing this much trouble. He sighed loudly, causing Pistol to half-turn his head at the sound. But knowing Delice, it might be as well if he didn't mention that she was causing him a lot of trouble – she was more than likely to take it the wrong way. He'd never figure women.

He only stopped twice, and that was more to rest Pistol than himself because he sure couldn't sleep. Instead he brewed coffee and chewed on some jerky, while Pistol grazed and dozed on his feet.

He continued to push Pistol hard the next day, promising the animal that he'd put him in the best livery once they got to Santa Fe. "I'll fix you up with a real comfy stall and the best bran mash. But for now you got to earn your keep. I know it's tough but we need to get there as fast as we can."

He was true to his word. As soon as they reached the busy town, Johnny installed Pistol at the most expensive livery stable. At least he was ten dollars richer, thanks to Stoney's reckless bet, and he could afford the high charges of the ostler.

But his next job was to track down Delice, and now, as he stood in the bustling street by the livery stable, he realized that there were a hell of a lot of hotels in Santa Fe. And boarding houses. And private homes offering accommodation. Shit. Maybe the best thing was to start at the hotel his father always used and then work out from there.

An hour later his feet were aching and he was no closer to finding her. He trudged from hotels to boarding houses and back to hotels. Looking down a quiet side street he spotted another hotel, set slightly back from the boardwalk with flowers trained against its neatly painted walls. It was the sort of place where a lady would stay. And even if Delice was a whore, he reckoned she was more of a lady than pretty much anyone he'd ever met.

He hurried up the steps, which shone like somebody spent a lot of time scrubbing them. There was a pleasant lobby with lots of big armchairs, and a fireplace with a polished brass grate filled with flowers as there wasn't much call for a fire at this time of year.

A woman, dressed in a high-collared and ruffled lace blouse, sat at the reception desk. She picked up a pair of spectacles attached to a long stick and inspected him through them. Judging by the briefest flicker of distaste on her face, he figured he must look pretty dusty.

He turned on his broadest smile and whipped off his hat. "Sorry, Ma'am, I've ridden a long way. But I was wondering if you could help me. I'm trying to trace a friend, a Miss Martin, and I wondered if she was checked in here."

The woman's mouth hardened. "I am sorry, young man, but we never reveal information about our guests."

Johnny felt a surge of hope. "So she is staying here then?"

The woman tilted her head and glared at him. "If you were paying attention, you would know that isn't what I said. Whether your friend is here or not is irrelevant. I will not check the register to find out. Good day, young man."

He was sure that if she'd had a ruler she would have rapped his knuckles. The only thing to do was check-in himself. Then the woman would have to get him to sign the register. "Well, Ma'am, I'd like to stay here anyway. I'll need a room for one night."

The woman pursed her lips. "I'm sorry, but we don't have

any rooms available."

Yeah, like he was going to believe that. He raised an eyebrow and held her gaze for a couple of beats before nodding and heading back out onto the street where he stood chewing his thumb.

It wasn't a small hotel, and he'd seen other staff through an open door of a back room. The woman was bound to leave the reception desk at some point and be replaced. He'd wait and check-in then, because he was certain that this was where Delice was staying.

He perched on a wall opposite the hotel so that he had a good view of the reception area. He didn't have to wait long. Within ten minutes a younger woman came out to sit at the desk and the first woman disappeared. Johnny grinned and moved swiftly to seize the opportunity.

He hurried to the front desk and smiled his most winning smile. "I'd like a room for the night, please."

The girl responded to his smile, patting her hair into place as she spoke. "That will be two dollars, please."

Johnny fished out some money. Delice must be making too much money out of the bordello if she could afford these prices every time she came to Santa Fe.

"If you could sign the register, please, sir." The girl pushed the book over the counter.

Johnny's smile broadened and he made a show of taking his time to sign while he scanned the other signatures on the page.

Yep, there it was, D. Martin in room twelve. He glanced at the board behind the girl on the desk; the key for room twelve was hanging up, so Delice had to be out in the town somewhere.

"You're in room eight, up the stairs and along the corridor on the right. Is there anything else that you'd like, sir?"

Johnny took the key and shook his head. "No, thanks." He paused and then gestured to the comfortable chairs by the fireplace. "Is it all right to sit down here and read?"

The girl nodded. "Of course, sir, and if you'd like a pot of coffee then let me know."

He nodded his thanks and hurried up to his room to dump his saddlebags before returning to the lobby. He sat in the corner, where he had a good view of the door, and picked up a newspaper so that it at least looked like he was doing something. Now all he had to do was wait. Sooner or later Delice would show up.

He sat watching the door for the next hour, apparently reading his paper but holding it in such a way that he could keep an eye on everyone who passed through the lobby. He was on the verge of heading out into the town to look for her when she walked in. She went to the reception desk to ask for her key and glanced around as she waited for the girl to hand it to her. Then she looked again. He laid the paper to one side and stood up, suppressing a smile at the look of amazement on her face. He chalked one up to himself – it wasn't often he managed to get a reaction from her.

Her eyes narrowed as he walked toward her. She moved away from the desk and hissed at him. "What the hell are you doing here?"

Johnny raised an eyebrow. "What am I doing here? Looking for you, that's what I'm doing. You and me, Delice, we got some talking to do."

CHAPTER NINETEEN

She pursed her lips briefly and then nodded.

He had to credit her for being so controlled. Most women would have fussed around, getting all sort of fluttery and demanding answers when something unexpected happened. But not Delice. She had class.

"You'd better come upstairs to my room, we can talk there." She moved as if to turn away.

"Heck, no, Delice." He lightly touched her arm. Dios, had she no idea of what people would think? "I can't be seen going upstairs with you. You're a lady, it wouldn't be right."

She furrowed her brow and an odd expression flickered in her eyes, but he couldn't read it. "Honey, I'm no lady, but this is a respectable hotel so maybe you're right."

He felt a pang of sorrow at her words. "You are a lady, Delice, and don't ever let anyone tell you different. I'll come up in about ten minutes, and I'll make sure that nobody's around."

She nodded. "My room's on the top floor. Number twelve." And with that she turned and walked away up the sweeping staircase.

He handed his key in at the desk and then ambled out into the street where he hung around on the corner for a few minutes. Then he slipped back into the hotel and asked for his key, saying he'd forgotten some papers in his room. He hurried up the stairs and then, pausing to make sure that nobody was looking, he sped silently up to the next floor where he tapped gently on the door of number twelve.

She opened the door immediately and he stepped into her room. Looking around he let out a low whistle as he took in the velvet drapes, and a vase of roses standing on a gleaming polished marble washstand. "Boy, this is a hell of a lot grander than my room."

She shut her eyes briefly, shaking her head. "You're staying here?" She sounded kind of stunned, like she couldn't believe what he'd just said. "In this hotel?"

He shrugged. "Had to. It was the only way I could sneak a look at the register to see if you were here. I been round half the hotels in Santa Fe looking for you."

"How touching." She didn't sound like she meant it. She folded her arms. "And exactly why were you looking for me?"

Was she really that dumb? He stared at her, trying to stop his mouth dropping open like he was planning on catching flies.

"Why was I looking for you? Well, heck, Delice, somebody had to come and stop you making such a big mistake, and to talk some sense into you. I mean you didn't even wait to see what the result of the vote was."

Her eyes hardened. "A big mistake? Talk some sense into me? Oh my! I can't wait to hear this." She sat down in an armchair in the corner of the room and sat back, raising an eyebrow, like she was waiting for him to keep talking.

He gritted his teeth. She was always tricky. Why couldn't she behave like other women? But then, she wasn't like other women and that's why he liked her. Still, she could be damned awkward at times – like now. He tried his widest smile; the one that always got the women eating out of his hand. "I came to tell you that they ain't going to close you down. The bordello can stay open."

He was hoping for her to look pleased at this piece of news, but he was disappointed. She shook her head, glaring at him. "You came all the way to Santa Fe to tell me that? But leaving that to one side, it might interest you to know that my decision to leave Cimarron had nothing to do with the town meeting. I told you before, if you'd been paying attention, that I have grown bored with Cimarron; it is dull and provincial." She paused, a small furrow appearing between her eyes. "They voted to allow it to stay open?" He could hear the disbelief in her voice.

Johnny nodded enthusiastically – what the hell did provincial mean anyway? "Yeah. It's good news isn't it?" He paused, and looked at her hopefully. She merely raised an eyebrow. "Well, I thought it was good news. I figured you'd be pleased." He kept his voice cheerful, but if he was honest, he was a little pissed that she didn't seem to appreciate this result – especially after he'd put so much effort into it.

She still didn't smile, she frowned instead. "Why would they do that, Johnny? There must have been plenty of people at that meeting who would want to see us closed down; all those prudish women for starters. And they'd make damn sure that their husbands voted to close it down. It makes no sense, no sense at all."

"The mayor decided to make it a secret vote, with only his committee voting. He said it would be more democratic that way..." Johnny trailed off. He had an uneasy feeling that this was taking him onto very dodgy ground.

Her eyes widened and she sucked in a small breath, like she was speechless for a second. But only for a second. She shook her head, closing her eyes briefly. "God preserve us from politicians! Only a politician could say that was democratic. How on earth is it democratic to reduce the number of people allowed to have their say?" She sniffed. And then gave him a sharp look, kind of like she was thinking things over. "Like I said, it makes no sense. So suddenly I'm getting the faintest whiff of a rat."

A rat? What the hell was she talking about rats for? And why was she staring at him that hard?

"You!" She snapped the word out so suddenly he flinched.

"It had to be you. What the hell have you been up to?" She was out of the chair now and pacing around the room.

"Nothing." He could feel heat flushing his face. "I—"

"Don't 'nothing' me. I am not stupid, Johnny, and I see your hand in this. You," she narrowed her eyes. "You have been meddling. How on earth did you persuade the mayor to make it a secret vote? There is no way that he would have made that decision without being pushed into it. Not with an election coming up. He's been very keen to show how he listens to his electorate. So something happened to make him change his mind. You must have threatened him in some way and yet, somehow, I can't see you threatening him with a gun." She stopped pacing and stood chewing on her lip, lost in thought. Her head jerked up and she gave him the full-on glare. The no holds barred one that made him squirm. "Sadie! Oh my God. Sadie told you about the mayor. That's the only explanation. That's the one thing you could threaten him with."

"Sadie didn't tell me nothing—"

He didn't get a chance to finish, she cut across him. Her voice was an icy cold hiss. "Don't lie to me. You have her wrapped around your little finger. She'll do anything you ask. And tell you anything. How dare you interfere in the running of my business! I am proud of my business, Johnny. Maybe that seems strange to you. But I built it up without any help from anyone. Just me. I did it all on my own, through my own hard work to make it what it is. And every one of my customers is entitled to their privacy. What they choose to do behind closed doors is nobody else's business. And now you've ruined it all. Thanks to your interference and arrogance, you have totally destroyed my professional credibility in one fell swoop."

Looking at her stricken face he felt about one inch high. Dios but he hadn't meant to upset her. "Delice, I'm sorry, I never meant—"

"So you admit it? You blackmailed the mayor?"

Johnny sighed. Seemed he'd have to confess. He couldn't bear to see her so hurt and angry. "I did it for you, Delice—"

"For me!"

Shit. That wasn't the right thing to say either. She was going a real funny color.

"For me? You did it for me." The hiss had turned into a snarl now. "Exactly how is ruining my business supposed to help me? Do enlighten me, Johnny, I'm obviously missing something here."

He shrugged and ducked his head. What the hell could he say? He couldn't think of a damn thing that was going to make this better. "I thought you'd be best off staying in Cimarron..." It didn't sound too good somehow.

"Because being a man you must know better than me?" There was a real edge in her voice now. "Your arrogance is quite breathtaking. What you mean is you didn't want to lose your access to a bunch of pretty whores. So, you wormed your way around Sadie and got her to tell you things she had no right talking about. She knows my rules about never, ever discussing our customers, and you know something, you just got her fired, Johnny. I hope you're proud of yourself."

Shit. He'd promised Sadie a job if this happened. An image of a furious Guthrie flashed through his mind's eye. "You can't fire her, Delice, it ain't her fault—"

"Not her fault! She revealed highly confidential information to you so that you could blackmail a customer. Do tell me, exactly how is that not her fault?" Delice paused for breath. He guessed she had to at some point. He started to open his mouth but damn it, she was off again. "Oh, God! The mayor's committee – did she tell you about them too?"

Johnny shuffled his feet, trying to think of something to say, but she didn't wait for an answer.

"You blackmailed them too, didn't you? How the hell did you get her to tell you so much? What did you threaten Sadie with?"

Johnny flushed. "I said I'd make one of the other girls my favorite and leave her for Jeb Lutz."

She was silent for a beat. Then she shook her head like she could hardly believe what he'd said. "And you were arrogant enough to believe it would make Sadie tell you what you wanted to know."

He bit his lip. He didn't think it would help matters if he pointed out that his tactics had worked perfectly.

She threw her hands up in the air. "And of course you were

right. Sadie gave in and told you exactly what you wanted to know. You were being totally selfish. You've gotten used to having some clean girls and you didn't want to go back to the rough ones. And yet you have the nerve to say you did this for me. This was about you, Johnny, because by no stretch of the imagination can I see how your actions were in my best interests."

Her words stung and he shook his head, angry and hurt that she thought so badly of him. "It was for you. You got a good place in Cimarron, you got friends there. Better friends than your Adam Smith—"

"Adam Smith?" She stared at him wide eyed, sounding like she didn't believe what she was hearing. "What the hell has Adam Smith got to do with any of this?"

"Yeah. Adam Smith. Where was he when you got beat up? I didn't see any sign of him coming around to help out, even though you reckon him as a friend." Johnny aimed a savage kick at the floor.

She shook her head, looking kind of dazed. "Leave Adam Smith out of this. The fact is you interfered simply because you didn't want to lose the bordello—"

"Damn it, Delice, I did do it for you."

She glared at him. "Oh yes? Like I'm going to believe that."

He hated this. Hated that she didn't believe him. Hated to see her looking at him like this. "I don't want you to leave, Delice."

"Because of the girls—"

"No, not because of the girls, damn it. You can't leave, I need you—"

He had a glimpse of her shocked face before she swung away to stare out of the window even as he tried to figure why the hell he'd said that. Where had it come from? He'd never told anyone he needed them. He didn't need anyone so why the devil did he say that he did? "I need you." It came out soft the second time. And it was odd, because he didn't mean to say it the second time either, but he felt lighter for saying it.

CHAPTER TWENTY

He shook his head in wonder. What the hell had possessed him? Telling Delice, of all people, that he needed her? But he hadn't been able to stop himself. The words had come out as fast as bullets from his gun. Hadn't even thought about it – and then, to top it all, he'd gone and said it again.

Furrowing his brow, he stared at her rigid back as she stood looking through the window onto the quiet street. He scratched his chin as he tried to figure it out because now he hadn't a clue what to say next. Especially when she was mad as hell at him. Dios, but he'd been dumb. He hadn't even stopped to consider that blackmailing her customers wouldn't do her business much good. She was right, he had been selfish. But not in the way she meant. He knew, if he was honest, that it was her he didn't want to lose. Thoughts of the girls hadn't come into it. Must be because he wasn't used to having friends he could trust. Yeah. That would explain why he knew he needed to keep her in Cimarron. Because he did trust her, more than anyone he'd ever known. And she always gave him good advice. And she always gave it to him straight. She didn't piss about sugar coating things. Yeah, that was why he needed her. But he could hardly tell her that he trusted her more than anyone he'd ever met. She'd think he was loco.

"I am sorry." He spoke softly. "I didn't stop to think about how what I was doing could affect your reputation." Hell, nobody knew better than him how important a reputation was. "All I could think of was stopping you leaving."

He saw her head tilt back, like she was staring at the sky, but she still didn't speak.

"I screwed up. And I'm truly sorry, because I wouldn't hurt you for the world. I value your friendship far too much for that." Was he saying anything right? She wasn't yelling, but then she wasn't saying anything either. He'd never be able to figure her, she was the most complicated woman he'd ever met. But maybe it didn't matter now because she was going to leave anyway. He swallowed the lump that seemed to have gotten stuck in his throat.

She took a handkerchief out of her pocket and blew her nose. But she still didn't turn around. Then she spoke, her voice muffled because of the handkerchief. "It seems that you rarely think about the consequences of your actions." She blew her nose again. "And if it wasn't enough you tried to ruin my business, I must be coming down with a cold."

"I'm sorry. Truly sorry." Maybe if he kept saying it she'd

finally believe him. He sighed softly. "Will you at least have dinner with me this evening? I mean you got to eat, don't you?" He paused. "If you can bear the sight of me, that is."

She turned toward him, still holding the damn handkerchief so he could hardly see her. "Dinner?"

He shrugged. "Yeah, dinner." He tried a smile but his heart wasn't in it. "Look at it this way, it'd give you a chance to have another go at me for being so dumb."

She sighed, and shook her head slightly, like she didn't know what to say or do. "Well, I have to eat, so yes, thank you, I will have dinner with you." She paused. "On condition that you stop telling me that you are stupid. You are far from that. Quite the contrary, in fact. You are manipulative and devious but you are most definitely not stupid. I only wish that occasionally you would stop to give due consideration to the consequences of your actions."

What was it with her and Harvard that they had to use long words all of the time? But heck, she'd said yes to dinner so at least she was calming down a bit. "I'll wait for you down in the lobby. There's a good place up the road." He tried another smile. "Well, leastways that's what I heard. It's real fancy food so at least you'll eat well, even if I come as a side order."

Although her face was half-hidden by the handkerchief, he heard what he could swear was a muffled laugh. A small one, but still a laugh. And the tightness in his gut eased a touch. He ducked his head before looking back at her. "I'll go clean up. I need to wash the trail dust off me. Then I'll go on down to the lobby. We can't be seen going downstairs together. I'll wait for you there." He opened the door a touch, to check that there was nobody around, and then sped down to his room.

He sloshed some water into the bowl on the washstand and had a quick wash. Then, having run his fingers through his hair in an effort to smooth it down, he ambled down to the lobby.

He sank into a soft leather chair and settled down to wait for her. He must be losing his touch. It was the only explanation. Because despite his efforts and planning, it had all gone horribly wrong. Delice was moving to Santa Fe and there wasn't a damn thing he could do about it. And he'd gotten Sadie fired, and that was going to cause fireworks between him and the old man when the girl turned up demanding a job. He shook his head. Shit.

And if all that wasn't bad enough, he'd still not made any progress on finding out what was eating Guy either. Could things get any worse?

He sighed. Yeah. Things could always get worse and in his experience they usually did. It was like one of those towers that people built out of cards, once one card went, the whole thing usually ended up falling down.

He glanced up as Delice swept elegantly down the stairs. She had a way of walking that made folk notice her. He jumped up as she walked toward him, noting that just for once she wasn't wearing that ugly grey dress she always wore at the bordello. Instead she was wearing a green one with fancy velvet trim. He smiled. He'd bet that her eyes would look even greener because of it. He watched as she stopped to hand her key in at the desk, and wondered how old she was. When he'd first met her he'd thought of her as an ugly old cow. The memory of that made him flush. But he knew her better now and he could tell that she wasn't nearly as old as he'd first thought. Maybe in her early thirties?

He pushed his thoughts to one side as she turned back to face him. He gave her a cautious smile. "So, shall we go to dinner?" He offered his arm which she slipped her hand through as he escorted her onto the quiet tree lined street.

She didn't speak as they strolled toward the hotel with the fancy restaurant. She looked about her while he tried to figure her mood. He wasn't sure if she was still angry or not. Damn, but he wished he was better at reading her.

His information was right – the restaurant was fancy. They were greeted at the door by a man wearing a black coat with tails. "Would you care to check your gun, sir, before sitting down?"

Johnny met the man's bland gaze. "No, I wouldn't."

The man inclined his head. "As you wish, sir. "I'll show you to a table if you'd like to follow me."

As he turned away, Johnny put his hand out to halt the fellow. "We'd like a corner table if you've got one, please."

The man nodded even as Johnny saw Delice's lips compress like she was trying not to laugh. She didn't speak until the waiter had left them settled in the corner of the dining room, with big ornate menus in front of them, all written on thick card.

"A corner table? Really? Are you worried that somebody will creep up on you in this place?" She waved her hand around indicating their luxurious surroundings.

Johnny grinned. "Old habits die hard. A man can't be too careful."

She raised an eyebrow. "I think it may be safe to let your guard down just a touch in here. I don't see any desperados waiting in ambush."

Johnny bit back a smile. She had him pegged. But, hell, she always had, right from the first time they'd met. Maybe that was why he liked her so much. "So," he spoke softly. "What would you like to eat?" He paused. "And I'm sorry, I should have asked what would you like to drink?"

Even as he spoke the waiter returned to ask the same question.

"I'd like a glass of white wine, please." Delice gave the waiter a charming smile.

"Chablis for the lady, please." Johnny enjoyed the look of confusion on her face. All those months with Harvard were paying off tonight. "And I'll have a bottle of the Lafite, please."

Delice's eyebrow was disappearing into her hair. "My," she spoke as the waiter wafted away. "I'm impressed. Not just by your knowledge, but your pronunciation. It's excellent."

He grinned. "I was in the Mexican army – briefly. Very briefly! We had a lot of French prisoners." Not that he was going to tell her just how some of those prisoners had been treated – it definitely wasn't something to discuss over dinner.

"The Mexican army? You do surprise me. Somehow I wouldn't have thought that you would have been the type of person to like taking orders." A hint of a smile quirked her mouth.

Johnny grinned. "You got that right. That's why my time there was brief. But it suited me for a while to join up." And no way was he giving away more than that. "Are you still mad at me?"

She narrowed her eyes. "You mean am I still angry with you for manipulating my staff for your own ends, blackmailing my best customers, destroying my reputation, and generally interfering in areas that are none of your business? Well, I really don't know, Johnny. What do you think?"

He bit his lip, and was relieved at the sudden reappearance of the waiter with their drinks. "I am sorry. Really." He waited till the waiter had gone out of earshot. "I know I'm a selfish bast—sorry, selfish fellow, but I couldn't bear the thought of you leaving." He shrugged his shoulders, smiling apologetically. "I mean, do you really think I'd still be at the ranch if it hadn't been for all your advice this past year? We both know I'd have fallen out with the old man and walked out months ago. I couldn't have done it without you."

The waiter came back. "Are you ready to order, sir, or would you like a little more time?"

Johnny shook his head. "Delice? Are you ready or would you like another minute?" He glanced across at Delice who was studying the menu intently.

"I would like the soupe de poisson, please, followed by the blanquette de veau." She smiled and handed the menu back to the waiter.

Johnny scanned the menu. "Um, yeah, I'll have the onion soup and then a steak, please."

The waiter made a brief note on his little pad. "How would you like the steak cooked, sir?"

"Just run it past the stove. I like it rare enough that a really good veterinarian could revive it."

Delice tried to smother a laugh.

The waiter's lips twitched. "Very good, sir. Bleu." The waiter hurried off and then Delice gave in to her laughter.

"That's a perfect way to describe wanting a rare steak!" She paused, eyeing him with a smile still quirking her mouth. "You never fail to surprise me, Johnny. I'm never quite sure what you'll do or say next. You are nothing if not unpredictable."

He felt a little more of his tension ebb away. She had spoken with warmth, like maybe she thought he wasn't all bad. Maybe she'd forgive him yet for his thoughtlessness over the bordello. But he still couldn't figure why she wanted to come to Santa Fe. This Adam Smith must have a real hold over her. He grimaced. Even thinking of that made the tightness in his gut come back. But he could hardly tell her that he'd be a better friend to her than Smith. Trouble was he didn't know how to deal with the fellow. Maybe she'd let something slip about the man during dinner.

"So, do you always stay at that hotel when you come to town?" He wanted to stop thinking about Smith for the time being. Push the man to one side.

She nodded. "It's quiet and very comfortable. I've used it for years."

"I didn't even know it was there. Guthrie always stays at one of the big ones on the main street. It probably costs as much but it sure ain't as comfortable."

She shrugged. "I find the large ones here rather vulgar and full of loud cattle men. I prefer a more discreet establishment."

"Loud cattle men? Like me?" Johnny grinned.

"Honey, you might be a cattle man but you're not loud. No, I mean those awful ranchers who stand in groups bragging to each other and swapping lies. And unlike you, very few of them are gentlemen."

His jaw almost hit the table. A gentleman? Him? He didn't like to say she was wrong, but that she thought he was one made him feel good inside. The arrival of the waiter with their soup at least saved him from having to reply. And that was just as well because he couldn't think of a damn thing to say.

"The soup is excellent." Delice nodded her approval. "And the bread is delicious. I love freshly baked bread and this is especially good. This was an excellent choice of restaurants, Johnny."

Well, leastways he got some things right. He ducked his

head before looking back at her. "Well, I'd heard it was good and figured you might like it." He wondered if this would be a good time to mention Sadie. He had to stop Delice from firing her. Guthrie really would go loco if the girl showed up at the ranch with her breasts bursting out of her dress and demanding a job. And he wouldn't blame Guthrie. Sadie hadn't been far wrong when she'd told him she was only good for poking. He sure couldn't see her as being good for much else.

"What's on your mind, now?" She was watching him, her eyebrow raised, like she knew he was worrying at something. He never could fool her.

He shrugged, unsure of what to say. "I was wondering if you really are going to fire Sadie." He swallowed. Was it his imagination or did her face harden a touch?

"Still worrying about your favorite girl?" There was a tone in her voice which he couldn't figure. "I don't see that it makes much difference to you, if I'm moving to Santa Fe."

He flushed, wincing a little at her words. But he might as well come clean and confess. Honesty was usually the easiest route in his experience. "It's nothing to do with whether or not she's my favorite girl. It's..." He paused. How the hell could he explain? He swallowed hard. Delice was watching him with narrowed eyes, kind of like she'd moved away from him again, and just when he thought things were getting easier. He shook his head. Spit it out, and get it over with. "The thing is, I told Sadie if you fired her we'd find her a job on the ranch and—"

He didn't get any further. Delice kind of choked on her meal and started coughing. Johnny leapt from his seat to pat her on the back, while she dabbed at her eyes with her napkin.

Once she stopped coughing, and he returned to his seat, she fixed him with a steely gaze. "You said you'd find her a job on the ranch?" She sounded like she couldn't believe what he'd said.

He pulled a face, embarrassed at how stupid he felt. "Well, yeah. I had to promise her something. Anything. She was real worried about telling me because she was so scared you'd find out. So I said if you did find out what she'd done, I'd find her a job. But." He could feel the heat flooding his face. "But somehow, I don't think my old man will be too impressed if she turns up—" He didn't get any further because Delice started laughing, kind of like it was the best joke she'd ever heard.

"Oh, Johnny! Don't ever change. You are quite incorrigible!" She dabbed at her eyes again while he tried to figure if being incorry-jabul was good or bad. But she sure didn't sound mad so it couldn't be too bad.

She shook her head, still laughing. "A job on the ranch? Sadie? Good grief, I can imagine your father's reaction if she turned up. I warn you, she has no real talents. She certainly can't cook, or knit, or sew, or—"

Johnny held his hand up. "Fine. Thanks, that's fine, I get the picture. But I was ready to promise anything at all in order to find some way of fixing the vote to stop you from leaving."

She started fiddling with her napkin, and he'd have sworn

she was blushing. Except this was Delice and he couldn't imagine that anything he said would embarrass her. She didn't say anything for a few minutes because the waiter arrived with their second course.

When the waiter had left them, she shot Johnny a curious glance. "How did you explain your coming to Santa Fe to your father? I'm surprised he was prepared to allow you time off to come here."

Johnny ducked his head before meeting her gaze. "I didn't exactly tell him."

She dropped her fork onto her plate and jerked forward. "What do you mean, you didn't exactly tell him?"

He shrugged. "I came straight after you. I didn't go home after the meeting. All I could think of was getting here to see you."

She stared at him, her eyes wide open. "You didn't even send him a note?"

He glared. "A note? Well, seeing as how I'm not leaving permanent, I couldn't see any point in leaving a note."

She shut her eyes briefly and muttered something to herself. If it wasn't for her being a lady, he'd have sworn that she was cussing. "Honey, what on earth will they be thinking now? You are a part-owner of the ranch. You have responsibilities. You can't simply up and go without any explanation whenever the fancy takes you. For all you know they'll be worrying themselves sick that you've either walked out, or that you're lying injured some place—"

He cut across her. "I got the stable boy to take a message saying I'd gone to Santa Fe."

She shook her head. "I don't think that will do much to appease your father. I imagine he will be incandescent with rage at your taking off like that. You should have told him what you were doing, or at the very least left a proper letter."

"I wanted to get here fast." He stabbed at the meat on his plate. "And... I didn't know what to tell him if I did go and see him. He'd have said no."

"So you were operating on the premise that it's better to seek forgiveness than ask permission." She tilted her head to one side, like he was some sort of problem she had to figure. "They'll be mad at you, but they might have been a little less angry if you'd taken the trouble to let them know what you were doing. I meant what I said. You can't simply take off whenever it suits you; you have to consider their feelings. I assume you're going straight back in the morning?" There was a questioning note in her voice, kind like she was hoping that he would agree with her. Seemed he'd be disappointing her on that score.

"Nope. Not yet. I was going to send a wire. There's something else I got to do now that I'm here."

"What else have you got to do?"

Johnny sighed. "I want to go to the library. I heard there's a library here. There is, isn't there?" He hoped she'd agree, but she was kind of looking stunned, like she'd been hit over the head with something.

"The library?" She sucked in a breath, like there wasn't enough air in the room. "I hate to say it, but I never really imagined you as an avid reader."

He glared. "What's that got to do with anything?" He paused. "I'm not, but I have read a book."

"A book? Just the one? Which book was it?"

"Ivanhoe." He was kind of proud of that, and even more so when he saw how taken aback she looked.

"Ivanhoe? Well, I am impressed. Scott isn't the easiest of reads. I always find him heavy going." Delice shook her head slightly, like she couldn't figure it all out. "Well, leaving Ivanhoe to one side, surely if you want a book you could ask Guy or your father to lend you one. If not, I have an excellent library myself and I'd be happy to lend you some books."

"I want to read up on the war."

That shut her up. She sucked in a breath and nodded slowly.

"Nobody will tell me anything about it, so I figured if I'm going to find out what's eating at Guy, I need to find a book about the war." His good mood had vanished. He could feel the tension coming back. And he felt guilty. He'd been so wound up over the bordello that he'd completely forgotten about Guy.

She tilted her head and he could see the sadness in her eyes. "Honey, like I said before, I think it might be best if you leave it alone. Some things are better left in the past and if Guy doesn't want to talk about the war, perhaps you should respect his wishes."

Johnny shook his head. She knew something too. It was damned obvious that she knew something about the war that she wasn't telling him. "You see, you're as bad." He spoke softly hoping she wouldn't hear the hurt in his voice. "You obviously know all about the war, but you won't tell me either. Everyone seems to know about the war except me. So, I'm going to have to go to the library and stay a few more days until I figure it out. And that's final."

She sighed heavily. "Honey, you don't need to go to the library. I think you'll find there is someone much closer to home who can tell you what you want to know."

CHAPTER TWENTY-ONE

"Closer to home?" He narrowed his eyes and dropped his knife and fork on the plate with a clatter. Who did she mean? "Do you mean you? You're going to tell me what I need to know?" He couldn't keep the note of hope out of his voice.

She shook her head. "No, not me, Johnny. I was building up my business back then. To be honest I didn't have much to do with it. I mean, I followed the reports in the newspapers but for the most part the war passed me by. If I'd been in the east or the south at the time, it would have been different, but I was already in Cimarron."

He furrowed his brow. "So, who?"

She shrugged. "Daisy."

"Daisy?" For a second he wondered who the hell she was talking about.

"Yes, honey. Daisy. The same Daisy who you so

thoughtfully sent to me for a job when you were in Abilene." She paused. "If you'd ever bothered actually talking to her, instead of just poking her, you'd know that she comes from the Shenandoah Valley. She was raised on a farm there."

Daisy. Damn it, Daisy with the broken nose who he'd felt sorry for when he'd met her at the end of the cattle drive. "She's from the Shenandoah Valley? But that's where Guy was..." He paused trying to get his thoughts into some sort of order even as he breathed a sigh of relief that he wouldn't have to go through all the books in the library.

Delice nodded. "Exactly. It's where Sheridan's men were in the fall of 1864. Doubtless Daisy will be only too pleased to fill you in on that aspect of the war." She stared down at her hands, fiddling with her napkin. "The thing is, honey, just allow for the fact that Daisy's view of that period of the war will be no more objective than your brother's account. They'll see it from different angles. I suspect there will be no shades of grey. They will have vastly differing opinions on what happened there."

Johnny raised an eyebrow and sighed softly. "I guess how you look at things, depends on where you're standing. A mountain sure looks different from one side to the other."

The faintest hint of a smile quirked Delice's mouth. "That is a very good way of putting it, Johnny."

Trouble was he wanted to know now what it had been about. He didn't want to wait until he talked to Daisy. "What did happen there?"

"Like I said, I wasn't there and I certainly don't feel qualified to comment on it. To be honest," she paused and shrugged. "I know I've said it repeatedly, but I might as well reiterate the point, I think you should leave it alone. Civil wars are the worst type of wars. They rip families apart and turn brother against brother and fathers against sons. But people have tried to move on since those events. Guy obviously wants to put his war experiences behind him. I think we're all striving for something better, looking for different things. To sail beyond the sunset, if you will." She paused. "Yes, to sail beyond the sunset. That's a line from one of my favorite poems, Ulysses by Tennyson. In it he says that *'we are one equal temper of heroic hearts, made weak by time and fate, but strong in will to strive, to seek, to find, and not to yield.'*

"I always felt that summed up how the soldiers in both sides of that tragic war must have felt, as well as people like Daisy who were damaged by the events of those dark years." She paused, looking like she'd gone someplace else far away for a few seconds. Then she shook herself, like she was dragging herself back to the present. "But if you're really not going to take my advice and let matters lie, the least I can do is try to prevent you from making matters worse with your father. I shudder to think what he would say if you stay away even longer. So, you can hear an account much closer to home instead of spending hours or days in the library here." She shook her head as if despairing of him. "I mean, just when things were going better between the two of you, you go and do this."

He wished he was better at explaining his actions, but he'd never been much of a talker, and he always found it tricky putting things into words. "I have to try to help Guy. I hate seeing him like he is right now. And he's stood by me in the past so I reckon I owe him. I want to see him more like his usual self so I guess I didn't stop to worry too much about what the old man would say." He flushed. "And like I said before, I sure didn't hang around to tell him about coming here. I wanted to get here as fast as possible to see you." He bit his lip, watching her sip her wine. He might as well ask her about Smith; it was eating away at him. "Are you moving to Santa Fe because of this Adam Smith? I mean are you in love with him or something?"

Delice gave a very unladylike snort and some of her wine sprayed over the table as she started coughing. She hastily dabbed at her mouth with her napkin. "Adam Smith?" The amazement in her voice was clear. And his spirits soared because he got the feeling that she wasn't in love with the fellow, although why he was pleased he couldn't fathom. It wasn't like he was interested in her. She was simply a good friend.

"Are you still going on about Adam Smith?" She stared at him with wide open eyes.

He ducked his head. "I'm guessing he lives here. He don't live in Cimarron. I asked Stoney about him but he'd never heard of him."

"Why doesn't that surprise me?" She muttered it more to

herself than to him.

"I asked Alonso, too."

She raised an eyebrow. "Alonso?"

Johnny nodded. "Yeah, Alonso, our segundo. I mean he's lived around there for most of his life, but he'd never heard of Adam Smith neither. So I guessed he must be from Santa Fe."

Delice's eyes widened. "All of this because I mentioned him once? And since when did the world revolve solely around Santa Fe and Cimarron?"

Damn it, but she was being tricky again. And it was like she wanted to avoid telling him anything about Smith. Who the hell was he? He glanced across at her; she looked as if she was trying not to laugh.

"Maybe you should try asking Guy about him." Her voice was quite gentle.

"Guy? He ain't lived around here any longer than I have. Well, apart from when he was a kid. But he was gone a long time in Boston. Why should he know about him?" He paused, as another thought struck him. "Is this fellow anything to do with the war?"

She tilted her head to one side and gave an irritated sigh. "No. Nothing to do with the war. Like I said, ask Guy. I suspect he will know who Adam Smith is."

Johnny shot a quick look at her before glancing away like he wasn't bothered by anything she said. He tried to keep his voice casual. "So, is he the reason you're moving to Santa Fe?"

Her mouth quirked. "No, honey. This is nothing whatsoever to do with Adam Smith. Although," her voice took on a thoughtful tone. "I suppose there is a faint connection seeing as how you've probably destroyed my business in Cimarron."

Damn it, but she was like a dog with a bone. Didn't look like she was going to forgive him for that any time soon. "I said I'm sorry. And I am. If you like I could have a word with the mayor and his committee, and kind of persuade them to keep bringing you their business—" He got no further.

"No!" She narrowed her eyes. "You have interfered enough already. Don't you dare say anything to any of them. I will speak to them myself."

He wondered why she was going to bother. If she was leaving Cimarron there wasn't much point in speaking to them. He pushed his glass around in circles as he tried to figure her mood. Was it worth asking about Sadie again? He guessed he might as well. Nothing to lose, because if the girl turned up at Sinclair, Guthrie would go loco.

"About Sadie." He paused, to try to gauge her reaction. But she didn't look mad, more like he'd said something funny.

"Yes? What about Sadie?" She tilted her head to one side like she was waiting for him to carry on.

"Well, I reckon Guthrie's going to be mad enough at me over taking off for Santa Fe, without Sadie showing up wanting a job. And to be honest I can't think of any work she could do on the ranch."

Delice bit her lip. "I suppose she could be employed to offer the ranch hands fringe benefits. A dollar a day and a weekly poke." She sucked her mouth in. He had the feeling that she was trying real hard not to laugh.

"Oh honey, for heaven's sake, I won't fire her. I'd hate to have your death on my conscience. Because I really do think your father might murder you if she waltzed up asking for a job." Delice sat back in her chair laughing. "Although goodness knows how I'm going to maintain discipline among the girls if Sadie thinks she got away with breaking all my rules."

Johnny grinned. "Thanks, Delice. I reckon you've probably saved my life, and maybe my old man's too. He'd have had a fit if she'd shown up."

"So, you'll head back, and go and beg your family's forgiveness?" She shot him a sharp look.

He nodded. "Yeah, I'll head back in the morning and I'll go and talk to Daisy too." He hesitated, sighing softly. "The girls were packing up when I left town. It ain't going to be the same without you. Seems a real pity. I mean you had a good business there. A real smart place, done up all fancy, and you'd got it exactly the way you wanted it. And even allowing for losing the mayor and his friends, you got lots of really good regular customers."

She was staring down at her hands again, back fiddling with the damn napkin. "Actually, I've been thinking about that." Her voice sounded odd. Kind of strained. "I've been reflecting on the logistics and financial considerations and everything."

Logistics? What the hell were logistics? He stared at her blankly. He couldn't say anything if he didn't know what the hell she was going on about.

"It occurs to me that maybe you have a point." She still didn't look at him.

"I have?" What point was that? He knew she never paid him much heed – even when he was right. Not that that happened very often.

"Hmm. I was thinking it would be very expensive to move."

He jerked his head up, and a tiny seed of hope took root somewhere deep inside of him. "Well, yeah. That's what I said. And moving all your things, some of them will get broke. It's not the easiest journey to Santa Fe. And then you got to build up a good name from scratch all over again."

She nodded. "And of course there is a great deal more competition in Santa Fe. And although we would naturally be a far superior establishment, it still takes time for word to spread. I do think you have made a very valid argument, Johnny."

He sucked in a breath. He certainly wasn't going to point out that he wasn't saying anything that he hadn't already said to her about it back in Cimarron. No. Keep encouraging her to think this way – that was the line to take. "Yeah, it always takes time for word to get around. And, like I said before, it's more expensive in Santa Fe. You know; the charges for businesses and things. And the girls might not settle. And you might not find a doctor as good as Ben to keep a regular check on the girls."

Delice nodded solemnly. "Yes, indeed. Those are all very serious and weighty considerations. I pride myself on the high standards of cleanliness in my establishment. Ben looks after the girls well."

He took a deep breath. "So, maybe you should stay put in Cimarron." And he said it like he knew that she would agree, even though he was holding his breath now, waiting for her reply.

She stopped playing with the napkin and looked him straight in the eye. "Yes. All things considered and having weighed up all the ramifications of such a move, I do believe that you are right. I will see my lawyer tomorrow and tell him that I have changed my mind."

He couldn't stop the smile from spreading across his face. It was as if a heavy load had been lifted from him and he'd grown a few inches taller. He felt warm inside like the sun had lit him up. "That's great news, Delice. Definitely the right decision. Yeah, no doubt at all, you're doing the right thing."

Her mouth quirked into a smile. "Perhaps, as you'll be back in Cimarron before me, you would be so kind as to let the girls know that they're to start unpacking."

"Hell, yes. I'll do it as soon as I get back." He scratched his chin thoughtfully. "You sure you don't want me to have a word with the mayor and—"

"No!" She held up her hand and for a second he would have sworn she was counting under her breath. "Thank you, but no thank you. I think you have done more than enough in that direction. Leave it alone."

He shrugged. Hell, he could take a hint. Although he couldn't see that it would do any harm to apply a little pressure to the likes of Tandy and Carter. But he sure wasn't about to risk pissing her off even more than he had done. Last thing he wanted was for to change her mind. "Whatever you say, Delice, whatever you say." The grin was back. He just couldn't stop himself from smiling. Dios, but he felt good. And it was odd, but he felt like he could handle anything now. Whatever was bothering Guy, he'd be able to deal with it better now. "I'll head back in the morning and go and see Daisy, and give the girls your message." He paused, noticing that the waiter was approaching. "Would you like a dessert? Or a cup of coffee?"

She shook her head. "No, thank you. But it was a delicious meal. And an excellent choice of restaurant. I love French food and that was especially good. Thank you."

They strolled back to the hotel, stopping occasionally when something in a shop window caught Delice's eye. The air was warm, and once they were away from the main street the scent of lavender and roses hung heavy in the air. And although there were lamps lit to guide their way, the moon added a soft light which lit her face as they talked.

It felt good. And he felt more relaxed than he could remember. Funny how he'd got so wound up over the thought of her leaving; it only went to show how much he'd changed. Time was he never let anyone get close to him, and now he counted her as his closest friend. What with her, and Guy, and Ben, and Stoney, his life sure was changing.

He walked her up the steps into the hotel lobby. He took hold of her hand. "I guess I'll have already left before you're up in the morning, so have a safe journey home. And I'm real glad you changed your mind, Delice." With a gallant bow, he kissed the tips of her fingers. "Goodnight. I'll see you when you get back to Cimarron."

Delice shook her head and rolled her eyes, but he noticed that her cheeks were flushed pink. "Goodnight, Johnny. I was right; you really are incorrigible." And with a slight wave of her hand she hurried off up the stairs.

CHAPTER TWENTY-TWO

Guthrie paced around the room, feeling angrier than he could remember in a long time. The boy was totally irresponsible. There was no other word to describe him. Except, of course, there were plenty of other words to describe him. Irresponsible, thoughtless, and reckless. Those three came to mind right away. Doubtless he could find a few more if he put his mind to it.

They'd waited dinner, but of course Johnny hadn't graced them with his presence. And then the boy from the livery stable had shown up with a message. His son had apparently taken off for Santa Fe without any explanation or apology. Typical of the boy. He never stopped to consider anyone else; just went on his way without a thought for other people – exactly like his mother. She had obviously made no effort to bring him up properly. Look at his table manners. And his surliness with fellow ranchers. And how he avoided shaking hands with people. And now this latest rudeness.

But what if Johnny didn't come back?

"Pacing around won't bring him home any sooner." Guy's calm voice dragged his attention back to the present, away from the fear which had suddenly taken root in his gut.

Guthrie licked his lips, his mouth suddenly felt very dry. He hesitated, uncertain whether to voice his fear to Guy. But no, anger was the easier option. It always was. "He's downright selfish, thoughtless, and irresponsible. What was he thinking of? He knows how stretched we are at the moment with so much work on our plates. And in case it's slipped your mind, it means you will have to cover for him. It's not only more work for the hands, it is for you too." That was the way to play it. His elder son was always too quick to cover for his brother. It was time to make Guy realize how thoughtless Johnny was.

And yet. And yet... If he was honest, nobody worked longer hours than Johnny. He'd noticed how the boy pushed himself, almost as though he thought he had something to prove. But heaven only knew why he should think that.

"It's not that he's irresponsible." Guy sounded as though he was musing aloud. "He always does his share when he's here."

"And there's the rub. When he's here!" Guthrie couldn't resist the riposte.

"More than his share." Guy carried on as if Guthrie hadn't spoken. "But sometimes I think he forgets that he has other people to answer to now. He sees a problem and rushes off to deal with it. Because that's what he has always done."

"A problem. What problem? For all we know he's gone off to see a woman. You know how he is with women." Guthrie stomped to the liquor cabinet to pour himself a whisky.

Guy laughed. "I think there are more than enough girls for him in Cimarron. One thing's for sure, he certainly won't have gone to Santa Fe because of a woman."

"He didn't even leave a note." Guthrie snapped the words out. But he felt the icy grip of fear coiling around his guts. What if Johnny didn't come back? He often had the feeling that his son wasn't happy. If he was honest he'd rarely seen Johnny look happy. What if Johnny had finally had enough and walked out. What if the message was a ruse to allay any suspicions? Or what if he was gunned down in Santa Fe, drawn into some pointless gunfight...

"I don't believe that he's left for good, if that's what's worrying you." Guy's voice sounded surprisingly gentle.

"I didn't say I thought he'd left." Guthrie knew he sounded defensive but Guy's perceptiveness had startled him.

Guy raised an eyebrow, the hint of a smile pulling at his mouth. "The two of you have been getting on so much better of late. You know that. And he's far more settled since we returned from Utah. He wants to be here, I'm sure of that." Guy paused and poured himself a hefty measure from the decanter. "When we were away on the cattle drive he told me how much more settled he's feeling now, and I believe him."

He felt a pinprick of hope, maybe his fear was unwarranted.

Not that he'd allow Guy to suspect that's what was really bothering him. "Hmph. You and he haven't been getting along too well of late." Attack was always the best form of defense. But now he came to think of it, Guy was right. He and Johnny had far fewer arguments these days. And when they did argue their fights were far less vitriolic than they had been in the early days when Johnny had first come home.

Guy stretched his legs out, leaning back in his chair. "I guess the cattle drive has thrown everyone off kilter. It was a long and tiring trip. And then there was the fight we had with the Comanches."

Guthrie viewed him over the top of his glass. That was an evasive answer if ever he'd heard one. It seemed that Johnny and Guy had a lot in common. Neither one would talk about anything that they didn't wish to discuss. It was odd, but he'd never noticed that about them before. "Johnny is worried that this relative of Hausmann will cause trouble for us. You know that's worrying him."

Guy shrugged. "The man has no reason to cause trouble. Johnny is a suspicious devil at the best of times, and never thinks well of people. You know that."

"You don't think it has anything to do with why he's suddenly taken off to Santa Fe?" In a way he hoped it had. It would excuse Johnny's disappearance as being justified "family" business. The trouble was, he didn't really think that was the reason. He suspected that it was more a case of Johnny being irresponsible, or wanting a break from the ranch after all of the bookwork over the weekend. He wanted to believe that. He had to stop worrying that Johnny had walked out for good.

"No." Guy's voice was cool, discouraging further conversation. "I don't." Guy stood up and went to the shelves and selected a book. "I think I'll have an early night and a read. I'll take my drink with me. Goodnight."

"So why do you think he's gone to Santa Fe?" Damn it, he wasn't done talking with Guy, the boy could at least stay a few minutes longer.

Guy's shoulders tensed briefly and then slumped down as he gave an audible sigh and turned back to face his father.

"I have no idea why Johnny has taken off; he didn't think to notify me of his intentions. But I don't believe he has walked out."

"But you can't be certain of that, can you? Maybe he's had enough of hard work and returned to whatever it is in his previous life that's so important to him." Guthrie waved his hand toward the window and the gathering darkness.

Guy closed his eyes briefly, shaking his head. "No, I can't be certain. But I have every confidence that he will come back. I just told you that he admitted to being more settled now. The most important thing will be not to lose your temper when he does come home. Surely you can make the point that it was a thoughtless thing to do without shouting. That always pushes him farther away from you. And let's face it; relations have often been strained between the two of you, although, as I just said, they've been better of late." Guy paused and scratched his neck while he chewed on his lip as if considering some problem. "The ridiculous thing is that neither of you sees how alike you are. You're both stubborn to a fault, far too quick to judge, and neither of you is ever willing to compromise over anything. Things are either black or white with no shades of grey."

"Alike! The boy is just like his mother - he doesn't favor me at all."

"Physically, maybe not. But he is so obviously your son. You might not have raised him, but never was there a son more like his father!"

Guthrie made a snort of derision. "All I know is that he is returning to his old habits of not showing any consideration to this family. He puts himself first and that's it."

Guy shrugged. "I think you are being particularly obtuse. Johnny will have had a reason for taking off like he did, he always does. But I can't for the life of me think what it might be."

Guy's voice carried conviction. Guthrie turned to stare into the darkness. Could Johnny have got wind of something to do with Hausmann's relative? Could that explain his sudden departure for Santa Fe? But Johnny had seemed so positive that there was a threat to Guy and if he truly believed that, Guthrie couldn't imagine Johnny taking off and leaving Guy to face some unseen danger alone. If he was certain of one thing, it was that Johnny had a genuine affection for his brother. They couldn't be more different in upbringing but they seemed to be forging a strong tie. Guthrie turned back to face Guy, who still stood at the foot of the stairs. "Maybe his visit to Santa Fe does have something to do with Hausmann."

"Hausmann and his family have no reason to cause trouble." Guy snapped the words out, running a hand through his hair in irritation. "I have had no association with them in the past or in the army. I have done nothing wrong." Guy paused seeming lost in thought and then flushed a dull brick red. "In Boston. Nothing wrong at all."

It was that afterthought – in Boston. The words jarred on Guthrie, forcing him to wonder when and where Guy had done wrong. He pushed the thought away, irritated with himself. All men had done things they regretted; there was no reason for Guy to be different. And doubtless anything Guy had done paled into significance if it was measured against the wrong doings of his younger brother. God only knew how many times Johnny had done the wrong thing.

"Anyway," Guy stood a little straighter. "I have every confidence that Johnny will return when he's ready. But it's unfortunate that he is totally selfish and fails to consider the consequences of his actions. He certainly never appears to consider his family. He couldn't have chosen a worse time to take off, not when we are so very busy. And as you said, I will have to cover for him. Again."

Guthrie eyed him curiously. There was no doubt in his mind that Guy's words had been selected to move the conversation away from the Hausmanns and the war. Still, that was hardly surprising, few fighting men wanted to dwell on such things. Even so, Guy was normally Johnny's staunchest defender, and for Guy to perform such a sudden *volte face* and so openly criticize his brother was an indication of how reluctant he was to come anywhere close to discussing his past.

Guthrie shook his head. He suspected that he was never going to come close to understanding either one of his sons. He swallowed hard. Always supposing that Guy was right and that Johnny hadn't walked out to return to his old life. He didn't want to think about what that could mean. It was easier to change the subject. "Speaking of Hausmann, I have some news. I heard from the bishop again. Hausmann is being asked to retire. It appears that my strongly-worded complaint about him was the final straw. So at least he will be deprived of his pulpit for the opportunity to make slanderous comments about his parishioners. Doubtless he will continue to be poisonous in private, but he will lack the tacit support of the church."

Guy nodded. "Well, that's one bit of good news. I found him thoroughly unpleasant. The sooner he leaves the better. And now I really am off to bed. Goodnight, Father."

"Goodnight." Guthrie turned away, listening to the steady sound of Guy's footfalls up the stairs and along the corridor to his room, before returning to his vigil at the window. In his heart what he wanted most was to see Johnny riding in, and strolling into the house as if nothing had happened.

Damn the boy.

Guthrie slumped into his chair, still staring into the darkness. He was sure he'd gotten more grey hairs since Johnny had returned home. Hell, every time Johnny went into town Guthrie feared that it might be the last time he saw him. A name like Johnny Fierro was not easily forgotten and surely it was only a question of time before some young, hungry gunfighter arrived to seize his son's reputation.

He pushed himself out of his chair, and moving slowly, went to pour himself a large whisky. He was also sure that he'd been drinking more since his boys had come home, but then Johnny was enough to drive any man to drink.

The morning dawned bright with the sun already hot by the time he'd finished his early breakfast, but he felt far from sunny. He'd waited up long into the night but Johnny hadn't returned, so presumably he was either still in Santa Fe or he'd walked out. All he could do was hope that the truth was the former, and he vowed not to lose his temper with the boy when he returned. He liked to think that he was picking his battles far more carefully these days and he had no intention of providing Johnny with ammunition or an excuse to leave for good.

Guy had been up and breakfasted early before setting off with a small work crew to clear a stream which was damming up. It was a job that Johnny should have been doing. Despite his resolution, Guthrie's jaw tightened at the thought. There was no denying that he was angry with his son, but it was certainly tempered by his fear that this would be the time that Johnny didn't come back.

His spirits soared as he heard hoof beats, and squinting against the sun, he strained to see who was riding in. Maybe, just maybe it would be... But no. Damn it, it was Hausmann in a buggy. What the hell did he want at this time of the morning?

He leaned against the gate of the corral watching as the preacher pulled up alongside. Guthrie gritted his teeth as he saw the expression on the man's face. Judging from the scarlet color and the veins almost popping out of his forehead, this was not a social call. Had the man already found out that he was to be fired?

Guthrie sighed softly. This was all he needed. He took a deep breath and stepped forward, resting a hand on the buggy. "Welcome to Sinclair Ranch, Reverend. Will you step inside the hacienda out of this heat?"

Hausmann's cheeks puffed out, his eyes bulging as he pointed a pudgy finger at Guthrie. "You have the audacity to ask me inside? I wouldn't set foot in that refuge of Satan's spawn. I hold you and your family responsible for the evil that has taken over the town."

Guthrie raised an eyebrow as Hausmann waved his arm dramatically in the general direction of Cimarron. Whatever was eating the man, it had nothing to do with being fired. Guthrie forced a smile. "I'm afraid I don't quite follow your meaning, Reverend."

"Your son. That is who I am talking about."

"Guy?" Guthrie tried hard to look innocent, even as he wondered what the hell Johnny had been up to now.

"Don't toy with me, Sinclair. You know that I am referring to the product of your mixed race marriage. Your half-breed has spread his influence among those people so that they do his bidding."

Guthrie stepped closer to the buggy, a sour taste in his mouth, and clenching his fists. "How dare you speak to me like that? I'm not going to stand here while you heap insults on my marriage and my family. I'm proud of my son and as to 'spreading his influence' as you put it, I don't know what the hell you're talking about."

Hausmann leaned forward, one vein standing out more prominently in his forehead. "That den of iniquity in the town, that's what I'm talking about."

Guthrie took a step back as a drop of spittle land on his sleeve. Hausmann was mad, quite mad. He'd suspected it, but now the man had definitely gone over the edge of reason. "I take it that you're referring to the bordello. But I really don't—"

"Yes, that den of iniquity." More spittle flew as Hausmann spat the words out. "Those fools in town voted to keep their whorehouse. Those Jezebels bewitch good men, leading them into sinful ways, corrupting them, and then they spread their disease to infect them. Good God-fearing men, like my own brother, in purgatory because of those harlots. That house of shame should have been razed to the ground but it still stands, and I know that your whoring half-breed had a hand in it. He's the devil's own—"

Guthrie's jaw tightened as he struggled to hold his temper in check. "If the people of Cimarron voted to retain the bordello, I imagine that is their affair. Now I would thank you to—"

"He had a hand in it. And you are no better than your son. The good book says that if thy right eye offend thee, pluck it out and cast it from thee. You should throw that miserable half-breed off this land and send him as far away from here as possible. He will corrupt everyone he comes in contact with. And your other son isn't much better. I know all about his exploits in the war. His sins shall ensure his place in hell"

Who on earth had Hausmann been talking to? Guthrie stepped forward. "I am not prepared to stand here and listen to you heap abuse on my family. This is my home and my land. Now take your poisonous thoughts elsewhere and get the hell off my property."

Hausmann picked up the reins, and urged his horse toward the road to Cimarron, even as he turned to call over his shoulder. "You haven't heard the last of this, Sinclair. I'll make sure that the vengeance of the Lord descends upon your family. I'll see that justice is served."

Guthrie took a deep breath and tried to unclench his fists which had again curled into tight balls. What the hell could

Hausmann know about Guy's war service? And could that mean that Johnny had been right all along? He felt a flicker of unease – Hausmann was mad, but was he also dangerous?

And what on earth had Johnny been up to? Guthrie could have sworn that the bordello would be closed, and he'd have been delighted to hear it. Johnny spent far too much time there and anything that would curb his son's behavior in that respect would be welcome.

He swiped his hat off and whacked it hard against the corral gate. Where the hell was Johnny and why had he gone haring off to Santa Fe? There was no doubt about it; the boy was just downright irresponsible.

CHAPTER TWENTY-THREE

Johnny left before dawn, determined to get back to Cimarron as quickly as possible. He wanted to hear what Daisy had to say.

And yet...

There was a chill deep inside of him, because although he wanted to hear what Daisy said, a tiny part of him was afraid of it. There'd been something in Delice's manner that warned him that whatever had happened in Virginia was not going to reflect well on Guy's army. But no, that couldn't be right, could it? Guy would never be involved in anything less than honorable, would he? Shit. The best thing was not to think about it. Wait and see what Daisy had to say. Yeah. Wait and see.

Even so, it was odd. Guy had been real reluctant to talk about the war. But maybe it was because of the killings. Yeah. That would be it. Nobody would want to talk about the killing. He of all people knew that.

But Delice had sounded kind of strange.

Oh hell, he should stop brooding about it. Wait and see.

He made camp for the night about thirty miles south of Cimarron. If he made it into town by mid-morning the bordello would be quiet and he'd be able to talk to Daisy without any interruptions.

Shivering in the chill night air, he hunched over the small campfire and brewed some coffee. It was sure different from how he'd spent the previous evening, wining and dining Delice. A smile pulled at his mouth as he remembered the look of surprise on her face when he'd kissed her hand. And how easy it had been to talk with her. Why couldn't he talk like that with his family? He never knew how to talk to the old man; maybe it was the look of disappointment he saw in his father's eyes all too often. Johnny knew he wasn't much of a son. There wouldn't be many men who'd want to own to him, particularly when they'd got a son like Guy as well. Hell, Guy was a son that a man could be proud of, not like Fierro.

He pushed his collar up, trying to keep the cold air off his neck. Clasping his mug of coffee in both hands for warmth, he settled himself down by the fire, leaning against his saddle. He tilted his hat back and glanced up at the night sky. The scudding clouds obliterated the moon and a fair number of stars. He sighed softly, hoping it wouldn't rain. Still, it would probably be God's way of getting even. The previous evening with Delice had been so good that something had to come back and bite him – it usually did.

Even so, the smile quirked his lips again as he recalled how elegant she'd looked in that green dress – it sure was different from the ugly thing she wore in the bordello. And her eyes had looked even greener; more vivid somehow. She ought to wear green more often; he must remember to tell her that sometime. Women always liked to know if they looked good in something. Although maybe she'd take offence if he did – she sure was tricky. She had to be the only woman he'd ever met who he couldn't charm. How old was she? And who the hell was Adam Smith?

The knot in his gut was back, so he rolled a cigarette. Maybe a smoke would take his mind off Smith.

But she'd sure been cagey about Smith – he was no nearer to finding out about the fellow. Ask Guy, she'd said. But why the hell would Guy know who he was? Guy hadn't been back home at the ranch much longer than he had. But leastways he'd found out where he could learn a little more about Guy's war. That was progress.

He blew a smoke ring which drifted away on the breeze. He grinned. And Delice had changed her mind about leaving Cimarron. Now that was real progress.

But who was Adam Smith?

He stubbed out his cigarette and tipped the dregs of his coffee out of his tin mug. If he didn't stop worrying around everything like a dog on the scent of a bitch, he'd never get any sleep. And he had a feeling he was going to need all his energy for the day ahead. Hauling himself to his feet, he shook out his bedroll close to the fire and shuffled down inside it, even as he wondered how many times he'd slept rough like this.

He slept badly. His night was disturbed by the ghosts of the men he'd killed, and by Guy angrily telling him to mind his own business, and by a pair of green eyes. He awoke bathed in sweat, wishing that just once he could get a decent night's sleep. Still, it was better than dreaming of his mother's men. Even so, it would be real good to get one night of unbroken sleep. Dreamless sleep.

Stiff as hell and cursing his aching back, he'd have loved a cup of hot coffee. But there was no point in building another fire. Instead, he chewed on a piece of jerky before hefting the saddle onto Pistol and heading back toward Cimarron.

He couldn't have faulted his timing; he hit town at mid-morning. He left Pistol pulling at a hay bag at the livery stables; the horse deserved a good feed and a rest after the few days of hard riding.

He hurried along the main street to the bordello, relieved that at least the dull ache in his back had gone. He was getting too old to be sleeping rough. Or, more likely, he was getting damn soft. He'd been living in luxury for too long; that was his trouble. He was getting used to a soft bed. And clean sheets.

He pushed open the heavy door of the bordello, relieved to

see how peaceful the place was. Clem and Bob were still sitting playing cards – he wondered if they'd actually moved at all in the past few days. And it looked like the same girls perched by them giving advice on how they should play their hands. He grinned. Would Delice keep them on once all the trouble died down? They sure looked like they'd settled in well, kind of like they were part of the furniture.

Clem looked up and waved at him. "Johnny, where you been? Sadie was mad as hell with you for taking off like you did. She's been going around biting everyone's head off."

Whatever else he was going to say was drowned out by a screech from the stairs. "Johnny!"

Sadie came tearing down the stairs and flung herself on him, attaching her lips to his with an agitated humming sound, a bit like a bee buzzing round clover.

Then she slapped him.

Johnny staggered back, his cheek stinging and his ears ringing. "What the hell was that for?"

Sadie pursed her lips. "You walked out on me, Johnny. Without a word. You just upped and went. And we haven't got much time left. Us girls will be moving to Santa Fe and then I won't see you at all."

"Shit, Sadie! You don't damn well own me." Johnny shook his head, wondering if the girl had gone crazy.

"I'm your favorite girl." She put her hands on her hips. "You said so. And I told you stuff I shouldn't have told you. But I trusted you, because I'm your best girl. You said so!"

He shut his eyes briefly. This was his own damn fault; he only had himself to blame. It wasn't the rain that had come back to bite him for having had a good evening with Delice, it was Sadie. Grabbing hold of her arm he pulled her, none too gently, into Delice's office. "Sadie, let's get one thing straight; you may be my favorite girl in the bordello but it ain't nothing more than that. So don't you go thinking it is." He glared at her, unmoved by her wobbling lower lip. "Now, I was real grateful for what you told me. And I went to Santa Fe and saw Delice. And you ain't moving to Santa Fe. Delice is keeping the bordello here. But if you push me—"

She flung her arms around his neck, almost knocking him off his feet. "We ain't moving to Santa Fe? You did that for me?"

He untangled himself from her embrace. "Sadie, did you listen to anything I just said? Anything at all?"

Sadie grinned, pushing herself forward at him so her breasts almost popped out of her dress. "I know you're sweet on me. I mean I know you can't do nothing about it, me being a whore an' all, but you're sweet on me, Johnny Sinclair." She reached down and made a grab for his balls, fondling them through his pants. "See, that proves it."

He pulled away, trying to ignore the stir in his dick, wondering what she'd say if he explained that pretty much any hand fondling that part of him would get results. Hell, he wasn't no different to any other fellow of his age. His dick wasn't too picky.

"See!" She pushed her hand back toward him as he skipped back a step to out-maneuver her.

"Sadie! You're only one of the girls. I like you, but it ain't nothing more." He eyed her warily, poised to avoid any more attacks on his dick. He hadn't got time for that right now.

She tilted her head and scowled. "Well, I know that ain't so, because why else would you go rushing off to Santa Fe?" She licked her lips like she was trying to tempt him. "We could go upstairs now, or,"—her eyes lit up—"you could take me here in madam's office; she'd never know."

Any urges he might have had vanished instantly. "Damn it, Sadie. I couldn't do that. Hell, it wouldn't be right."

Sadie pulled a face. "Sometimes, Johnny Sinclair, I think you care more about what Madam says than you do about me."

Johnny furrowed his brow, wondering if maybe she didn't have a point. He shrugged. "Anyway, Sadie, I ain't got time for that. I need to talk to Daisy. And while I'm talking to her you girls can start unpacking. Delice said to tell you to get the place back to normal before she gets back."

Sadie narrowed her eyes. "What do you want with Daisy? I'll give you a much better time than she will."

"Damn it, Sadie, I ain't going to poke her. I need to talk to her."

Sadie sniffed. "What do you want to talk to her about that you can't talk to me about?" She raised her eyebrow in a flirty way. "I can talk real dirty if that's what you want."

Johnny shut his eyes briefly, thinking what a lucky escape the ranch had had. If Sadie had turned up for a job... Shit!

"I want to talk to her about the war, Sadie. And Delice said I could talk to her in here. So, you push off and start unpacking and leave me to talk to Daisy."

Sadie made a sort of hmmmph noise and flounced off, banging the door as she left the office. Johnny opened it again and called to Daisy who was sitting in a foaming swirl of petticoats next to Bob, pointing out which card he should play next.

With one last instruction to Bob, she ambled across the room, brushing her skirts down and looking very different from the ill-kempt whore she'd been when he'd met her in Abilene. He bit back a smile. Best advice he'd ever given a girl, telling her to come here. And Delice hadn't let him down. She'd taken Daisy in and scrubbed her up, and leastways the girl didn't have to worry about getting her nose broke no more.

He beckoned her into Delice's office, as she furrowed her brow thoughtfully. "Something bothering you, Johnny? I thought you'd be off with Sadie by now. She's been carrying on something awful since you walked out the other day." She rolled her eyes. "She made one hell of a fuss. She should have been an actress. She loves a bit of drama."

Johnny rubbed his ear which was still stinging from Sadie's slap. "Yeah, she did seem real worked up. Dios, it was like she'd gone loco."

Daisy smiled. "Well, she's got a bit of a thing about you. It ain't surprising; most of the customers are either grubby cowhands, or fat middle-aged men. You're a mite prettier than them. And mostly you smell better."

Johnny grinned. "Only mostly?"

Daisy raised an eyebrow. "Trust me, when I met you in Abilene you didn't smell too good."

Johnny bit back a smile, and then looked back at her. "I'll let you in on a secret, Daisy, neither did you!"

She laughed at that. "Nope, I don't reckon I did." She paused, chewing on her lip like she was searching for words. "I reckon I owe you, Johnny. I'm not sure I ever really thanked you for sending me here, but I'm grateful." She paused and sighed softly. "More grateful than you can know. And to Madam. To be honest, I don't really know why she took me in. I mean I'm a fair bit older than the others, and I sure didn't look good when I showed up. And with my nose being broke too often an' all." She shrugged. "Well, it was real good of her. I told her you sent me and she took me in. She's a very kind woman. I mean, the girls all joke about her being as hard as nails, but she's good to us girls. And thoughtful. There aren't many like her in this business."

"No." Johnny spoke softly. "I don't reckon there are."

"So, what was it you wanted?" She tilted her head. "It can't be to poke me – Sadie would scratch my eyes out."

"I wanted to talk to you." He paused, uncertain of how to put it. "I really need you to tell me something."

Her eyes widened a touch. "What on earth do you want to

talk to me about?"

He sucked in a breath and then let it out slow. "About the war. About the Shenandoah Valley and what the hell happened there."

CHAPTER TWENTY-FOUR

The color drained from her face and she staggered as if her legs were giving way. Afraid she was going to faint, he leapt forward to catch her but she waved him away as she stumbled to a chair.

She turned accusing eyes on him. "What do you want to know about that for? The war's over, Johnny. Over!" She spat out the words, and half-turned away rubbing her eyes with the back of her hand.

He knelt down in front of her, pulling her around gently to face him. "Daisy." He spoke softly, placing a finger under her chin and tilting her face up. "I didn't mean to upset you, but I really do need to know what happened there. Delice said you'd be able to tell me about it."

Daisy sucked in a breath, shaking her head, even as Johnny flinched at the despair in the girl's eyes.

She jerked her head up suddenly. "Why don't you ask your

brother what happened?" There was defiance in her voice, but not in her eyes. "He was part of it all. One of Sheridan's men, wasn't he? Or that's what I heard..." Her voice tailed off as a tear rolled down her face and she looked down at her hands clasping and unclasping in her lap.

Johnny shook his head slowly. How to answer her question? Hell, she deserved an honest answer. "I tried asking him, Daisy. But he won't talk about it. And that makes me wonder why." He shrugged. "I don't really know nothing about that time. I was too busy selling my gun down along the border, even back then. Hell, we had our own war in Mexico. I wasn't interested in a Gringo one."

"Yeah, well, I ain't surprised he doesn't want to talk about the burning." Her voice was bitter and she bit her lip hard, kind of like she was trying to stop herself from sobbing.

"The burning?" Johnny squeezed her hand gently. "Daisy, what do you mean? What was the burning?"

Her eyes widened with surprise. "You really don't know anything about it, do you?"

He shook his head. "No, I don't and that's why I want to hear about it from you. Delice said you came from the Shenandoah Valley and that you'd be able to tell me what went on there. Will you do that? Please, for me?"

She sucked in another breath, brushing a tear away as she tilted her head back and stared up at the ceiling. Then closing her eyes, she nodded. "Yeah, I'll do it for you, because I owe you and

Madam. But that's the only reason why." She opened her eyes and looked at him. "But I don't think you're going to want to hear it."

He ducked his head briefly. He was fast thinking the same thing and the chill inside of him was spreading through his body, numbing him all over. "Maybe not, Daisy, but I need to hear it if you can stand the telling."

She sat staring down, wringing her hands, as if she'd forgotten he was even there. "I guess you've never seen the valley." He had to strain to catch her words, they were so soft.

"No, Daisy. I ain't never been to Virginia."

A tear trickled down her face but she gave a strange sort of half-smile that tore at his heart.

"It was the most beautiful place you ever saw." She paused, her face contorting like she was in pain. "I mean it's got everything a body could ever want. Lovely lush river valleys, and high, rolling grazing-land, and then there's rocky wasteland and deep dark ravines. And there're mountains either side stretching into the distance, all soft and blue."

Johnny shut his eyes trying to picture the land. "Sounds real pretty, Daisy."

She nodded slowly. Her eyes had a far-away look, like she'd gone back to her valley. "Yeah, it sure was pretty. And that summer of '64 was the best wheat crop we'd ever seen." She turned and looked at him. "Folks grew wheat and corn and fruit. And we raised all sorts of stock. The land was that fine we could grow pretty much anything in the valley. It was real pretty, the prettiest place on God's earth, until they burned it."

He furrowed his brow. "What do you mean, they burned it? What did they burn?"

"The valley." Her voice sounded as far away as the look in her eyes. "They burned it, Johnny. All of it. Sheridan's men came through and burned everything. Crops, barns, houses. They killed our stock, they killed everything. All that was left was a black wasteland."

He tried to grasp what she was saying. But she couldn't mean they burned the whole valley. That was crazy. He knew all too well the methods used in range wars where fields and barns could be burned, so maybe she only meant a village or two? "You mean they burned the area you lived in, Daisy?"

She shook her head, seemingly lost in the past. "No. They burned the whole valley. All of it. They went marching through burning everything. They set all the fields ablaze. You could see smoke rising up for miles around. And all you could smell was the stench of dead and burned livestock.

"It got into everything, the smell. I won't never forget the stench. Got in your clothes and your hair. You couldn't escape the smell or the burning. And the cavalry." She shook her head and made a noise like she was disgusted. "The cavalry, they loved carrying out them orders. The infantry, they weren't so bad. Sometimes I heard tell that the infantry spared a barn or stock. But not the cavalry. Not them. Bastards they were, if you'll pardon my language. They'd swagger in on their fancy horses and torch everything. And then ride on out to burn the next farm. They acted like they owned the world.

"Sheridan set out to destroy our valley. He burned houses, barns, corn cribs - and his men seized the ploughs and the harrows. They weren't going to rest till they saw us starve."

Johnny shook his head, bewildered by the way men could treat those weaker than themselves. To march through destroying everything in their path? What sort of people made war on women and children? But Guy wouldn't have been involved in anything like that. Would he?

Guy was a good man. An honorable man. Wasn't he?

"Why, Daisy? Why did they do it? It makes no sense starving folks."

"The Yankees said it would stop us from feeding our army. It would make the war shorter they said." She took a scrap of handkerchief from inside her sleeve and dabbed at her eyes. "But they starved us too, not just our army. It was a dreadful hard winter. Even the few animals they left us were starving that winter. The horses were that thin they looked like fence rails with legs. Pitiful it was to see them."

She bit her lip and started clasping and wringing her hands again. "I come from a decent family, Johnny. You might find that hard to believe, to see me now..." A tear coursed its way down her cheek and she scrubbed at it with the back of her hand. "We was poor, we only had a small parcel of land, but we was decent, God-fearing folks, and we worked hard."

He took her hands in his, crouching in front of her and speaking real soft. "I believe you, Daisy. What happened to you? How did you end up here? What went so wrong for you?" But he had a sick feeling that he knew exactly what had happened to her.

Her face contorted again and she chewed on her lip. "I was fourteen, Johnny. Not a child, but not a woman." She swallowed. "We heard that the cavalry was getting close; coming to burn our crops and barns. My brothers were away fighting in our army. The cavalry came galloping into our yard. I was upstairs when three of the men came into the house. There was a fire burning in the hearth and one of them lifted a log from the andirons and flung it onto the bed while the other two caught hold of me to stop me trying to put out the fire. The bedding caught in no time.

"My Ma was out by the chickens, pleading with one of the men to leave our house and barn alone, but he pushed her aside. They never liked to hang around long, they was scared our folks would attack them. So most of the men moved on. But the three from upstairs." She lifted her hand to stifle a sob. "They took me out the back and... and... had their way with me." She fell forward with a gulping wail even as Johnny pulled her into his arms.

He held her tight as she wept and shuddered against his chest. He could feel the red heat of rage growing inside of him at men who could treat a young girl in such a way. Three of them! He wanted to kill the bastards. Kill them slowly. Pieces of shit like that deserved nothing else. He pulled her tighter to him as if by doing so he could undo all the damage they had done.

He rubbed her back gently, like a mother might soothe a crying child, but knowing that there was nothing he could say to make this better. There were too many rotten people in this stinking world, and war made them even worse. But to treat their own countrymen in such a way. To wreak such devastation. Madre de Dios!

Her sobs subsided as he rocked her slowly in his arms. "Sorry." Her voice was an indistinct mumble. She pulled away, scrubbing again at her eyes and nose with a handkerchief. She forced a weak smile. "That was the first time my nose got broke."

He went to Delice's drink cabinet at the back of the office, pulled out a glass and poured some of her best malt into it. "Here," he proffered the glass. "Drink this."

Daisy took a sip, pulling a slight face at the taste. "Guess I'm more used to rough rye whiskey." She sighed. "We lost the house and the barn. And my brothers never came home from the war. It broke my ma's heart. And then I found I was going to have a baby." Her lip wobbled again, and she bit it hard, kind of to try to keep control. "I was so scared. And I didn't want some Yankee bastard's child. Anyway, it was born too early. And then Ma got sick. Like I said, I think my brothers dying just broke her heart. And so I ended up on my own."

"But didn't anybody take you in? Surely a neighbor or a relative..." He trailed off. He knew all about people who wouldn't take an orphan in.

She shrugged. "They'd all lost pretty much everything too.

They couldn't hardly feed their own families. And let's face it. Wasn't nobody who was ever going to want to marry me. Not being soiled and all."

Johnny swore softly. It was one rule for men and another for women. And it wasn't fucking fair. It was all right for men to have had a woman before they married but girls were supposed to be pure? How crazy was that! Like whores and girls were two separate species. What the hell did it matter if the woman wasn't a virgin? Dios, but people were shit. And most of them were hypocrites.

"I moved away looking for work. But you know how it is, if you're cold enough and hungry enough." She flushed.

And yeah, he knew all about that. Whore out your body. Whore out your gun. But the girls kept their souls. Not like him, he'd sold his a long time ago.

She sucked in a breath. "But I tell you one thing, Johnny. If it wasn't for those men, I wouldn't have ended up like this. I wasn't born bad. And maybe if they hadn't burned our farm, Ma might have been all right. But there was so little food that winter, anyone weak got sick. Little children and old people, all starving. And those Yankees treating us like dirt." She paused. "And if your brother was with Sheridan's men, he wasn't no different from them."

He flinched. There it was, laid bare for him.

Guy's sin.

No wonder Guy didn't want to talk about the war.

But he was going to talk about it now. Even if Fierro forced it out of him at gunpoint. He wanted to know what Guy had done in that valley. What part had he played in the destruction of people's lives?

And it hurt. It damn well hurt to think that all this time when Guy had been pushing Fierro for more details of his past, he'd kept this huge sin covered up, hidden away. And all the while he'd been making Fierro feel guilty and ashamed. But Fierro had never made war on women; he'd never sunk that low.

Johnny gritted his teeth. It was always the same; people betrayed you, or disappointed you. Sooner or later they always let you down. And Guy wasn't no different.

He shouldn't have broken his golden rule; never trust anyone. But damn it, he'd trusted Guy. He'd believed in him. He'd thought Guy was better than other men.

He'd think on it later, for now he needed to comfort Daisy. She was watching him, a small furrow between her eyes.

"I told you that you wouldn't want to hear it." Her voice was so soft he had to strain to hear her.

He reached out and gently touched her cheek. "I needed to hear it, Daisy. And I'm grateful to you. I know that was tough for you to tell it. And I'm truly sorry for dragging up the past. Do you know what happened to those soldiers?"

She laughed bitterly. "Oh, my Ma complained to their officer but he just made out that I was a cheap whore and got what I deserved." She sighed heavily. "And now, I am just a cheap whore. But this is a lot better than where I was in Abilene, so I am grateful to you, Johnny. I feel safe here. You did good to send me here and life is much better than it was."

But what he'd done wasn't enough. Not nearly enough. Her life should have been so different. Could have been different if it hadn't been for Sheridan's men. Guy's men.

He shrugged. "Well, if it's any comfort you ain't going to have to move to Santa Fe. Delice is staying put. She told me to tell you all to start unpacking."

Daisy's mouth broke into a smile. "That's good to hear, Johnny. None of us was looking forward to moving. Do we have you to thank for talking Madam out of her plan?"

Her question surprised him. He reckoned he'd underestimated Daisy; she was sharp. Too sharp to be working as a whore. He pushed the thought away – it was too late for Daisy, her life course had been set the day the men had raped her. He ducked his head before looking back at her. "I don't know about that. All I did was tell her how expensive it would be to move. Anyway, I'd best get on home, leave you to unpack." And he could go and search out Guy and demand some answers.

He dug down into his pocket and pulled out a handful of notes. "Go buy yourself something pretty, Daisy." He shoved them into her hands before leaning forward and giving her a clumsy kiss on the cheek. And he wished he could do more. Give her something of her life back. Something. Anything.

He hurried out of the bordello into the bright street and walked straight into the Reverend Hausmann.

CHAPTER TWENTY-FIVE

Shit! He really didn't need to have words with this interfering, puffed-up windbag. And although he was starting to wish he'd taken Delice's advice to leave well alone, right now he was more concerned with finding Guy to discover what part he'd played in the burning of the Shenandoah Valley.

Johnny sidestepped to pass the Reverend but judging from the wild look in the man's eyes, he wasn't going to let things go with Johnny. Probably still sore over the town's decision to let the bordello remain open.

"You son of Satan!" Hausmann stepped in front of Johnny. And damn it but there was no pushing someone that big out of his way.

Johnny narrowed his eyes. "I ain't in the mood for a friendly chat, Reverend." Johnny moved again to step around the man, but Hausmann shot out his hand, grabbing Johnny's arm.

Johnny turned an icy glare on the man. The full-on kind of glare that made most men blanch. Hausmann seemed unmoved. But looking into the man's eyes, Johnny could see why. They were wild with a sort of crazy, intense stare - totally loco, like he'd fallen over the edge of reason. There was spittle at the corner of his mouth which was working like an engine under a full head of steam. Johnny sighed softly; there would be no reasoning with a man in this state. Best let him have his say and get it over and done with.

"You have bedazzled the people of this town." Hausmann gestured wildly toward the main street. "They are tainted by your presence. It's the devil's work you have been doing, and that this whorehouse still stands proves the evil hold you have here." The spittle was flying and Johnny swayed backwards to avoid a glob landing on his shoulder. "You have turned this town into a ruined heap, a Gomorrah. The good Lord will smite you down. He has ordered me to oversee the destruction of your power."

Johnny shook his head. If Hausmann thought God was giving him orders, he really had gone crazy.

Hausmann drew in a huge breath, ready to launch into another attack when the door of the bordello swung open. Clem and Bob stepped out onto the street, their guns drawn, and looking mean enough to deal with a whole army, never mind this crazy old coot.

"You having trouble, Johnny?" Bob could sound mean too when he had a mind to. Johnny almost smiled at the transformation. Gone were all traces of the halfwit that Delice had dubbed him. Yeah, he always knew Bob and Clem were the right fellows for a place like this to have around.

"And there are two more sinners!" Hausmann pointed a finger at them. "Doing the Devil's work!"

Bob stepped forward, with narrowed eyes. "Who you callin' a sinner? We're honest men doing our job. And part of our job means stopping troublemakers like you crossing this line." He gestured vaguely to where Delice had originally drawn the line which she'd told him and Clem not to cross.

Johnny bit back a grin, even as he waved them back. "It's fine, Bob. I can handle this. Go on back inside."

Bob and Clem holstered their guns but made no move to leave; they folded their arms and stood watching. It seemed they took their duties seriously and they were going to guard Delice's line come hell or high water.

Hausmann turned his crazed eyes back to Johnny. "I will see your family destroyed; every last one of them is corrupted by you. I am being sent from this place because of your father's pernicious influence. And your brother is no better than you."

Johnny gritted his teeth. "Leave my father and brother out of this. They're both good men." And heavens, but he hoped that was true.

Hausmann snorted. "Your father thinks he can buy anything. Like all rich men, he buys influence and he has bought my removal – don't tell me it's not so. I can read between the lines.

I see his hand in this. And that brother of yours, he's responsible for the deaths of too many good young men. He was one of Sheridan's men. He was with them when they came marching through the south, destroying everything in their path. If it wasn't for the likes of them, my boy would be alive. My nephew wouldn't be maimed."

"My brother didn't know your son or your nephew. He ain't responsible—"

"It doesn't matter!" A vein was pulsing in Hausmann's head and his face was scarlet as he spat out the words. "They're all guilty! All of them! Rich, spoiled young men playing at soldiers. But I've done for your brother. And you'll be next. And then your father. I will bring down the wrath of God—"

Johnny grabbed hold of Hausmann's arms, shaking him roughly. "What do you mean you've done for my brother? What the hell are you talking about? What've you done? Ain't nobody hurting my family."

Hausmann threw back his head and laughed. "Oh, you're too late to stop it. My nephew, he's taking care of your brother now, as we speak. He's gone to find him. And he'll send him to Hell, where he belongs."

Madre de Dios, what had Hausmann done? Johnny pushed Hausmann to one side and raced to Pistol. He had to find Guy. Bob chased behind him. "Johnny, hold up. I'll come with you."

Johnny shook his head as he vaulted into the saddle. "No. Stay with the girls. I don't trust that bastard. And tell Stoney that

Hausmann's gone loco. And get Ben too. Tell him about Hausmann."

He set his spurs hard and took off out of town at a gallop. But where would Guy be? And could he get to him before Hausmann's nephew did?

Crouching low and urging Pistol on, he tried to remember what Guy's plans for the week had been once the books were finished. Guthrie and Guy had discussed it over lunch, before Johnny had left for the town meeting. Shit. He had to remember but he hadn't really paid much attention.

They'd been droning on about something. What the hell was it? Guy was going to take a work party to clear the river near the forest to the east – wasn't that what they'd said? But then Guy was going to do something after that. What the hell was it?

Fence posts. He should have known; everything always came back to those damned fence posts. Guy was going to survey the area below the forest. He was to calculate what they'd need to do to improve the area for grazing, and how much material they'd need to fence off a part of it.

He swung Pistol off the track and headed east. Thank God Guy wasn't working out at the northern boundary; that was a hell of a distance. And he didn't know how much of a start Hausmann's nephew had gotten on him. Maybe the man had been watching Guy's movements to work out the best time to attack. Mierda! Johnny kicked Pistol on, even as he felt the icy clutch of fear at his guts. The area was remote. If the man had been watching Guy, then it would be a great place for an attack. A man could pick anyone off with a rifle from the safety of the lodge pine cover above. Shit.

Maybe he should have simply killed him when he'd discovered that he was working at Hausmann's place. He'd always planned to kill him for hitting Delice, but he should have done it sooner. If anything happened to Guy... He tried to push the thought away but all he knew was that if something happened to Guy it would be his own fault for not acting earlier.

Pistol was slowing, so he set his spurs harder, urging the horse on to clear a wide ditch. Pistol stumbled on landing, almost unseating Johnny, but then regained his balance and they charged onward with Johnny almost lying along his neck to avoid the low branches overhanging their route.

Johnny reined him in as they crested the ridge. He had a good view of the hillside overlooking the land east of the mesa. Screwing his eyes up against the sunlight, and breathless from the wild ride, he peered at the slope. There was enough pine, scrubby brush and rock to give a bushwhacker plenty of cover. He'd lay money that the fellow would try and pick Guy off from a distance – he sure as hell wouldn't be the type of man to give Guy a fighting chance.

He slid from Pistol and studied the hillside, methodically scanning each section. He sucked in a breath as he thought he saw a glint from the hillside. Was it his imagination? Shielding his eyes he stared intently at the spot. And yes! There it was again.

Someone was using a spyglass.

Johnny nodded slowly. "Got you, you bastard." But where the hell was Guy? The watcher had a better view of the valley, and maybe already had Guy in his sights. Johnny gritted his teeth. The only thing he could do was fire his gun and hope that it served as a warning to his brother if he was down there working. At the very least it would get his attention. Drawing his gun, he fired off a volley of shots even as the crack of a rifle shot echoed around the valley. He reloaded so fast that he dropped half of them, what with jumping on the horse and spinning him around to head across the hillside. Pistol scrambled to keep his footing, sliding sideways on the loose scree and almost unseating Johnny as he struggled to load another bullet.

He was almost on a thick clump of trees when he heard the crashing sound of breaking branches. Someone was riding through fast, so Johnny headed straight toward the trees just as the big, fair-haired man appeared. The asshole lifted his rifle fast to point it straight at Johnny.

The man's finger moved to the trigger.

Johnny smiled. A hair trigger was a real advantage at times like this.

The explosion sent birds flying up in alarm, even as Guy appeared at the edge of the clearing with his gun cocked. His eyes went straight to the bloodied body lying flat out on the bed of leaves and then his eyes widened as he saw Johnny. "What the hell's going on? Someone took a shot at me." He was breathing hard and he flinched, looking first at the body and then back at Johnny. "Who the hell is that? Was it he who was shooting at me? He only just missed me too. It was too damn close for comfort. Far too close…" He paused, and looked at Johnny with a frown. "And what on earth are you doing here?"

Johnny holstered his gun, before looking back at Guy. "What I'm doing is saving your skin. And this is the fellow I told you about. Hausmann's nephew. God knows why, but he was fixing to kill you. You're lucky that shot of his missed."

Guy stared at him. "Fixing to kill me? Him?" He pointed at the body. "I've never seen the fellow in my life. Why would he want to kill me, for heaven's sake? It's crazy. It makes no sense, no sense at all."

Johnny laughed humorlessly. "Reckon being crazy is a family trait. I saw Hausmann in town and he was ranting and raving like he'd gone loco."

Guy took his hat off and beat if against his leg before running his fingers through his hair, still breathing heavy. "But it's mad. Totally mad! What on earth have they got against me? What have I ever done to them? I don't know this fellow." He gestured wildly toward Hausmann's nephew.

Johnny shrugged. "I reckon it's something to do with the war."

Guy glared at Johnny. "There you go again. You keep harping on about the war. I can't believe that this has anything to do with that. It was years ago, and it's over."

Johnny raised an eyebrow. "Is it? You ain't been acting like it's over. You been acting like you got the weight of the world on your shoulders. But from what Hausmann said, it wasn't over for him. And seeing as how his nephew just tried to kill you," Johnny jerked his head toward the body, which stared at them through unseeing eyes. "I reckon it wasn't over for him, neither. And it sure as hell ain't over for people like Daisy."

Guy frowned. "Daisy? Who on earth is Daisy?"

Johnny eyed him coolly. "One of Delice's girls."

Guy threw his hands up. "A whore? Tell me, Johnny, exactly what has the war got to do with some girl in a bordello? Sometimes, I don't understand you at all. Like you rushing off to Santa Fe with no explanation—"

Johnny cut across him. "What's the war got to do with Daisy? Well, I'll tell you, Guy. She was in the Shenandoah Valley during the war, and she told me a real interesting story about what happened down there. And Hausmann was down in that area too. So ain't neither of them happy about it, and that makes me real curious. So now I want to hear your telling of it."

Guy swallowed hard, and then gestured toward the body, blanching as he did so. "We should deal with him. We need to get him into town. We'd best go and see Stoney and explain what happened. Never mind the war, we can't leave him lying there."

Johnny laughed softly. "He ain't going anywhere. He'll keep. Right now I want to hear about the burning. And I tell you, brother, I ain't taking no for an answer."

CHAPTER TWENTY-SIX

Guy didn't say a single word at first. Opened his mouth and then shut it again, like he'd thought better of whatever he was going to say. Then he sighed heavily. "You won't let this go, will you?"

"Nope." Johnny shook his head. "All this time you been getting me to spill my secrets, but you've never said anything about your past. Not a word. And if what Daisy told me is true, about what your army did down there, I ain't surprised you didn't want to talk about it." Johnny paused, trying to keep his temper under control. But the heat of rage was burning him up, so he might as well get it said. "Women and kids, Harvard! Women and kids! Hell, I know what a bastard I am. And I know I've done wicked things in my lifetime. I've made a shitload of bad choices and I ain't got no illusions about where I'm headed. I know I'm going to hell for all the men I've killed, but I never stooped that low. I never made war on women or kids. Never!" But he'd known enough men who had. And he hated the thought that Guy might be one of them.

Guy sucked in a deep breath, his lips tight and his eyes narrowed. Then he sank down onto a tree stump like his legs wouldn't hold him up no longer. "What did this girl tell you?"

"She's got a name, Guy. She ain't just some girl, she's got a name. Daisy."

Guy shut his eyes briefly. "What exactly did Daisy tell you?"

Johnny kicked at the leaves around his feet. He was still shaking from his outburst; he needed to get a grip of himself. Wouldn't do no good to yell. He took in a deep breath, trying to calm himself. "She was raised on a farm in that valley. She said your army went marching through it burning everything. That you burned their crops, their barns, even their houses, and you killed their stock. And she said the people starved that winter. Women and children starved and the few remaining animals that your army didn't kill, they were starving too. And I'll tell you something else, Harvard." The heat was building up inside of him again, spilling out, like the words. "Something else your fucking army did. They raped her. She was only a kid, Harvard, and your fucking army raped her."

Johnny's hands were making themselves into fists; it was like he couldn't stop them, and his breath was coming in short bursts. Hell, where was the Fierro cool? He had to get a grip.

He stared down at Guy. He was sitting with his head bowed, and not giving anything away. Johnny took a deep breath. "I mean, I wasn't born yesterday, I know what happens in wars.

Bystanders always get hurt." And wasn't that the truth. He tried to block out a memory of his mother with two men from the Guardia Civil who thought they had some God-given right to rape her. He bit his lip and dragged his mind back to the present. "But to burn the whole fucking valley? All of it?"

Guy looked up. "It was supposed to make the war shorter—"

"That's what Daisy said your army said." Johnny spat the words out. "But women and kids suffered, Guy. If soldiers want to kill each other that's one thing, but to make all those other people suffer, innocent people, little kids, that's something else!"

"Are you going to let me say anything?" Guy was looking straight at him now, his face creased up like he was hurting.

Johnny sucked in another breath, closing his eyes briefly before nodding. "Yeah, Harvard, go on. I've done yelling for a few minutes."

"You've got to believe that I joined the army because I believed we were right; that I was fighting for a just cause." Guy paused, his brow furrowed like he was remembering things. "And, if I'm honest, a part of me wanted to rebel against my aunt and uncle. They certainly didn't want me to join up; the thought horrified them. They contacted Father, so my joining up got everyone's attention and that did make it seem more appealing. I saw the war as a wild adventure, a cause worth fighting for. And a break from the monotony of Boston society. But I wouldn't have joined if I hadn't believed in the cause.

"But by the time the Shenandoah was burned, we'd been at war for more than three years. Obviously I wasn't in it from the start, I was too young at first, but I joined up at the first opportunity. But by the fall of '64 it had been three and a half years of battles and suffering. Everyone had had enough of the killing by then. Thousands of men on both sides were dying. And so, it was decided that the quickest way to end it all would be to starve the Rebs' army. And that valley was incredibly verdant and a very bountiful larder for their soldiers. They grew pretty much everything they needed, so the answer was to make it unusable. What was it Sheridan said?" Guy rubbed his chin, frowning. "That the people must be left with nothing but their eyes to weep with over the war; that was it. And so we went through there like a plague of locusts, destroying everything. Sheridan's promise was that by the time we finished there would be little left in the valley for man nor beast."

Johnny opened his mouth but for a second it was like the words wouldn't come. And how to say what he felt? He knew what it was like to go hungry. Especially after Mama died and it had felt like all his hope had died with her. "But all of it? God almighty, how can anyone do that to their own people? Because you're all part of the same country." Johnny shook his head. Hell, he'd seen enough of war, and range wars, to know what men could do their fellow men, but it was the scale of this which made it somehow even more shocking. "Why? Why did you do it, Guy?"

Guy jerked his head up. "What do you mean, why did I do

it? I didn't like my orders, Johnny. I hated what we had to do. But I was a soldier, an officer. My duty was to follow orders, whether I liked them or not."

"No!" Johnny paced up and down. "Fuck duty! Nobody should follow orders if they're bad orders."

Guy laughed, like he couldn't believe what he'd heard. "Not follow orders! If we all pick and choose what orders we want to follow, it would be chaos! You can't run an army like that. A soldier follows orders."

Johnny took a step toward Guy, his fists clenched. "Even when they're bad ones? That ain't no defense, Guy."

"What would you have had me do?" Guy snapped out the words.

Johnny shrugged. "Well, here's a thought; you could have ignored them."

Guy's mouth dropped open. "Ignore them? How the hell could I ignore orders? Unless you would have liked me shot for mutiny. Because that's what happens to soldiers who don't obey orders, in case you're not aware of that."

"You could have left."

Guy was staring at him like he'd gotten two heads or something. "Left? You mean desert? You have no idea of military honor do you? I had a duty to my men, my family, my friends and comrades."

"Duty!" Johnny shook his head. "What sort of excuse is that?"

Guy huffed in a breath. "Well, you wouldn't understand about a soldier's duty, not having been in the army."

Johnny quirked an eyebrow. "But that's where you're wrong, Harvard. You don't know everything about me, for all your digging. You see I was in the army – the Mexican army." If he'd wanted a reaction he certainly got one. Guy looked stunned – and was speechless for a few beats.

"You were in the army?" He sounded like he couldn't believe it. Probably wondered what the hell the army had been doing letting the like of his brother enlist. Guy swallowed hard and then shrugged like it didn't matter none. "Well, you should understand then, what it's like. You'd have taken orders."

Johnny laughed humorlessly. "Trouble is I never was much good at doing what I was told. In or out of the army. And I didn't like following orders. Especially bad ones, so I sure as hell wouldn't have followed your army's orders."

Guy cocked his head. "Then you would have been shot. That is what happens to soldiers who don't obey orders – in any army! But luckily you've never been in a position where you've been faced with having to disobey orders, otherwise you wouldn't be here."

Johnny scuffed the toe of his boot against a rock, and looked Guy in the eyes. "But you're wrong again, Harvard. I was faced with fucking awful orders, so I left."

Guy's eyes opened real wide. "Left? Left! You mean you deserted? You walked out?" He leapt to his feet. "Does that mean the Mexican army is looking for you? They shoot deserters, Johnny. And anyway, how could you just leave? What about your comrades? Did you not think of them?"

Johnny rubbed his chin and leaned back against a tree. "I doubt the Mexican army's looking for me. And even if they were, I sure as hell wasn't using my own name back then. I was trying to lie low for a while, and disappearing among thousands of men seemed a good way to do it." And it had been a good way too. Nobody had thought of looking for him there. The army had been his escape – as far as everyone knew he had simply vanished off the face of the earth.

Guy was still looking at him like he was a stranger. "But why did you desert? What could have been so bad that you just walked out on your comrades, and your duty?"

Dios! There he went with the duty thing again. What about a man's duty to himself, to his own conscience? Johnny shrugged. "I was only a kid."

Guy narrowed his eyes. "So, being only a kid as you put it, someone gave you an order and you walked out. What could have been so bad that you deserted?"

Johnny sighed softly. They were supposed to be talking about Guy's war, not his.

"Or was it the hard work that made you up and leave?" Guy's tone was scathing.

Johnny narrowed his eyes, flinching at the insult. And damn it, but his hands were making fists again. "No, Guy, it wasn't hard work that I couldn't take. It was being told to take three French prisoners out into the woods, get them to dig a trench and then shoot them. That's what I didn't like."

Guy paled and hissed in a breath.

Johnny shrugged. "I guess I was only about fifteen at the time. And I reckon those soldiers weren't much older than me. I mean everyone knew that the French treated Mexican prisoners like dirt, but even so..." He paused, shaking his head slowly. "Even so, that didn't make it right for us to do the same. It's one thing shooting a man who's packing a gun, I got no problem with that. But unarmed kids who were a hell of a long way from home, fighting in a war they didn't understand? No. I couldn't do that, Harvard. So I walked them out into those woods and I let them go. And then I walked away. Like I said, I know what a cold-hearted bastard I am, but some things... Well, it was a step too far and I got to live with myself."

Guy sat down heavily onto the tree stump again. "You and me. Sometimes it feels like we're a million miles apart. Could our lives have been more different?"

"So what would you have done in my boots, Guy? Would you have followed those orders?"

Guy didn't say anything, simply sat shaking his head.

"Well?" Johnny stepped in front of him, his fists clenching again. "Come on, tell me. Would you?"

Guy ran his hand through his hair. "God only knows! I don't know what I would have done. I'm merely thankful I never had to make a decision like that. But as for ever contemplating deserting? It wouldn't have entered my head. Where would I have gone? I couldn't have spent my life running. I had a life in Boston. People who thought well of me there, and our father, who had expectations of me. My whole life, Johnny, I've been raised to accept discipline and an ordered way of doing things. A line of command if you like. Even in school we had that, a pecking order. Duty to others is as much a part of me as breathing. It's about responsibility and being part of a civilized society. It's engrained in me."

"You think what you did in the valley was civilized?" Johnny scoffed. "I figure in this life there's them that gets kicked and there's them that does the kicking. And you and me? We were on different sides."

Guy's jaw tightened. "No, Johnny, I don't think what we did in the Shenandoah was civilized; it was anything but civilized. Some of our officers treated Reb prisoners appallingly; they were simply used as pawns. If any of our forces fell victim to bushwhackers, there were often terrible repercussions for the civilian population. And before you say anything, yes, there were some cases of rape. I don't know why but there are always some soldiers who seem to think that raping a woman is the spoils of war. You must have seen similar things in your army."

"The difference is we were fighting the French, not our own people, Harvard. And there weren't any French women hanging around to be spoils of war as you put it."

"Don't try and tell me that your army never raped. I won't believe you." The tips of Guy's ears were red, just like the old man's always went when he knew he was wrong footed.

Johnny eyed him sadly. "Nope, I ain't claiming anything about the Mexican army. There were a lot of shit soldiers in it; hell, they were shit men. Being a soldier don't turn a man into an animal if he ain't part of the way there already. But there were always men to deal with anyone who did that sort of thing. We had our own type of justice. But you want to know what happened when Daisy's ma complained to one of your officers?"

Guy nodded slowly. "Go on."

Johnny paused, kicking at the ground again before looking back at Guy. "She was only fourteen years old, Guy, and that officer said she was just a cheap whore who got what she deserved."

Guy's head drooped, and he stared down at the ground for what felt like forever.

"So." Johnny had to break the silence, it was grating on his nerves. Setting them on edge. "We seem to have talked all about my war, but we still ain't talked about yours, Harvard. What did you do in that valley? What part did you play?"

CHAPTER TWENTY-SEVEN

Harvard.

Guy frowned. It was strange how Johnny always reverted to using that name when he was trying to put distance between them. He'd noticed that. And now he could feel himself coloring up under his brother's angry gaze.

Angry? No. Not as much angry as disappointed.

He sighed softly, turning slightly so he didn't have to see Hausmann's nephew's eyes too, accusing even in death.

And how to explain? How to explain his actions to someone like his brother who had the oddest moral code he'd ever encountered. A man who could desert because he was required to carry out an execution, but who killed regularly in gunfights.

"Well?"

There it was again, that tone of voice which would brook no arguments. No, there was no getting out of this. And if he was honest, he couldn't blame Johnny for wanting answers. God only knew he'd demanded enough answers from Johnny since they'd been home. Now it was his own turn to explain – if only he could. And could he tell him the worst of it?

He drew in a deep breath and then exhaled slowly. "When I was at school, my closest friend, William, was from an old New England family. I used to spend a lot of time with them. I loved visiting them and having the chance to join in with what I viewed as real family life. It was always so lively. There were lots of them, and I envied him all those brothers and sisters. They'd all be arguing and squabbling, or laughing and teasing each other. I liked his parents too. They were very forthright, strong minded and persuasive. And they were very fervent abolitionists."

Johnny narrowed his eyes. "Abolitionists? What the hell are they? And what has that got to do with what happened in that valley, Harvard?"

Guy closed his eyes briefly. "I'm trying to explain why I felt I was fighting for a just cause, if you'll let me."

Johnny shrugged and then leaned back against a tree with his arms folded, his face impassive.

"Abolitionists held the Puritan notion of collective accountability. That means they believe every man is his brother's keeper. They saw slavery as the worst of social sins. They believe that everyone is equal in God's sight and the souls of Negro folk are as valuable as white souls. Believe me, coming from an environment where everyone worshipped money with as much fervor as they worshipped God, I found their beliefs very refreshing.

"My aunt and uncle, and their friends and relations, like most people at the time, supported the war for purely financial considerations. They considered that southern businesses had an unfair advantage because they were able to make use of free labor in the form of slavery. That was the real reason the Government went to war – war nearly always comes down to concerns over money or land. Moral sentiments rarely enter the minds of politicians.

"There was a song called The Battle Cry of Freedom, and I think that title very much describes how I felt. For me, the battle cry of freedom seemed to polarize around the cause of slavery and the belief that all men should be free. That was the moral justification for me joining up. Annoying my uncle was a bonus."

Johnny leaned against a tree and slid down into a squatting position. He picked at a stalk of grass, and broke it into tiny pieces. "So you believed you were right when you joined up, fair enough. That's fine. But what happened in that valley, that don't sound fine to me."

"We'd been fighting our way down through the south. I told you about the Battle of Trevilian Station in the June of '64, where I first encountered those men we met in Abilene. That battle was the bloodiest cavalry action of the entire war." He could feel his heart pumping faster even as he recalled the battle. He took a deep breath. "Christ! Bloody doesn't even come close to describing it. It was hell on earth even getting there. We were enveloped in a huge dust storm in choking heat and many of our horses collapsed under the strain. And then, when the battle started in earnest, we lost more than a thousand men over the course of only two days. It was carnage. Men blown to pieces..." He faltered, biting his lip hard before carrying on. "You think you've seen blood in gunfights; you've seen nothing. Nothing! Friends cut in half by cannon fire. There were bits of body flying through the air. And a young boy bugler, only a kid really, standing so close to me when he took the full brunt of cannon fire..." His hands were shaking now. And oddly they were brushing at his clothes as if to brush the blood off himself, just as he had that day. He swallowed hard; he couldn't talk about that.

No. Describe it in simple military terms. That was what he needed to do. He sucked in a lungful of air. "We were trying to hold the Rebs at bay while we tore up the railroad. It was partly a diversionary tactic. While we were busy doing that, the plan was for Grant to march 100,000 men to the south across the James River. They were to take control of the rail hub at Petersberg to try to cut off supplies to the Rebs. And yet, after all of our fighting and dreadful losses, it turned out to be all for nothing – the Rebs repaired the railroad within two weeks and supplies carried on reaching their army."

Guy leaned forward, wrapping his arms around his knees to stop himself shaking, before looking back at Johnny. "So, I was back with my unit, but we felt as though we'd hit rock bottom.

We'd lost so many friends and comrades. We'd seen so much blood, so much suffering and horror." Guy shook his head. "Hell, even the songs we sang were about longing for peace. Our favorite was 'When This Cruel War is Over' which tells you all you need to know about how we felt.

"Everyone wanted peace. We'd had enough. Enough of the killing, enough of what seemed like rivers of human blood. We'd reached a stage where we would have done anything to bring that terrible time to an end. And it was against that background that the powers-that-be decided the swiftest way to end it all was to starve out the Rebs' army. And that meant destroying that valley."

Guy bit his lip and then glared across at Johnny. "And I jumped at the chance to shorten the war, but if you think I enjoyed what we did down there you're damn well wrong."

Johnny met his gaze, before ducking his head and then looking back at him. "No, I would never think that you would enjoy war, or killing, or anything that made people suffer. I just can't understand you being part of it all, I guess."

"Because you think what exactly? Why wouldn't I be in the army fighting for something I believed in?" Guy shook his head, frustrated. He couldn't understand what exactly was bothering Johnny most. "I mean is your fury about Daisy and what happened to her? Or the fact that we destroyed the valley? If you were in the army, for however short a time, you must understand that it works because men follow orders, exactly the same as children are subject to rules and boundaries." But even as he said the words he remembered something Stoney had told him about Johnny as a child. About how he'd probably never been a child, he'd been left to fend for himself with no-one to take care of him. And that was the crux of their differences – how could Johnny understand about rules and orders when he'd never been subjected to the normal background that most people had?

Johnny picked at another stem of grass, and took a while to answer. "What you said about this family you knew, and how you liked their ideas. Well, I can understand you joining up, thinking it was for a good reason. For something just and right. That makes sense, and if I'm honest, I admire you for that. I think," Johnny pushed his hat back, "I think what I find hardest to accept, is the thought of you and all the cavalry riding down through part of your own country destroying everything. Peoples' homes, their property, their animals, their lives. And not just a small area, it was the..." Johnny paused, his brow furrowed. "The scale of it. Yeah, the scale of it. Like you had some God given right to destroy everything they had, because you were all so fucking certain that you were right.

"I mean, I wasn't born yesterday. War is shit. Hell, most men are shit too. And men do what they need to do, or have to do to survive. It's just... I don't know; it's that somehow I figured you to be different. That you wouldn't be involved in something like that – making war on women and kids. Something that dirty. I thought you were better than other men. More... honorable."

Guy opened his mouth to reply. And then closed it. What

the hell could he say to such a ridiculous notion? Why should Johnny think him better than other men in some way? He frowned while he tried to formulate an answer but then threw his hands up. "Why? Why on earth do you think I'm different?"

Johnny's mouth twisted into a kind of rueful, wistful smile. "I guess it's because you've stood by me. Ever since I came here, you've backed me. Hell, even in Utah, with everything you heard in that courtroom, you still backed me. And no ordinary fellow would want to know me, I know that. Shit, I know that nobody ever wants me around because of what I am, and who I am. But you, with all your education and fancy background, you claimed me as a brother. Why? Why would you do that if you weren't different to other folk? Better than other folk."

Guy found he was doing it again; opening his mouth to answer but nothing was coming out. It felt as if his brain and mouth had lost contact with each other. Maybe it was because he felt a wave of sadness that Johnny should have felt so isolated in his life that he couldn't really accept affection and support. And it struck him how extraordinary it was that Johnny had opened up and talked to him over the past few months. He reckoned he might be the first person that Johnny had ever allowed himself to get close to. And whatever he said now, he didn't want to destroy what they had.

"Perhaps," he spoke softly. "I claimed you as a brother because I saw a man who doesn't make war on women. I saw a man who has his own moral code, granted a rather bizarre code, but still his own moral code which he applies consistently. You have an innate sense of justice for the downtrodden – that's what I admire. For most of my life I have been surrounded by men who were full of empty rhetoric. You were different. Are different!"

Johnny flushed, as though embarrassed, so Guy hurried on. "But much as I hate to disillusion you, I'm not especially honorable. In the war, like everyone else, I was merely trying to survive.

"I hated what we did. Even though I felt I'd lost sight of why I joined up in the first place, the thought of deserting never crossed my mind. All I wanted was for the war to be over. I wanted an end to the suffering. And my fellow officers and men felt the same. We'd have done anything to see it end. And believe me, burning barns and crops, and occasionally burning homes, was very hard to justify." He shook his head. "Is hard to justify; never mind was! It's easy for politicians hundreds of miles away, sitting in safety, to agree to such things. They don't have to carry out the action. Or live with the consequences."

He bit his lip. He didn't want to dwell on how men like him felt almost morally bankrupt as a result of some of those actions. "But as to what my part was in that campaign... We started slowly in the valley. The Union had a long record of disasters there, so we sparred with the Rebs initially. We didn't really drive them any farther south than Winchester in the first six weeks. But then that's where we made our first real strike against them. It was terrifying. And thrilling too, I suppose. We were two full divisions of horsemen and we thundered down on General Early's left flank in a sabre charge like something out of olden days. You can't imagine the noise and the speed of it, all of us with drawn swords. It must have been a terrifying sight to Early's men. There were 2,000 of them and they surrendered. Some of them made their escape but we captured most of them.

"But then we had the second part of the plan to carry out, which was to turn the valley into a wasteland. Grant had told Sheridan that it should be such a barren waste that crows flying over it should have to carry their provender with them. We were playing for keeps. We didn't make much distinction between rebel farmers and those who claimed to support the Union. We knew the grain and fodder would go to the Rebs, so we destroyed it all. And yes, civilians suffered. It didn't bother some men, but for some of us it was a hard burden to carry. Our own countrymen."

He paused, furrowing his brow, lost in the memories of the heat and dust, and the fires and smoke. Ash blowing for miles. And the stench of burning. A man could never forget that. It had pervaded everything. He dragged his mind back to the present, conscious of Johnny still squatting, watching him intently. Watching him for what? Some sign of weakness? A sign that his account was not truthful? He couldn't tell. Johnny was a hard man to read.

"And yes, there were rapes. There will always be rapes in war. But any man under my command would have been horse-whipped for such an offence. However, it did happen within some units. And worse things than that happened. Much worse." He swallowed hard, knowing his voice was faltering. But he wanted to tell it all.

Johnny leaned forward, tilting his head like he sensed something bad. "What? What else happened?"

Guy took another deep breath. He owed Johnny the truth. After all they'd been through together since coming home, after all that Johnny had shared with him, it was his turn. So yes. The whole truth.

"We used to divide up into small units. We'd each be allocated an area to clear. Mostly we'd be told to spare the main house, and only burn the barns and the crops. But sometimes we'd be specifically instructed to burn the house too. I hated those most. I always used to try and ensure that the family could at least get their belongings out. They'd carry out their belongings... Their treasures all piled up in the fields amid the smoke." Guy screwed his eyes tight for a second, if only he could blot out the memories.

And still Johnny squatted there watching him. What was Johnny thinking?

Guy shook his head hard, as though by doing so he could dislodge the memories. "There was one farm we went to early one morning. It was deserted. There was no sign of the family anywhere although I called out repeatedly, and we banged on the doors. I ordered one of the men to search the house, to check that it was empty before we burned it. And in the meantime we set light to the barn. Then the corporal returned and told me the house was empty. He said he'd searched thoroughly, so we burned it."

He tried to quell the rising nausea. He gritted his teeth; he needed to get this said. "The only thing was... it wasn't empty. There was an elderly man in there. I spotted him at an upstairs window, trying to get out. The flames were all around him. And then I saw the child with him. A small girl..."

CHAPTER TWENTY-EIGHT

The leaves around his boots were damp and decaying. All dead. They'd lain there through the winter moldering on the ground. He scuffed at them while he tried to get his thoughts into some sort of order. Because, right now, he didn't know what the hell to think. He'd wanted this so bad. Wanted Guy to open up. And he'd wanted Guy to tell him that he'd played no part in what happened to the innocent in that valley somewhere the other side of this huge country.

But Guy hadn't told him what he wanted to hear.

He hadn't told him anything he wanted to hear.

Instead he'd told him everything he didn't want to hear. An old man. A small child.

He'd been so sure that Guy would have taken no part in such actions. He thought Guy was better than other men. Better than Fierro. But Madre de Dios...

"Children? Women and children, Guy. Old men." His voice faltered. So many people who'd suffered. He could picture the building and the old man and small girl burning up. Their mouths wide open as they screamed. Flames leaping around, snapping and crackling. Madre de Dios. And he could picture the terrified young girl that Daisy would have been. And he could see matchstick-thin children scavenging for food in a long, cold winter.

"It shortened the war." Guy's voice was wooden.

Johnny stumbled to his feet and paced around, shaking his head. "That don't make it right, Guy. It can never, ever be right to make little kids suffer. They can't protect themselves; they just have to take all the shit that people heap on them. We're supposed to protect them. Not burn their homes. Not fucking starve them." He gulped in some air but the tightness in his chest didn't go away. "But you wouldn't know what it's like to be starving." Johnny tried to unclench his fists, but they wouldn't do what he wanted. "Hell, I remember those fellows in Abilene saying how well you all ate in your campaign."

Johnny turned toward him. "But to a little kid... You don't know what it's like to be a hungry kid. Not to understand why some people have so much that they throw food away and yet you're starving and it feels like rats gnawing at your insides. And it's all you can think about every waking minute, that hole in your belly. And you have to scavenge in the garbage with the rats just to stay alive." The words were spewing out. He couldn't stop them. "But yeah, your soldiers were fed. You officers were fed. You didn't go hungry. You were living it up, feasting, and you took the food off the plates of the people who lived there, who'd sweated growing that food, sweated harvesting that food. And you left them with nothing. You left women and kids to starve." He shook his head, he knew all about what it was like to be that hungry.

"I don't doubt that you had good reasons for joining up. I can see that. That's fine. I ain't got a problem with that. But for all that talk about slavery, I reckon people like you were played for fools. I ain't never noticed anyone treating them better now that they're free men. Seems to me they still get treated like shit by an awful lot of people." Johnny paused and shrugged. "Like half-breeds get treated like shit. Like Indians get treated like shit. There's an awful lot of white folk who reckon themselves better. Better than them colored folk, and better than half-breeds or Indians."

"I don't think myself better." Guy's voice was soft, almost like he was talking to himself.

Johnny closed his eyes, trying to calm his racing heart. "I know that. I know that much about you, Guy. But... I still don't see how you could do what you did in that valley. And I know you say it made the war shorter. But little kids? Old men? It ain't right. It can't ever be right to do that, whatever the reason."

Guy jerked his head up, his jaw clenched as tight as his fists. "If you'd seen your friends cut in half, been splattered by their guts and brains, maybe then you'd have some sort of idea. It's all very well for you to stand there and say it can't ever be justified. Saying that the end doesn't justify the means. Those are easy words, Johnny. Easy for you, standing here now. You weren't there among the blood and the chaos." Guy paused, he was shaking all over. "I thought I was fighting for justice. For an ideal. But really..." He shook his head. "You want to know how it feels now? It feels dirty. I feel dirty. And not a day goes past when I don't relive it all. When I don't want to scrub at my hands to wash the blood away. Are you happy now?"

"No!" Johnny kicked hard at a tree stump. "No, I ain't happy, Guy. I really thought you were better. Better than me. I mean, shit, I know I'm damned. The things I've done made sure of my place in Hell a long time ago. God only knows I got plenty of blood on my hands. I got to live with the things I've done. Things I did when I didn't give a damn who I killed because all I cared about was building a reputation. Becoming someone who other folk would be too scared to trample on. I'd had enough of being stomped on; had it for too many years. It reached a point where as long as I got me a reputation I didn't care what sort of reputation it was; not when I started out. And I sure as hell ain't proud of that now. But you..." God, it hurt. It was like his guts were being torn out. "But you." His voice was more of a whisper now. "You're better than that, Guy. You got to be better. Better than me. The old man thinks you're so perfect. And we all know what he thinks of me. But God help me, if you're a sinner, if you got that much dirt on your soul..." He couldn't voice the thoughts. Not out loud.

"Damn it, Johnny. I'm human. I'm not a bloody saint. I'm

simply a man who tried to keep his sanity in a totally insane war. I'm no different from most other men." The tips of Guy's ears were red. And the vein was pulsing in his temple; just like the old man's did. "I don't want to be on some crazy pedestal that you've put me on. I'm surprised you haven't asked about the man and child in the burning house. Don't you want to know all about that?" Guy was shaking.

Johnny closed his eyes briefly. "I don't need to ask. I know you'd have done your best to help them. If I'm certain of anything, and God knows I ain't certain of much anymore, I'm certain you'd have done everything you could to help them."

Guy bit his lip, and sucked in a breath. "Thank you for that at least. But." He shrugged his shoulders in a hopeless kind of way that ripped another bit from Johnny's guts. "I failed. I couldn't save them. I tried, but there was nothing I could do."

Johnny turned away to stare down at the body. "I can't talk about this now, Guy. I need to think things through. I guess I don't know what to think of it all. Of you. All I can see right now are those kids left to starve. And Daisy raped by three bastards wearing your army's uniform. God, I hate people." He sucked in another gulp of air. "I should have known not to believe in anyone when I came here. That's always been my rule, and I forgot it. But in the long run it sure as hell saves a lot of disappointment."

He stooped to get hold of the dead man's feet and dragged him toward Pistol. "I'll take him into town. God only knows where his horse went – it bolted. I'd best go tell Stoney what happened.

Not that he'll believe me. He knew I was out to get the son of a bitch."

Guy moved to help him.

"No!" Guy flinched at the tone of Johnny's voice. "Leave him be, Harvard. I'll do it. He's my problem. I killed him, I'll deal with him. You can go look for his horse." Grunting with the effort, he heaved the body up and laid him across Pistol, who snorted and tried to swing away from the dead weight which Johnny secured with the rope from his lasso. "Ssssh. Steady, boy." Johnny stroked Pistol's neck to soothe him before swinging himself up into the saddle. He pushed his hat down so his face was in shadow. "I'll see you later, Guy. Right now, I want to get things straight in my head." With the lightest touch of his spurs he turned the horse toward the town, leaving Guy standing, his arms hanging limp by his sides and staring at the ground.

He couldn't go fast, not with the body on board, but right now he'd have liked to have made the trip at a flat out gallop to put as much distance between him and Guy as possible.

And he knew Guy was hurting. And he knew, deep down, that Guy had been trying to level with him. Had finally tried to tell his story without making any excuses or trying to defend his actions. But how could he have been a part of such brutality? He was better than that. He was an honorable man. Or leastways that's what Johnny had always thought. A good man. A man who accepted a breed gun-hawk for a brother. That had to make him different from other men.

Johnny shut his eyes to try and block out the memory of Guy brushing at his clothes like he was trying to wipe something away. God almighty, what a thing to live with. But people like Daisy were living with memories too, and nobody gave a damn about the Daisies of the world.

He reached behind him to steady the body as Pistol slipped on the loose scree of the hillside.

Hausmann's nephew.

The man would have put a bullet in Guy if he'd had the chance. And all for something that Guy didn't do. Nothing to do with what he did do. What a crazy world.

Maybe God had washed his hands of the world, same as Guy wanting to wash the blood off his hands. Maybe that was why wars happened and men were cruel. He couldn't blame God if he'd taken a look at his creation and been disgusted by the lot of them and decided to have no more to do with mankind. Couldn't blame him at all. Men were shit whichever way you looked at them. Except...

Except somehow he'd always thought Guy was different. He kept coming back to that. Look at how Guy had stood by him in Utah. Anyone else would have walked away. And how he'd always defended Johnny to the old man. And how kind and patient he always was with Peggy, even when she was being a pain in the butt.

He couldn't deny he respected Guy for joining up to fight for a cause he believed in. But to go through that valley doing what they did? How could his brother ever have allowed himself to do that? Johnny sighed heavily, for that was what he kept coming back to.

He rode slowly into town, reining in outside the undertakers. He unhitched the lasso from the body, even as Ike Cousins came out of his shop, all bug-eyed and a face full of questions.

"Got a body for you, Ike." Johnny hauled the fellow over his shoulder. "Where d'you want him?"

Ike swallowed hard, his eyes glancing nervously toward the gun on Johnny's hip. "Um, er, inside, on the slab." He held the door as Johnny stumbled through, glad to dump the weight on the cold marble table.

"What happened?" Ike licked his lips, glancing again at the iron on Johnny's thigh.

Johnny stopped in the doorway, resting his hand on the wall. "What happened? What the hell does it look like happened? He ran into a bullet." Johnny glared. "Don't go fretting yourself. I'm off to see Stoney now, not that it's any of your damn business."

Ike put his hands up, kind of like he might if Fierro pulled a gun on him. "Didn't mean nothing by it, Johnny. I was only asking."

"Yeah, sure, Ike. You was only asking." Johnny stalked out, letting the door slam shut behind him.

He hurried along the street, grateful that at least there

weren't many people around to have seen him ride in with the body and who would have been asking him damn fool questions. He pushed open the door to Stoney's office but there was no sign of him; only the usual mess of papers and cigar butts. And there was no sign of Hausmann in the cells neither, which is where Stoney should have stored him if Clem and Bob had done as they were told.

Johnny gritted his teeth. Seemed if he wanted something done right he had to do it himself. He walked swiftly to the edge of town where Bob and Clem slouched against the bordello wall, chatting. "Can't you two follow a simple order?" He snapped out the question. "Why the hell isn't Hausmann in jail where he should be?"

Clem furrowed his brow, and Bob stared, with his mouth slightly open.

"You didn't say nothing about putting him in jail, Johnny." Clem scratched his head. Dios, did men really scratch their heads when they were thinking hard? Or maybe he was trying to feel if he had a brain in there.

"Yeah, I did, Clem."

Bob shook his head slowly. "Nope. You didn't say nothing about locking him up. You didn't say nothing like that. What you did say was for me to get Stoney and tell him about Hausmann and to tell Ben. But Stoney's out of town, and apparently the doc is off delivering a baby some place. Hausmann said he'd got a funeral to prepare for, so we figured we shouldn't interrupt that. I guess he's gone off to get ready for it."

"A funeral?" Johnny tilted his head. "I didn't know anyone had died of late." Well, besides the nephew, and Hausmann didn't know about that – yet.

Bob shrugged. "I don't know about that, Johnny. But it wouldn't have been right to mess with a funeral. Not fair on the family."

"Not fair at all." Clem nodded solemnly. "There might be some grieving widow, some kids."

Johnny clenched his jaw shut. No point in yelling. 'Specially if they were right and he hadn't said anything about locking Hausmann up.

"D'you find your brother okay?" It seemed that Bob reckoned a change of subject was a good idea.

"Yeah. My brother's fine. But that crazy son of a bitch, that Hausmann sent out to kill him, ain't doing so fine. I shot him."

Bob let out a low whistle. "He really was going to kill your brother? He ain't the only crazy one. That Hausmann is crazy too. Really crazy. No knowing what a man like that could do."

"Anyway," Clem sounded hopeful, and had that sort of eager spaniel look on his face. "I know where Hausmann went. I saw him go down the alley round the back of the bordello a few minutes ago. So leastways we know which way he went."

Johnny furrowed his brow. "Well, that ain't anywhere near the church, not if he's doing a funeral. I think I'd best go see what the old devil is up to. I don't trust him an inch."

Johnny sped down the alleyway which led to the back of the buildings facing the main street. Peering each way he couldn't see anyone at first. Not a soul. So where the hell had Hausmann gone?

He turned again toward the back of the bordello as he heard a door open. He heard Daisy calling out. And then he glimpsed her mouth opening to scream, even as Hausmann jumped forward, holding something which was flaring and spitting.

Johnny went for his gun but didn't even clear leather before he was hurled onto the ground by a deafening blast, and glass and splintered wood flew everywhere.

He tried to scramble to his feet but his legs didn't work and his head was ringing. All he could see was smoke and dust and something rolling toward him. He reached out to stop it, and his hands were suddenly drenched in warm pulp. And as the smoke cleared, he saw one of Daisy's favorite pearl earrings swinging from the half of her head he held.

CHAPTER TWENTY-NINE

He gasped as he dropped it, staring down at his hands, wet and covered with blood, and splinters of something hard and white like broken china.

Still kneeling, he shook his head to rid himself of the eerie moaning sound filling his ears, but it carried on. And all he could focus on was the carnage of mutilated bodies around him. Fragments of Daisy's frothy skirt were floating in the breeze and he stretched his hand out to grasp a piece, only to recoil as he saw again the bits of humanity sticking to his fingers.

And rocking back and forth he could still hear the low moan. Was it him?

There were voices now, but they sounded a very long way off.

Maybe that was Clem he could hear? Calling at someone to keep back. And other voices too.

He stared down at his knees – there was stuff on his knees. Some of it was red, and some was a dirty sort of white. And there were other bits... He tried to brush it off but it stuck to his fingers. He rubbed his hands down the front of his jacket to wipe it off but there was more of it on his jacket.

He jumped at the light touch of a hand on his shoulder. A voice saying his name but it was muffled and far away. He turned slowly, looking through dulled eyes to see Bob squatting next to him.

"Johnny." Bob's voice sounded gentle. Different from usual. "Come on, Johnny, let me help you up. Lean on me."

Johnny didn't move. He stared back down at his hands. So much blood. Like the blood of all the men he'd killed was swirling around him.

Almost numb, he felt hands holding him under his armpits, hauling him slowly to his feet.

"Come on, Johnny. Let's get you away from here. Away from all these people. We'll go to Stoney's office."

What people? He hadn't noticed the people. But he allowed himself to be guided away, with Bob grasping him tight each time he stumbled. His feet didn't want to walk. He wanted to fall back to his knees and rest but Bob hefted him against him so that he took the weight while Johnny felt his feet dragging reluctantly in clumsy shuffling steps.

He couldn't keep from looking down at his boots. They were dusty. And the dust was streaked red and there were sort of strange grey blobs sticking to them too.

Bob covered a chair with an old blanket and eased Johnny down onto it. The sort of chair that felt like it could swallow him up. He wanted to be swallowed up. Like Jonah. But he didn't want to get spat out again. He stared around, still dazed; Stoney's office. He didn't remember getting there.

Bob.

That was it. Bob had taken him there.

Where was Bob now?

By the stove. Could see him now. He was doing something with a pan.

He sniffed, scenting the smell of coffee. That was it. Bob was making coffee.

He stared down at his hands, rubbing them across his thighs. But it wouldn't come off.

He turned dazed eyes toward the door as it opened. Stoney. Stoney was back. He'd take care of everything. He looked worried though. His brow was all screwed up and he was saying something. Maybe talking to Bob.

"You drink this coffee, Johnny." Bob was pushing a mug into his hand. But he didn't want to hold it. He'd make the mug red too. And there was too much red.

"Come on, Johnny." Stoney sounded sort of gentle. Just like he had when he'd first met him and was only a little kid. Stoney took him for a meal back then. Filled his belly. "Let me help you with that. I'll hold the mug, all you got to do is sip it. It'll do you good."

The mug was pressing against his lips, so he sipped. Didn't want to upset Stoney. He sipped again even though it was too sweet. He could feel the heat travelling through him, coursing its path down to his belly. But he was shivering. Weather must have turned colder.

"Have another sip. Come on." Stoney was pressing the mug to his lips once more, so he sipped at it. But it didn't warm him up. Felt like every bit of him was shaking. Yeah, must have turned really cold. He sipped again.

"That's it. You're doing good, boy." Stoney still sounded gentle.

The door opened. More voices. Ben? Was that his voice? Ben shouldn't be here. Daisy needed Ben.

Daisy? He sucked in a breath hearing the strange noise it made.

"Daisy? Ben. Daisy..." Johnny reached out to touch the doc. But his hands were red.

"Get some water and wash his hands!" Ben sounded real pissed. "And then, let me have a look at him."

He was vaguely aware of Bob and Stoney busying themselves with water and trying to soap his hands and wiping his face. It seemed an odd thing to be doing. But his head hurt so it didn't seem worth the effort of thinking too hard on it.

Ben was pulling at him now. Dragging Johnny's eyelids down and peering in, getting way too close. Johnny tried to pull back, wrenching his head away from Ben's hands. "I'm fine, Ben." He paused. His voice sounded kind of strange but at least he had a voice. Earlier he hadn't been able to find it. "I'm fine." Yeah. It sounded stronger now.

Ben gave a grunt, kind of like he was irritated. "Will you sit still, Johnny, and let me check you over."

"Daisy. Daisy needs you." But there was something wrong with those words. Something very wrong. He stared down at his hands again. They were red. Stoney and Bob had washed them but they were still red.

"Johnny. I'm sorry, I can't do anything for Daisy." Ben was crouched real close. "But we do need to check you over. That was one big blast. I need to check whether there're any fragments of wood or glass in you. All right?"

"Daisy?" But he knew. He shuddered suddenly remembering the warmth in his hands. And the earring. It was coming back now. Hausmann. Hausmann with the dynamite fizzing in his hand. "Hausmann?"

"He's dead, Johnny." Ben's voice was gentle too. Kind of like Stoney's and Bob's voices had been. Why were they all talking odd?

And then the biggest coldest hand of fear he'd ever felt clutched at his guts. "Delice? What about Delice." He shook Ben's arm. "Delice. Is she okay?" The words sounded odd. Like he could barely say them and he was fumbling again, trying to get to his feet to push past Ben. "Delice."

"She's out of town, Johnny. She's not here, I think she went to Santa Fe."

He fell back in the seat, sucking in a huge breath of air. And then sighing it out just as hard. She was OK. She was safe. His Delice was OK.

He leaned forward again. "The girls? What about the girls?" Johnny tried to haul himself up out of the chair, but Ben pushed him back.

"The girls are fine, Johnny. Shocked, but fine. Clem's looking after them all. The back of the building's a bit of a wreck though."

But nothing else was. Because now it was all flooding back. The warm pulpy feel of Daisy's head. The stuff all over him – it was Daisy and Hausmann.

God almighty.

Why? It was crazy. Why poor Daisy? She'd never done anyone any harm. Never hurt nobody.

Ben was doing something to his arm. Dabbing it with something that stung, and picking bits of something out of it with some pincers. White splinters. And wooden splinters and the occasional bit of glass. He stared wide-eyed at the white splinters as he realized, with a sick feeling in his gut, exactly what the splinters were.

He tried to suck in another bit of air because his chest felt all tight, like nothing would work right and he couldn't hardly breathe. The creak of the door opening was a relief. It gave him something to look at besides those tiny slivers of white.

A wave of relief flooded him as he looked at the man standing in the doorway. A man in a thousand. A man to lean on when things got too hard to bear. A man who stood by him come what may.

"May I come in?" Guy sounded uncertain, like he thought he'd be turned away.

A shard of guilt pierced Johnny, like Ben's damn pincers. He nodded, flinching slightly as Ben dug a touch deeper.

Guy came and squatted down next to the chair. "Mother of God, Johnny. Are you all right? Damn it, I'm... I mean... What a terrible thing, it's crazy, insane. Hausmann did all of this? I came into town, I wanted to see you to try to clear things up. I heard... I heard the explosion when I was still some way out..." His voice tailed off.

Johnny reached out his hand to touch Guy's arm, almost to check it really was Guy; that he wasn't imagining it. "I'm glad you're here, Guy." He pulled his hand back quickly. Was there blood on it? They'd washed it but yeah, there was blood on it. He could see if, even if nobody else could. Like the blood on his soul. Nobody else could see that. But he knew it was there.

Same as Guy really. He'd been trying to brush the blood off. That's what he'd been doing when he'd mentioned... what was it? A bugle boy that was it.

And Madre de Dios! He shuddered, biting his lip hard. Guy had seen sights like this all too often. Sights like Daisy.

Johnny tried to move forward but Ben pushed him back. "I'm not done yet, Johnny. You just sit still."

"I'm fine, Ben."

Ben smiled, but it was a sad smile. "No, Johnny. You're not fine, and for the time being you're staying put, until I say otherwise."

He hadn't got the energy to fight, so he sat back shutting his eyes and let Ben carry on. And all the while he could feel Guy watching him. Kind of ready to help but also like he still expected Fierro to yell at him.

Finally Ben stood up and stepped away. "I think that's the lot. You've got a hell of a bad concussion there, it'll take a while to settle down. But otherwise, I don't think there's much else wrong with you physically." Ben shook his head, a deep line showing between his eyes. "I think the best thing you can do is go home, and have a quiet few days. I know you hate it, but I want you to rest up for a while. It's important."

Going home had a good sound to it. Except... Except the old man would be fit to bust over the way he took off to Santa Fe. And right now it felt like his head would split open if anyone yelled at him.

"Don't worry about Father, I'll talk to him." Guy's voice was calm. How did Guy know that he'd been thinking about the old man?

"I'll get him home, Ben. Come on, Johnny." Guy helped him gently out of the chair. "Do you want me to rent a buggy from the livery?"

Johnny shook his head vigorously, and then wished he hadn't. "No, I'll ride. Might warm me up. I can't stop shivering."

Guy shot a quick look at Ben, his eyebrow raised and his eyes all serious. "Maybe he shouldn't be riding."

"Just get me home. Now." Johnny stumbled slightly but recovered his footing, and pushed Guy's arm away. "I'll be fine. Let's go home."

"Get him home, Guy, and I'll come out later to have another look at him. Keep him warm and make sure he has some peace and quiet." Ben held the door open as Johnny took a couple of faltering steps into the light.

He leaned against the door frame while Guy busied himself preparing their horses. Johnny fumbled his way to Pistol and heaved himself into the saddle before turning the horse toward home.

They took it slow, a real steady walk. And that was as well, because he reckoned he might have fallen out of the saddle if they'd gone any faster. He glanced at Guy whose face seemed older somehow. Lined and drawn.

Johnny drew in a shuddering breath. "I had part of her head in my hands. It was warm."

Guy turned his head sharply and looked at him. "Johnny, try not to think about it. I know that's easier said than done, but believe me, it's the only way to deal with it."

"You saw things like that every day, didn't you?" And

there it was. His brother had endured that horror every damn day of his war.

Guy sighed softly. "Not every day, thank God. But every battle. It haunts a man. You try to harden yourself to it. And in some ways it works. You can tell yourself that it's war. And you're used to it. You can keep up the pretense during the sunlight hours. But at night—"

"That's always when our demons come to visit." Johnny shook his head slightly. He had lots of demons.

Guy nodded. "Yes. That's when they come visiting."

Johnny stared down again at his jacket. The blood had dried, making dark stains like the ones on his soul. But he'd never figured on Guy having them too. He hated to think of Guy having been part of what happened in that valley. The way Daisy had described it before the soldiers had come, it had sounded real pretty. He flinched as he remembered the dreamy look on her face when she'd told him how beautiful it was, even as he tried to block out the memory of how she'd looked after Hausmann... What a pointless waste. Such a fucking waste of life.

And how the hell did men cope with seeing sights like he'd just seen? What would that do a man if he had to see that more than once? To see it often, like it was almost a normal part of life. He fingered Pistol's mane twisting the coarse hairs in his fingers. What had it done to Guy? Shit.

He remembered the look in Guy's eyes when he'd said he'd jumped at the chance to end the war, that he'd have done anything to bring it to an end. Johnny twisted the strands of mane harder. And he now knew why that chance must have seemed so appealing to men like Guy, worn down by the blood and the horror.

He looked across at him, wondering how to tell Guy that he thought maybe he understood even though he could never approve. Not when little children had gone hungry and women were raped. But he had a glimmering of how desperate Guy must have felt.

He swallowed hard. He needed to say something. "Guy, I, I think I kind of understand what you meant now. About why you'd have done anything to end it. I can understand how..." He paused. "I mean, I'll never think it was right what they did, taking the war to those people in that valley. But after seeing Daisy this afternoon and all the..." He paused again, pushing down the urge to spew his guts up. "All the mess. I sure as hell understand why you thought the way you did.

"And that house you burned? What happened to that old man and child, I don't see as that was your fault. Although I got to tell you, I'd have fucking shot the fellow who said he'd searched it. But, Dios, Guy, I wish to hell you'd told me all about this when I first asked you. It would have been a damn sight easier if you'd told me about this straight off."

Guy stared at him. "I thought you would condemn me. If I can't forgive myself for it, why should anyone else?"

Johnny hunched himself down into his jacket. He was still shivering. "You know, I was right about you. You are honorable. Most men would argue that sort of thing away, telling themselves that it was war, and just one of those things. But not you. You go carrying it around blaming yourself. See what I mean? You were a good man who got caught up in a terrible war." Madre de Dios. A terrible war – that was putting it mildly. To see the stuff like what happened today.

He needed to try to explain how he'd felt; he owed Guy that. "I was really mad at you because you wouldn't talk to me. I'd told you so much. And I guess I was hurt that you didn't trust me. And then, when I talked to Daisy." He screwed his eyes shut for a second, before swallowing hard and carrying on. "When I talked to her and heard all about what happened there, I got really mad. I felt let down by you. But if I'd stopped and thought about it, I'd have realized that you'd have had to have had some sort of good reason for being part of it all in the first place, and I reckon your—" Johnny paused, furrowing his forehead in concentration as he tried to recall the words. "Your battle cry of freedom, as you put it, was a pretty good reason for joining up. Not that I'll ever understand your ideas of duty. I sure as hell don't feel guilty about deserting. And I still fucking hate your generals for taking their war to women and children. But, at least I can see a little bit of how you must have felt at that stage."

Guy smiled sadly. "For what it's worth, I hated what we did in that valley – all of it. Every second of it. Innocent people suffered, and I have to ask myself if the end justifies the means. I'm not sure that it does. I tell myself that what we did made the war shorter. I tell myself that I was doing my duty and following orders. But deep down, I know that we did a truly terrible thing. We caused the innocent to suffer, not just the opposing army. And now, I have to live with it."

Johnny tilted his head. "It's kind of strange really. We always come at things from different directions, you and me. But we always end up in the same place. I think it was shit what was done there. Hell, I'd like to string up your generals and all the fucking politicians who play their games and use little people like pawns. And so do you. But I needed to hear it from you. I don't understand your world of duty and honor. But I guess in some ways we got common ground."

Guy looked across at him. "Yes, I think we do." He paused, and frowned. *"We are one equal temper of heroic hearts, made weak by time and fate, but strong in will to seek, to find and not to yield."*

Those words. He'd heard them before. Delice. In the restaurant. Was it only a couple of days ago? It felt like a life time ago now. "Tennyson."

Guy stared at him with his mouth open. "You recognize that poem? Where on earth did you hear that? You never fail to surprise me, Johnny."

Johnny shrugged. He didn't want to share the memory of his evening with Delice. He wanted it untouched by everything that had happened on this dreadful day. It was his own memory to cherish. "I know all sorts of things, Guy." He reined Pistol in; they could see the ranch from here, it looked calm and welcoming. If only Guthrie would be too.

Guy nudged his horse forward. "I'll go on ahead and talk to Father. You take it easy and ride in slowly. It'll be fine; I promise he won't yell." And then Guy shot him a worried look. "Can you manage riding in alone?"

Johnny nodded. "Yeah, I can manage. I've had a lifetime of practice."

CHAPTER THIRTY

He was mending. He knew he was mending and feeling more like himself – in his body at least. The headaches had gone and his hearing had returned to normal. He'd even stopped shivering.

But he couldn't get rid of the memory of Daisy's head in his hands.

It brought him gasping for air from sleep at night. It invaded his thoughts at the oddest times. He'd be standing talking to Peggy about what was for supper and it came flooding back. Or when he was shifting uncomfortably as Carlita scolded him for being untidy... Or listening to Guthrie droning on about blood lines or water holes or those damn fence posts. But there it was – that warm and pulpy thing in his hands.

He'd find himself staring down at his hands and seeing them colored red.

He wondered if he was going loco – like Hausmann.

In some ways it wouldn't have seemed quite so bad if it had been a man who'd been blown to pieces. But things like that weren't meant to happen to women. Never to women. And certainly not to girls like Daisy.

Poor damaged Daisy who'd never harmed nobody in her all too short life.

And the guilt that kept gnawing away at him was if he hadn't sent her to Cimarron, she'd still be alive. Still be breathing, and laughing that way she had when she threw her head back and laughed like something was the best joke ever. She'd still be looking down all demure like and then flashing a glance with a kind of half-smile which had a way of hardening a man's dick.

Ben hadn't let him go to the funeral. Guy had gone. But that was something else to feel guilty about. Another bit of dirt on his soul. He should have been there. But damn it, Ben had made so much fuss. And then Guthrie and Guy had joined in. He would have gone regardless but he'd felt like shit, kind of dizzy and sick. Hell, he had been sick. Been puking everywhere. And they'd said he might puke over the coffin. That had stopped him in his tracks. He couldn't risk doing that to poor Daisy. Not that there was much of Daisy in the coffin...

Guy had said he'd go and "represent" Johnny, whatever the hell that meant.

But he had to give the old man credit; he hadn't had a go at him over anything since he'd gotten home. But that was kind of unnerving in itself because he knew he'd behaved badly. It felt like he was permanently on a knife edge just waiting for the old man to bring up the trip to Santa Fe. And yet, all the old man had said was could he leave a note the next time he took off?

Surely the old man should have yelled at him? Maybe Delice would explain it to him. She seemed able to figure things better than he could.

He knew that was simply an excuse to go see her. The truth was he wanted to see her. Needed to see her. He needed to check that she was all right after coming back to the nightmare of everything that had happened. And... Mierda, if he was honest, he was terrified that this would have been the last straw and she might have decided to move to Santa Fe after all.

So when Guy had suggested that he ride into Cimarron with him, he'd leapt at the chance.

Guy had looked at Johnny real thoughtful. "I have to run some errands for Father, why don't you come into town with me?"

And that had been welcome. Because part of him, just a tiny part of him, had been dreading that first ride into town alone.

It was a real nice day. All the scents of summer were heavy in the air. It was warm and still. The birds were busy feeding on insects and intent on flying to their nests to feed their young. And the land had long lost that newly washed look which it had in the spring, when everything was so green it looked like it was fresh from Peggy's laundry. But now there was an added warmth to the air and the start of that drowsy feel that hot summer days had when it was like only the lizards had enough energy to haul themselves out to soak up the sun.

"Will you come and see the lawyer with me?" Guy's question jerked his mind away from the sight of a litter of snowshoe hares frolicking together.

Johnny stared down at Pistol's neck, before shaking his head. "No. I thought I'd go and check on Delice. I'll have a drink and see how she's doing."

Guy sucked in a breath, a small furrow creasing his brow. "Are you sure you want to go there yet?"

Johnny raised an eyebrow and shook his head slightly. "Nope. But I'm going to go anyway. I want to see if she's all right."

Guy pushed his hat back. And then fidgeted with his reins, making his horse edge sideways. "Well, I'll see you after. I may wait for you."

Johnny nodded. "Fine. But I must check up and see how she's doing." He paused, trying not to flinch at even the thought of walking in there. "It must have been a hell of a shock to her coming back to all of this." He waved his hand vaguely around, like it was meant to mean something. And because he couldn't voice exactly what it was Delice had come back to.

Guy nodded. "I'm sure she'll appreciate a visit. I'll see you later."

And so Guy headed off to the lawyer's office and Johnny was left staring at the heavy front door of the bordello.

His heart was thumping in his chest, and his palms were damp. How pathetic was that? He'd been through this door so often, but hell. He choked the rising bile back down. Needed to get a grip on himself. He sucked in a huge gulp of air, and then pushed the door and stepped inside.

It was strangely quiet. Normally the girls would be lounging around chatting, or sewing, but none of them was there. A lamp was lit in the corner behind the bar, but none of the crystal things hanging from the ceiling had been lit. But through the gloom he could see a glimmer of light coming from behind the door to Delice's office. Looking past her door toward the back of the bordello, he could see it all boarded up, presumably waiting for the rebuilding work to start.

He walked softly toward the light, but his spurs gave him away and she peered around the door with a questioning look on her face.

Her eyes widened. "Johnny. I didn't expect you in." She gave him a sharp look over, the kind which didn't miss a trick. "Are you supposed to be riding yet?"

He whipped his hat off and shrugged. "Yeah, Ben gave me the all clear. I wanted to come and see how you were doing."

She opened the door of her office wider and motioned him inside. "I think how you're doing is more to the point, honey. Come on in and have a drink."

She went to the cupboard and pulled out two glasses and a bottle of malt, then shot him a quick look. "Maybe you'd rather have tequila?"

He shook his head and sank down onto a big leather chair. "No, the malt's fine, thanks." If truth be told, he probably couldn't have tasted the difference right now. He had to force food down and it all tasted like sawdust.

She poured him a hefty measure and then settled herself down in her chair. "So, how are you doing, Johnny?"

He stared down at the glass, pushing it in circles on the desk. The word 'fine' came to mind. It's what he would have said to anyone else. He sighed softly, shaking his head. "Not too good, really."

She didn't speak. She took a sip of her drink, and then quirked an eyebrow looking kind of thoughtful. "And there I was expecting you to say fine." Her voice was gentle. Like she knew that was what he always said, and kind of like she knew he wasn't fine at all.

He swallowed hard. "I'm sorry I couldn't make the funeral..." His voice trailed off. He didn't even want to say Daisy's name out loud.

"Honey, you weren't well enough to make it. I understood that. Ben was there, and Guy. Guy's having a headstone made for her. She'd have liked that." Delice gave a kind of smile, but it looked real sad. "Daisy was the type of girl who'd have thought only important people had headstones."

"Yeah, Guy mentioned that he was doing that." Johnny stared down at his boots. Not the pair he'd worn when Daisy... He'd thrown those out. But then he'd always thought it was dumb having two pairs. A man could only wear one pair of boots. He forced himself to look up. "It's my fault. All of this is my fault."

Delice took another sip before placing her glass down and steepling her fingers under her chin. "Your fault? You always seem to blame yourself for everything so I wondered how long it would take before you came out with that. And why exactly do you think this is your fault?"

"I sent her here. If I'd never sent her here she'd still be alive." And there it was. If he'd only left Daisy alone. If he hadn't interfered in her life. If he'd left her in the saloon where he'd first met her, she'd still be living and breathing. And not in pieces in a wooden box buried in the cold ground.

Delice shut her eyes briefly, and sighed. "Honey, you sent her here because you're a compassionate man. She was having a dreadful life in Abilene. Goodness knows how many times she'd had her nose broken. And because you are essentially a kind man, you gave her money so that she could come somewhere safer. For all you know, if you'd left her there one of those men might have killed her by now.

"You cannot hold yourself responsible for the actions of someone like Hausmann. To be honest, I'm not sure if Hausmann can be held responsible for his actions. The man had gone quite mad."

"But maybe if I hadn't pushed him. Maybe if I'd not fixed the voting over the bordello—"

"Johnny, it's not your fault. You did the best thing by Daisy in sending her here. That's it. What happened later was simply one of those crazy, awful quirks of fate. And Daisy was in the wrong place at the wrong time. If she hadn't been at the door at that exact moment she'd have been fine. His dynamite caused some superficial damage at the back of the building without making any real impact on the main area."

Johnny shook his head slowly. "When I saw Hausmann outside, after I talked with Daisy, he said his nephew was going to send Guy to hell. I—" He chewed on his lip. He couldn't admit to panicking, but it was what he'd done. "I didn't stop to give Bob and Clem proper orders. I told them to look after the girls. To tell Stoney and Ben that Hausmann had gone loco. But I didn't tell them to lock him up. If I had... If I hadn't gone rushing off." He shut his eyes briefly. "If I'd stopped to tell them to lock up Hausmann, she'd still be alive."

Delice sighed as soft as a breeze on a summer evening. "But does it not occur to you that if you'd stayed longer talking to Bob and Clem, Guy might have been killed. Johnny, this was a terrible event, but you cannot hold yourself responsible for it. Hausmann went crazy; you couldn't possibly know that he would attack the bordello. You can't keep blaming yourself like this. It wasn't your fault."

Johnny shook his head. He wished he could believe her. "And it ain't only me. Guy's blaming himself because of being in the Shenandoah Valley and Hausmann finding out about that. And Guthrie is going on about how he should never have written to the bishop because it got Hausmann fired."

Delice rolled her eyes. "So guilt is a family trait then. Heavens, and I thought it was only you." A sad smile pulled at her mouth. "Honey, I'm certain of one thing, Daisy wouldn't want you blaming yourself."

Johnny shrugged. "I know." He flashed a brief smile. "She liked you. She liked you a lot."

Delice nodded slowly. "I liked her. She was a really bright girl. And like all of the girls here, she didn't deserve to end up in this sort of life." She shot Johnny a quick look. "And how are things between you and Guy?"

"We're doing OK. Fine. We're fine now. We talked some. Sorted a few things out, I guess." Johnny chewed on his lip. "You... You ain't changed your mind about staying, have you? I mean after all of this happening? You ain't going to go to Santa Fe after all, are you?" She couldn't see the knot in his gut, but could she hear the fear in his voice?

She tilted her head to one side. "Well, after all your machinations, it would be a trifle mean of me to change my mind."

And what the hell were machinations?

"Honey, you want the truth?"

He nodded, despite the sick feeling forming in his gut.

"If you hadn't already succeeded in changing my mind over that, as a result of your very convincing economic arguments, I would have decided to stay as a direct result of Hausmann's action. I'm damned if anyone's going to force me out of anywhere! So, I'm staying put. It looks like I'm here for good."

A wave of relief spread warmly through him, washing away some of the tension. "What about Bob and Clem? Are you keeping them on?"

She narrowed her eyes a touch and made a sort of hmmmph noise. "I've told you before, I like to hire and fire my own staff. However." She paused and fiddled with a pen on the desk. "Old Clem, the barkeep, wants to go and live with his son in Colorado. So I do have a vacancy. And I felt that as I find it very trying having to go to the bother of learning names, I might as well keep young Clem on in that capacity. The girls tell me that he was very calm and kind to them when, when Hausmann... Anyway, it would save me the bother of having to learn a new name." She glared at Johnny like she was daring him to say a single word.

He bit back a smile. "Yeah, well, I can see the sense in that, Delice. Good call."

"And as for Bob." She sniffed.

"Bob was real good to me after." Johnny shut his eyes briefly. "Got me away and over to Stoney's office and things."

She made a small inclination of her head. "Yes, I believe I heard something about that." She shot him another fierce look. "Anyway, as you can imagine there is quite a lot of work needed doing around here now. Repainting and so forth. And because I really can't bear the thought of you and Stoney nagging me incessantly about having someone here to keep trouble at bay, and only because it would get on my nerves if the two of you start carrying on. Well, I thought he might as well stay too." She tilted her chin and glared at him again.

He nodded solemnly. "Well, as you say, entirely your decision, Delice. I sure as hell would never interfere in the way you run things. Ain't none of my business, but it sounds like a..." He paused while he tried to think of some way of putting it that sounded good. "A real sound business decision. Yeah, real good sense."

She narrowed her eyes slightly. "Hmmm. And yes, Johnny, I know it would never cross your mind to interfere in my business." She gave him a sharp look but he'd swear that her lips were twitching.

He could feel himself coloring up, and damn it, but he reckoned she was the only woman who'd ever been able to make him feel awkward and tongue tied. How did she do that? He sighed softly as the guilt came flooding back - he really hadn't thought about her business when he was busy turning the screws on the mayor and his committee. "Do you think your best customers will come back?"

She tilted her head to one side. "Oh I daresay he will."

"I meant all of them, the mayor and his committee." He ducked his head awkwardly.

"Honey." Her voice was very gentle. "You're my best customer."

He jerked his head up. It was real nice to hear her say that but he knew he wanted more than that. He wanted something deeper – he wanted her friendship. That was it, friendship.

"And," her mouth quirked into a smile. "You're also my best friend."

The warmth started deep inside of him, spreading through his veins and it all seemed to come bursting out into a huge smile and he felt taller and stronger. And some of the pain he was carrying kind of slipped away on the warm tide. Hell, he thought Ben was her best friend. Or that Adam Smith. He pushed the thought of Smith away. Wasn't going to spoil this moment.

She twiddled with the glass in front of her; pushed it in circles on the table. And she bit her lip like she couldn't decide whether to say something. "I, um, I decided it might be best, as far as the mayor and his friends are concerned, if, um, I let them think it was Daisy who gave away their secrets. Otherwise I really would have to, at the very least, give Sadie a real dressing down over it. And after all that's happened, I really haven't the heart to do so." She paused. "Not that I'm getting soft or anything, but—"

Johnny bit back the start of a smile again. "Soft? You? Never!" Daisy had been right about Delice – she really was a very kind person, even if she didn't like people knowing it. He frowned as another thought struck him. He'd have to have a word with her about Sadie and the way she'd been when he got back from Santa

Fe, before Hausmann— He swallowed hard and was surprised that his hand started shaking at even the thought of Hausmann. "But I wanted to talk to you about Sadie."

Delice raised an eyebrow, and her eyes narrowed a touch. "Yes? What about Sadie?"

Funny how Sadie was always a real tricky subject with Delice. "The thing is." He tried to avoid looking at Delice – it was the set of her jaw he found unnerving. "I wondered if maybe you could have a quiet word with her."

"A quiet word? About what?" Delice sounded kind of distant.

"Well, the thing is, I think maybe..." He paused and swallowed hard again. "She went kind of loco when I got back from Santa Fe. Before I spoke with Daisy. The trouble is, I think maybe she's kind of got the wrong idea about me. I think she's sweet on me." The words came out in a rush. "And she seems to think that because she's always been my favorite girl here that it means more than it does."

"And doesn't it?" Delice quirked an eyebrow, but looked real hard at him.

"Hell, no!" Johnny sat forward in his chair with a jolt. "No, it don't mean nothing, it's just she's good at her job, that's all. And she's a nice kid. But I tried telling her that and I don't think she listened to a word I said. And I guess it's because she's lonesome and maybe wants a man of her own. But the thing is, it ain't going to be me."

Delice turned away, reaching for the bottle to top up their glasses.

Johnny ran his fingers through his hair. "I mean I don't want to hurt her, Delice, and I told her straight that there wasn't anything more to it, but it was like she didn't hear what I was saying." He sighed softly. "And what with Daisy and all. Well, hell, she's had enough hurt these past few days. But I hate to think of her carrying on hoping for something that ain't going to happen."

Delice leaned over to top up his glass. A smile tugged at her mouth. "You've a kind heart, Johnny. I wish you recognized that. And yes, I'll have a quiet word with her and set things straight." She bent down to open a drawer in her desk and pulled out a package. "I have a gift for you that I bought in Santa Fe."

Johnny felt his jaw drop before he could stop it. "A gift? For me? It ain't my birthday. And it sure isn't Christmas."

Delice's mouth twitched. "I wanted to get you this as a small thank you for a lovely evening." She handed him the parcel which was neatly wrapped in brown paper and tied with string.

Dios, but she really had gotten him a gift. She'd been thinking of him after he'd returned to Cimarron, and that was real nice. It kind of made him glow inside, like the sun had come out after a long cold spell.

He fumbled with the string, feeling unusually clumsy. Pulling the paper away he saw a small, leather-bound book, etched with gold lettering on the spine. "The Poetical Works of Alfred,

Lord Tennyson." He spoke the words slowly, stumbling only slightly over the Tennyson. That was the fellow Delice and Guy had quoted from – and it was her favorite poem, she'd said. "That poem you liked, is it in here?"

"Ulysses? Yes, it is. I've marked it for you. But I think you'll enjoy a lot of the poems, not just that one."

He flicked through the book until he reached the marked page. He ran a finger over the page, below the title. "How did you say that?"

"U-li-sees. It's a strange spelling, but that's how it's pronounced. It's a beautiful poem and I think you will find that it moves you."

Johnny glanced at her. "It was odd, but Guy said some lines from this poem too; when he was talking about the war. Exactly like you did." He furrowed his brow reading the unfamiliar words. "Do you think there are any words in here that might be right for Daisy's headstone? I think she'd like something special like that; not just her name and some dates that don't mean anything to anyone. I guess it would be nice if someone reads it in years to come, when she's been forgotten by everyone, and the words make someone wonder about her."

Delice tilted her head to one side. "That's a lovely thought, Johnny. I'll read it through and decide which part is suitable. But you're right, she would like that. Poor Daisy, she deserved something better than this life."

"She sure did." He got slowly to his feet, and put the book inside his jacket. "Thanks for the book. And I'll tell Guy that you're going to find some good words to put on the stone."

"Johnny." Her voice was soft and he could see the concern in her eyes. "Please don't blame yourself for this. None of it was your fault. It was fate. And all we can do is carry on."

"And sail beyond the sunset?" He was pleased to see her eyes widen slightly.

"You remembered the words." Her lips quirked and he could see that she was pleased. "I was right, you will enjoy that book."

He took his leave, and headed back into the sunlight. Guy was sunning himself on a rocking chair outside Mayor Tandy's shop but he sprang to his feet as soon as he saw Johnny. He scanned Johnny, looking him up and down, almost like he was checking for signs of damage. "Are you all right, Johnny?"

Johnny nodded. It was kind of odd because he did feel better – he'd been dreading going in there, but seeing Delice and talking had eased things. "Yeah, I'm fine. Come on, let's go home."

They rode in silence until they reached the ridge where there was a good view of the ranch. And it was like they had some unspoken agreement because they both reined in at the same spot and sat looking down on the hacienda, basking in the late afternoon sun. It was familiar and comforting, and it made him feel good inside knowing it was home. It was his home and that was pretty amazing. All those years alone and never having anything to call his own. But suddenly he had all of this.

He chewed on his stampede string thinking back on all of the events of the past few days, before glancing at Guy who was sitting relaxed in the saddle and not even fiddling with his reins the way he normally did. "Guy, there's something I been meaning to ask you."

Guy hissed in a breath. "Something else about the war?"

Johnny shook his head. "No, I reckon we covered that, don't you?"

Guy's mouth quirked into a smile, and Johnny could see the relief in his brother's eyes. "I had hoped so. What is it you want to know?"

"Well, it's kind of dumb, and I don't suppose you have, seeing as how you ain't lived here much longer than me, but have you ever heard of a fellow called Adam Smith?"

Guy's eyes widened and then he laughed. "Adam Smith?"

Johnny narrowed his eyes. "Yeah, well, I didn't think as how you'd—"

"You mean THE Adam Smith?"

Johnny narrowed his eyes a touch more. "THE Adam Smith? You mean you know him? Or you've heard of him?"

"Well of course I've heard of him. His magnum opus was 'An Inquiry into the Nature and Causes of the Wealth of Nations.'"

Johnny kept his face blank. "The what?"

"He's considered to be the father of economics. He was a philosopher and a pioneer of political economy."

Johnny raised an eyebrow. "Economics, huh?"

Guy nodded. "Oh yes, it must be one of the most influential books ever written."

Economics. He tried to drag his mind back to the conversation he'd had with Delice that day. Something about giving her advice on running the business. What was it she'd said? Something about how Johnny was suddenly an expert on economics, maybe she should call him Adam Smith. "Does this fellow live around these parts, Guy?"

Guy laughed. "Hardly. He died about 70 years ago, Johnny. And he was a Scot, like Father's father. Not from around here."

"He's dead? You're telling me that this fellow is dead? Are you sure?"

Guy raised an eyebrow. "Quite sure. Why on earth do you want to know about Adam Smith? Where did you hear about him?"

Johnny flushed; he had the uneasy feeling that he'd been well and truly had. "Oh, it was just something Delice mentioned."

Guy grinned. "She is a remarkably well-educated woman."

Johnny gritted his teeth, trying to squash the laughter and the sudden feeling of relief. But he couldn't hold the laugh back and he leaned forward on his saddle horn, his shoulders shaking. "Yeah, I reckon she is at that, Guy. And you know, one day I'm going to take great pleasure in strangling her with my bare hands!"

Guy furrowed his brow, like he was real puzzled by his crazy brother. "I could get you a copy of the book if you like, but I'm not sure that you'd find it very entertaining."

Johnny shook his head still grinning. "No, I already got a book to read, Guy. But I'll race you home." And with a whoop he spurred Pistol on down the hill, leaving Guy trailing in a cloud of dust.

ABOUT *THE DEVIL'S OWN* SERIES

Gunfighter Johnny Fierro has been dealing with death all his life. Part Apache, he's never been welcome either side of the border, but his speed with his gun has brought him fame. Now, though, he's tired of the killings and tired of being used. Fate intervenes and gives him the opportunity of a different life. The *Devil's Own* traces his efforts to adapt and face up to a future he never expected to have.

The Devil's Own books, in order:

Dance With The Devil

Johnny Fierro's a gunfighter, maybe the best. He's hunted trouble and a reputation all his life. But the killings and the range wars have worn him out and brought him to a point where he would welcome death —until he hears that his estranged and hated father faces a battle to hold onto his land in the Cimarron Valley. Fierro has sworn to kill his father and this is too good an opportunity to miss. What he hasn't bargained for is a share of the ranch, or a brother he never knew existed. While his upright, authoritarian father and Harvard-educated brother struggle to come to terms with his violent past and vicious reputation, Fierro wrestles with the unwelcome realization that his mother didn't tell him the whole story about the past. He doesn't know what to believe, but he has to make a choice when the bullets start flying.

An Uneasy Alliance

Gunfighter Johnny Fierro is home at last. After years of hunting trouble and gaining a fearsome reputation along the Mexican border, Johnny is trying hard to settle into a new life as a rancher in the Cimarron Valley in New Mexico. He's also dealing with living with his family for the first time, adjusting to his uptight father and Harvard-educated brother. This proves hard enough after a life spent as a gun hawk, but his past just won't let him go. Whenever he turns around, something else is there to threaten his chances of making this new life a success. Whether it's gunfighters looking to settle old scores, or bushwhackers who'd like to put a bullet in his back, there's always someone out to get him. The neighbors—and maybe his father too— want him gone or dead. Until lawless drifters bring trouble to Cimarron, threatening the town's peace. Then the neighbors want to hire Fierro, want to hide behind his gun. When the drifters attack a woman in town, Johnny knows he's the only one who can stop them— but at what cost?

The Stacked Deck

Life for former gunfighter Johnny Fierro has never been easy. He and Lady Luck don t always see eye-to-eye. Some days he thinks she likes to turn the cards and stack the deck against him.

Fierro's returned to the Sinclair ranch, but feels like an outsider. And, even as he struggles to settle into a normal life and build relationships with his once-estranged family, his past comes back to haunt him. Lady Luck shows her hand, and his life is thrown into turmoil. Two lawmen arrive at the ranch with a warrant for his arrest, and take him to Utah to stand trial. For murder.

Fierro has dark, terrible secrets he'll share with no man. As the fates conspire against him, he fears that the trial might lay bare the man Johnny Fierro really is. And while he fights to avoid revealing the truth and escape the noose, newly forged family ties are tested to the limits as his brother, Guy, faces some unpalatable truths. Guy must question everything he thinks he knows about Johnny, and decide if he can not only live with what Johnny is capable of, but if he can continue to call him brother.

ABOUT JD MARCH

Adventurer and journalist JD March has tracked leopards in the Masai Mara, skied competitively, ridden to hounds, paddled dugout canoes on the Indian Ocean, and is an accomplished and experienced sailor. JD has lived in a series of unusual homes including a haunted twelfth-century house in Cornwall and a chalet in the French Alps. But a lifelong passion for the old west means JD is happiest in the saddle, rounding up cattle in the Big Horn Mountains in Wyoming.

Contact JD at www.jdmarch.com or jdmarchwesterns@gmail.com